M. E. M. (Mollie Evelyn Moore) Davis

An elephant's track

and other stories

M. E. M. (Mollie Evelyn Moore) Davis

An elephant's track
and other stories

ISBN/EAN: 9783742894311

Manufactured in Europe, USA, Canada, Australia, Japa

Cover: Foto ©Andreas Hilbeck / pixelio.de

Manufactured and distributed by brebook publishing software
(www.brebook.com)

M. E. M. (Mollie Evelyn Moore) Davis

An elephant's track

AN ELEPHANT'S TRACK

AND OTHER STORIES

BY

M. E. M. DAVIS

AUTHOR OF

"UNDER THE MAN FIG" "MINDING THE GAP"
"IN WAR TIMES AT LA ROSE BLANCHE"

ILLUSTRATED

NEW YORK
HARPER & BROTHERS PUBLISHERS
1897

Of the stories embraced in the following collection, the two entitled "*A Heart Leaf from Stony Creek Bottom*" and "*At the Corner of Absinthe and Anisette*," appeared respectively in "*The Atlantic Monthly*" and "*Romance*." By the courtesy of Messrs. Houghton, Mifflin & Company and of the Current Literature Company, I am permitted to reproduce them here.

"*The Cloven Heart*" and "*The Love Stranche*" were written for this volume. The other stories have all appeared in the publications of Messrs. Harper & Brothers.

M. E. M. DAVIS

CONTENTS

I
ALONG JIM-NED CREEK

II
FLYING THREADS

III
FROM THE QUARTER

ILLUSTRATIONS

I

ALONG JIM-NED CREEK

"It kin be done, Nance, an' I'm agoin' to do
it ef it busts me." Newt Pinson brought the
forelegs of his raw-hide-bottomed chair down on
the puncheon floor with a thump, and slapped
his knees emphatically with his hairy hands.

"Five dollars air a mighty heap to spen' fer
sech foolishness, Newt," replied his wife, turning the squalling baby over on its stomach and
pounding it vigorously on the back. "Mo'over,"
she added, after a pause, "I don't see ez ye've
got the five dollars, nohow."

Mr. Pinson stretched out one long leg and
thrust a hand into his trousers-pocket. "Ye're
mighty right, Nance, I 'ain't," he admitted, blowing the loose tobacco from the handful of coin
fetched up from the honest home-made depths ;
"I've got jes three dollars and a half lef' outn
what Sam Leggett paid me fer the yearlin'. But
me an' the childern hev been a-talkin' of it over,
an' they hev conclusioned to th'ow in ther aigg
money ; Dan fo' bits, an' Pete fo'; Joe an' Jed
hez two bits betwix 'em, an' Polly M'riar says
ez how she hev fifteen cents. I'm lackin' of a

1

dime, but I reckin I kin scratch thet up somewhers."

"Ther's my two bits up yan in the clock," Mrs. Pinson remarked, with pretended indifference; "ye kin take that ef ye air sech a plumb fool ez to pike the whole passel of us inter town to see the circus."

"Shucks, Nance!" he returned, indignantly; "I ain't agoin' to *tech* yo' two bits." Nevertheless he got up and fumbled about in the clockcase on the high mantel-shelf until he found it. "Anyhow," he added, as he reseated himself, "I kin pay it back when ye git ready fer yo' nex' bottle o' snuff."

"Will they be a el'phunt?" demanded one of the freckle-faced urchins gathered around the heads of the family, listening, breathless, to the discussion.

"A dollar fer Nance, an' a dollar fer me," Mr. Pinson counted, gravely, taking no notice of the interruption, "an' fo' bits apiece fer Beck an' Dan an' Pete an' Polly M'riar an' Joe an' Jed. Childern half price "—he glanced casually at the flaming circus poster tacked against the chinked wall in the chimney corner—" not countin' of the baby. An' fifteen cents lef', by jing!"

"Do ye reckin I kin git in fer half price, paw?" This question, which came from Becky, the oldest of the Pinson brood, who stood five feet six and a half inches in her bare feet, might have been meant as a bit of covert sarcasm, had not the eager voice belied any such intention. Her father's eyes travelled slowly up from the hem of her homespun frock, as she stood leaning against the chimney jamb, to her pretty round face framed in its shock of frizzly red hair. "Waal, I be dinged, Beck!" he exclaimed, in dismay, "I keep fergittin' ez how ye air growed up!" His face clouded, and he looked ruefully at the pile of dimes and half-dimes lying in his large palm.

"An' Sam Leggett's gone to Kansas on a cattle drive," murmured the twelve-year-old Dan, with a meaning leer at Becky. A vivid blush overspread her face; she dropped her eyelids and squirmed her shapely toes. But Mr. Pinson was absorbed in a mute recalculation, which ended presently in a beat-out whistle and a mournful shake of the head.

Mrs. Pinson, with the colicky baby laid over her shoulder, was jolting her rockerless chair to and fro, and singing, in a sweet, drawling undertone:

" Far-ye-well, oh, far-ye-well ;
When ye git to hev-ven ye will pa-art n-o-o m-o-o'!"

She interrupted herself to observe, quietly, "Ye kin tote the baby, Beck; an' I kin tote Joe; an' yo' paw *he* kin tote Jed, twel we git inside the tent. They ain't no charge fer children in arms. It says so."

"Lord, Nance!" exclaimed her husband, in an ecstasy of admiration, "ye air the beatenes' white woman on Jim-Ned Creek! Thet settles it oncet mo'! Fetch me a coal fer my pipe, Polly M'riar."

Becky heaved a deep sigh of relief, and sank down on her heels, reaching under her mother's chair at the same time for the snuff-bottle.

"Will they be a el'phunt?" persisted Jed, the tow-headed boy next to the baby, already in long trousers, which were hitched up to his shoulders with a single white cotton "gallus."

"Of co'se. They is al'uz a el'phunt with a circus," replied his father.

"I 'ain't nuver seen no circus," said Mrs. Pinson, in jerks between the long-drawn swells of her mournful lullaby.

"Nuther hev I," admitted Newt; "but I jes natchly know that ever' circus has *got* to hev a el'phunt an' a clown."

"Didn' I tell ye so!" cried Dan, triumphantly, following with a dirty forefinger the head-lines of the poster. "Ain't the el'phunts right here, a-dancin' an' a stan'in' on they heads, an' a-rollin' o' barrils? An' ez fer *clowns!* they is four mirth-pro-vo-king clowns in this here show. It says so. An' five beau-ti-ful and ac-com-plished lady bare-back riders;" and he continued to spell out laboriously the manifold and unrivalled attractions of Riddler's Mammoth Circus and Menagerie, billed—for one performance only—in Comanche at two o'clock P.M., Monday, the 18th of October. Come One. Come All.

Becky, struck by a sudden thought, stared at him, shifting the brush uneasily from one corner of her mouth to the other. "Like ez not," she broke out, abruptly, "Brother Skaggs 'll preach

agin it nex' Sunday. Sho's yo' bawn, Brother
Skaggs air a-goin ter preach agin it."

Mrs. Pinson stopped singing; Polly Maria and
the boys turned stricken faces upon their father.

His eyes twinkled under their bushy red brows,
but his voice was decorously sober as he drawled:
"Brother Skaggs hes gone to Confunce, an' he
won't be back twel Sat'day week. Ye min',
Nance," he continued, "it air thirty-one mile to
town, an' ef we lay to git ther in time fer the
show Monday, we got to camp somewhers 'bout
Blanket Sunday night."

"Jes to think o' me goin' to town oncet mo'!"
said Mrs. Pinson, meditatively, that night, when
she and Becky were getting supper in the brush
arbor behind the cabin. "I 'ain't been sence you
was a baby, Beck. Yo' paw an' me went to Wash
Dingwall's infair—he died with his boots on four
year ago; an' Tempunce Loo—thet's his widder
—she's married agin to Bijy Green. I rid behin'
him, an' he toted you on his lap. Town folks air
mighty bigaty," she added, warningly; "'n' ye
mus' do up thet pu'ple caliker o' yourn, Beck, an'
put on yo' shoes an' stockin's."

"Seems lak fo' days won't nuver go," fretted
Beck, "an' ole Baldy air sho to lame hisse'f, or
sump'n'. It's alluz that a-way whence a body air
plumb sot on doin' a thing."

But the four days did go, and when the event-
ful Sunday afternoon came, old Baldy, unusually sound and spirited, was with Jinny, the gaunt
gray mule, harnessed to the wagon; the patched
and dingy cover was drawn over the bows, a

bundle or two of fodder and a few ears of corn
were thrown into the hinder part, and Mr. Pinson drove gayly alongside of the rail-fence in
front of the cabin. The rickety house door was
drawn to with a rock behind it to keep it shut.
A couple of chairs were handed up for Mrs. Pinson and Becky, and they clambered in with the
baby. The yellow cotton poke, well stuffed
with corn-bread and bacon, and the battered coffee-pot and frying-pan, were stowed under the
chairs. Polly Maria and the boys sat on a quilt
spread over the sweet-smelling fodder; Rove,
Ring, and Spot, the lean, long-eared brown
hounds, yelped and whined against the wheels.

They jolted away, serious, as became a perfessin' fambly on a Sunday, but full of inward excitement. At night they camped on the pecan-
fringed banks of Rastler's, and were off betimes
in the morning. But not too soon to find the
road lively with friends and acquaintances from
all the settlements around, bound on the same
joyous errand as themselves. They passed Joe
Holder, with his wife and sister-in-law and the
thirteen children of the two families, creaking
along in a huge freighter's wagon drawn by five
yoke of gaunt, wide-horned oxen; they were
overtaken and outstripped by a noisy squad of
girls and young men on horseback from the Fork
Valley neighborhood; they kept within hailing
distance for a dozen miles or more of old Daddy
Gardenbrier and his wife, riding double on their
blind yellow mare. The Mount Zion folks, they
heard, were ahead of them by some hours, and an

impatient youngster who trotted by on a paint
pony threw over his shoulder the information
that the Big Puddle lay-out was coming on behind.

"Lord, Nance!" Mr. Pinson exclaimed more
than once that morning, "I wouldn't of took five
dollars to of stayed at home."

"Nuther would I, Newt," Mrs. Pinson as often
returned, with a kind of solemn delight on her
thin, sallow face.

The long reaches of post-oak "rough" were
heavy with sand; the shinn-oak prairies between
were a tangle of roots that zigzagged across the
road, and made progress slow and painful; the
abrupt banks of the frequent "dry creeks" were
steep; the October sun was hot; and by noon
old Baldy had become utterly dispirited. He had,
moreover, fallen a little lame, and he moved dejectedly along by Jinny, who long ago had flopped
her big ears downward in sign of weariness and
discontent.

The Pinsons under the dingy wagon cover were
wellnigh speechless with impatience.

Suddenly Dan stood up, knocking his head
against the low wagon bows. "Jes over yan,"
he declared, "pas' one little bit o' shinn-oak
prery, an' crost a dry creek, an' up a hill, is
town." Dan had been to town once with Sam
Leggett to lay out his long-hoarded egg money
in a four-bladed knife and a pair of store sus-
penders.

Polly Maria, slim and thin-legged, standing up
beside him, pitched backward into the fodder as

the wagon came to a sudden halt behind a group
of dismounted horsemen, who, with their bridles
over their arms, were squatting down, apparently
searching for something in a half-dried mud-pud-
dle to the right of the road. "Hullo, Jack!"
called Mr. Pinson; "what ye lost?" One of the
men looked over his shoulder. "Hy're, Newt?
Howdy, Mis' Pinson?" he cried, springing to his
feet and coming back to the side of the wagon,
where he shook hands all around. "We 'ain't
lost nothin'," he went on, putting a foot up on
the hub of the front wheel and resting his arms
on the hot tire; "we've found sump'n', though,
you bet! A genooine elephant track in the sof'
mud yonder, plain as daylight, an' no mistake."

Polly Maria and the boys scrambled in hot
haste over the tail-board. Mr. Pinson threw
down the reins, and held the baby while Becky
and her mother jumped out.

"Wish I may die ef it *ain't* a el'phunt track
sho!" he exclaimed, when he had joined the
wondering circle gathered about the huge foot-
print.

"It looks to me lak ez ef it were hine-side
afore somehow," said Mrs. Pinson, timidly.

"I have just been explaining to Mr. Jack Cy-
arter here and these other gentlemen, madam,"
said Mr. Tolliver, the old Virginian who taught
the school at Ebenezer Church, "that it is a fact
in natural history that the track of the elephant
always presents that appearance." He removed
his hat as he spoke, and made an old-fashioned
courtly bow.

"Ye don't say!" murmured Mrs. Pinson, overawed.

Jack Carter and his friends mounted their
horses and dashed away, followed at a more sober pace by Mr. Tolliver on his slab-sided plough-
mule.

The Pinsons climbed back to their places and
jogged on, across the bit o' prery and over the
dry creek—where they came near getting stalled
—and up the hill. On its crest Newt Pinson involuntarily drew up. "By jing! this beats *me!*"
he ejaculated, with widening eyes. The square
at the foot of the slope was in an uproar. Horses
stood nose to nose around the court-house fence,
and were hitched to the scraggy mesquite-trees
that shaded the town well. The dusty streets
leading away from the plaza were blocked with
wagons little and big, carts, ambulances, dilapidated hacks, high-swung red-bodied stages—
every imaginable kind of vehicle — and all the
intervening spaces, as well as the irregular side-
walks in front of the four infacing rows of stores,
were alive with men, women, and children, who
elbowed one another, whooping, laughing, gestic-
ulating—surging about in a state of the wildest,
best-natured excitement. Beyond the unpainted
little Baptist church, on the farther side of the
square, the circus tents were visible. Flags and
streamers were flying from their poles, and a vanishing burst of music came floating from them
up to the top of the hill.

"This beats *me!*" insisted Mr. Pinson again.
With a deep-drawn breath he gathered up the

ragged, homespun lines and drove down into the
square, picking his way dexterously through the
crowd until he halted alongside the shaky platform in front of Bush Gaines's store. "Holloa
agin, Newt—that you?" grinned Jack Carter
from behind the counter within, where he was
helping himself to a plug of tobacco. "You're
jest a minit too late to see the procession. It
cert'nly is a fine show. The elephant was there,
mighty nigh as big as Ebenezer Church. An'
such a clown! You'd ha' laughed yourse'f to
death to ha' seen him. His breeches are more'n
a yard wide, and he 'ain't got a hair on his head!"

"Ef we hadn't of stopped to look at the el'-
phunt's track—" began Newt, regretfully; "but
nuver min', Nance, it air a heap better to see it
fust off fum the inside."

"Oh, a heap better," responded Mrs. Pinson,
with cheerful alacrity. Bush Gaines, measuring
off some jeans for a Mount Zion matron, called
to Newt to bring his fambly in the sto' an' set
down, an' pass the time o' day. But after a
brief consultation with his wife, during which
Becky took mental note of some town girls in
looped overskirts and bangs — an observation
which bore fruit at the next Quarterly Meeting—
Mr. Pinson declined with thanks, and drove on
to the town well—all but gone dry from the ex-
cessive strain put upon it—where Dan and Pete
watered the team.

Afterwards they crossed the square and stopped
by the Baptist church, in full view of the circus
tents, whence arose at that moment a prolonged

and sullen roar. "They're feedin' of the nan-nimals," explained Mr. Pinson, in a familiar, off-hand sort of way, whereat Mrs. Pinson shuddered and hugged the sleeping baby closer to her bosom.

Old Baldy and Jinny were unhitched and fed from the trough at the back of the wagon; the panting dogs lay down in the shade of the church; the children had a snack all around out of the yellow poke, and Becky and her mother fetched out the chairs and sat down to "have a dip."

"It air a haff'n hour yit twel the do's is open," said Mr. Pinson, finally. "Jes you an' the chil-dern stay right here, Nance. I'm goin' to tramp down to the pos'-office an' git the las' 'lection news, an' sich. I'll be back the minit it air time, an' min' you all be ready, less'n we don't git no seats."

Mrs. Pinson nodded, and he strolled away. "This here beats *me*," he kept saying to himself. Comanche was indeed in an unwonted state of excitement. Riddler's was the first circus that had ever quitted the line of railway and vent-ured across the long sandy reaches of post-oak rough to the little isolated town in West Texas. And the whole surrounding country had pulled to its doors like the Pinsons, and responded to the invitation of the huge posters: "Come One. Come All."

Newt's progress was slow, owing to frequent encountering of neighbors and the necessity of inquiring after the health of their families. He did at last, however, reach the post-office, a ramshackle building next to the blacksmith shop. As he turned the corner he came upon a cake-and-lemonade stand. His hand went instantly down into his pocket, and came up with the extra fifteen cents, which he exchanged for three solid slabs of mahogany - colored gingerbread. "Fer Nance an' the childern," he explained, as the woman in charge wrapped up his purchase. The bleary old creature looked at him with a sudden kindly smile, and slipped a stick of peppermint candy into the parcel.

With one foot on the post-office step he paused to look at a man who had planted a gigantic yellow umbrella out in the dusty square, and standing bareheaded beneath it, was yelling some unintelligible jargon at the top of his lungs. Mr. Pinson hurried over and joined the ring of gaping spectators. On a bit of board in the shadow of the umbrella a couple of odd little marionettes of colored metal were circling in a kind of grotesque waltz. "*Lots* of fun for twenty-five cents!" shouted the showman, stopping now and then to touch up the figures with a stubby forefinger. "Lots of fun for twenty-five cents! The greatest toy invented in this age or any other. So simple that a crawling child cannot fail to manage it! Those who know the trick will please say nothing. *Cheap*, gentlemen, for *twenty-five* cents. Oh, I see the gentleman is going to buy!"

Newt grinned and shook his head regretfully.

"One for *one*, two for *two*, three gets the half a *dollah*!" bawled another individual who had set

up a table near-by covered with wooden ninepins.
Jack Carter and his crowd were throwing at these
with little painted balls. A cigar, Jack explained
to Newt, was the reward for one pin knocked
down at a throw ; two cigars went to the player
who knocked down two ; while the lucky thrower
who succeeded in knocking down three received
fifty cents. "One for *one*, two for *two*, three gets
the half a *do*llah," went on the proprietor, mo-
notonously. "Three throws for *five* cents. Step
up, gentlemen, and try your luck ! For a *nickel!*
One for *one*, two for *two*, three gets the half a
*do*llah !"

"Lord ! ef I hadn't of bought this durned
ginger-cake !" groaned Mr. Pinson in spirit, gathering the paper parcel more securely under his
arm and moving on with the crowd.

A step or two brought him to an open wagon
from which a patent-medicine man was holding
forth. "*Try* the remedy," he whined, flourishing a stout black bottle and a pewter spoon.
"Cures all diseases ! *Try* the remedy ! Admin-
istered free of charge to any one in the crowd.
This sup*erb* bottle filled with the remedy, only
fifty cents. The wise man tries, the fool dies.
Try the remedy !"

"This here beats *me*," murmured Newt, mechanically wiping the perspiration from his forehead and backing against the court-house fence,
where he leaned, fairly exhausted with the varie-
ty and novelty of his emotions. "The haff'n hour
mus' be nigh 'bout up. Dinged ef I ain't glad,"
he continued, letting the crowd drift on with-

out him to where the health-lift man was exhort-
ing the cautious ranchmen to " try the machine;
try the *wonderful* machine, gentlemen. Excel-
lent for the constitootion! Only five cents a trial.
Try. the machine;" and the reckless cowboys
were emptying their pockets at the invitation of
the vender of prize-boxes.

" Curious game that, sir," said a smooth voice
at his elbow. He looked around, startled. A
seedy but respectable - looking personage was
standing by him with his arms crossed on the
low fence. He jerked his head as he spoke towards a little knot of men hanging around the stile-
steps leading into the weed - grown court - house
yard.

Newt walked over and looked on. It was a
simple-enough-looking game at cards. An in-
nocent-faced little fellow with black hair and
curly mustache was manipulating the greasy
deck. The bet was five dollars. Two country-
men, unknown to Newt, with suspiciously stiff
white collars above their coarse hickory shirts,
and scrupulously clean finger-nails, won succes-
sively five dollars, and the dealer, much chagrined,
seemed on the point of giving up.

Newt made half a step forward. His heart
was beating violently and the blood was surging
in his ears. "I'm a perfessin' member," he
argued mentally with himself, while the cards
were once more shuffled and spread out, " yit
it air jes' 'bout the easies' thing in creation to
tell which one of them cyards air the right one.
An' Nance an' me 'll hev mo'n time to trade

out the five dollars whence the show air over.
Shucks!"

And he counted out and laid down his handful of dimes and nickels, and hazarded a bet.
He bent forward eagerly, and unconsciously
stretched forth a hand. "This here monty air
a mighty deceivin' game," remarked the blacksmith, with an air of conviction, as the dealer
raked Mr. Pinson's money into his own pocket
and walked jauntily away.

Newt turned about, half dazed by the sudden-
ness of the whole transaction, and bewildered by
the jeers of the by-standers. Just then, however, a noisy burst of music from the circus tents
gave the signal for the opening of the doors; a
wild rush immediately began in that direction,
and in a few moments the square was deserted,
except by the patent-medicine man and the
owner of the big umbrella. These joked each
other loudly, and slapped significantly their sil-
ver-weighted pockets.

Newt passed them with his head bent, heedless of the sneering laugh which they sent after
him. As he approached the church he saw that
Becky had the baby; she was holding him up
and smoothing the pink calico skirts over his
fat white legs. Mrs. Pinson looked at him with
an unwonted sparkle in her solemn black eyes as
he drew near, and lifted the chunky Jed in her
arms. "She looks lak she did whence I war
a-courtin' of her," he thought, with a sore pang.
Joe plunged towards him with a joyous whoop.
"Hurry, paw, hurry!" screamed Polly Maria;

" we ain't agoin' to git no seats less'n we hurry."
He put Joe aside roughly and strode on to his
wife. His face was set and hard, though his
mouth twitched convulsively.

"Lord-a-mighty, Newt Pinson, what ails ye?"
ejaculated Mrs. Pinson, letting Jed slip from her
arms.

"Nothin' ain't ailin' me ez I knows on," he
returned, in a dry, harsh voice; "we got to go
back home 'thout seein' o' the show, thet's all.
I done bet away ever' cent of ourn an' the childern's circus money on a fool game o' cyards—
yander. Oh Lord!" he ended with a groan. A
single wild wail burst from Polly Maria and the
boys. Then they huddled against their mother's skirts in mute agony.

A faint flush passed over Mrs. Pinson's thin
face and the light faded from her dark eyes.

" 'Tain't no diffunce, Newt," she said, lightly,
catching the baby from Becky's limp and nerveless arms. "Jes ye hitch up, quick ez ye kin,
an' le's get outn this here bigaty town. Me an'
the childern air plumb beat out wi' these stuck-
up town folks, anyhow!"

Newt stared at her in silence, and slouched
away. Her gaze followed him to the rear of the
wagon; when he was beyond the reach of her
voice she whirled around and blazed in a threatening half-whisper: "Ef ary one o' ye says a
word to yer paw 'bout this here misfortin o' hisn,
or 'bout hankerin' a'ter the show; er ef ary one
o' ye ain't thet gamesome an' lively, lak ez ef they
wa'n't no sech a thing ez a circus, er a clown, er

a el'phunt in this here livin' worl'—sho's ye bawn
I'll shet the do' in Sam Leggett's face an' cow-
hide the balance o' ye twel ye can't set down fer
a week !"

Becky's ruddy cheeks grew pale. " Yes, maw,"
she returned, in a subdued tone.

" Yes, maw," echoed Polly Maria and the
boys, stolidly, not without squeezing back some
ungamesome tears, however, as they stood in a
row against the Baptist church and watched
their father bring around Jinny and old Baldy.

Had they only known it, they might have seen
while they waited, the Liliputian Lady and the
Fat Woman go by in a shaky hack with torn
curtains, and descend before the painted flaps
of one of the side shows. But they did not
know.

The wagon was turned around ; they climbed
over the wheels and settled themselves under the
dingy cover. As they moved slowly across the
silent square a tremendous shout from the spectators within the tent, and a pompous fanfare
from the brass-band, announced that the Grand
Entry had begun.

Newt stalked along beside the tired team
downcast and miserable. " I've even fergot
wher' I lef' the childern's ginger-cake," he muttered to himself, as his mind went over and over
the incidents of that fatal haff'n hour.

A curious hilarity prevailed that night around
the little camp-fire. Mrs. Pinson, usually silent
almost to taciturnity, had become all at once
loquacious. She painted to the family circle in

2

glowing colors the pride and wickedness of town
folks; she pictured the denunciatory wrath of
Brother Skaggs when he should learn that perfessin' members of Ebenezer Church had been inside of a circus tent; she related the experience
of sundry sinners who had been overtaken by
divine vengeance while in the very act of laughing at the antics of a clown; she even lifted up
her voice and sang some particularly flame-and-
brimstone-promising hymn tunes. Becky, mindful of Sam Leggett away off in Kansas, seconded
her efforts to keep the general cheerfulness up
to a proper pitch. If it showed signs of flagging,
however, a warning look, shot from beneath their
mother's drooping eyelids, acted like a charm on
Polly Maria and the boys.

Newt, who at first sat mournfully hugging his
knees and gazing into space, presently caught
the infection himself, and when, finally, he un-
rolled a patch-quilt and threw himself thereon,
closing his eyes in peaceful slumber, it was almost with the conviction that the five dollars
had been well lost in keeping a perfessin' fambly
out of the worldly and soul-destroying circus
tent.

Mrs. Pinson, sitting alone by the smouldering
fire with the baby in her arms, looked at his unconscious face upturned in the dim moonlight;
her gaze travelled slowly from one muffled, indistinct form huddled under the shadow of the wagon, to another; she sighed heavily, and her face
relapsed into its usual sombre expression. "I
wisht—" she muttered; then after a long pause,

as she stretched herself on the quilt beside her slumbering spouse and wrapped the baby's feet in an old shawl, she concluded with a little touch of triumph in her whispered tones, " Anyhow, I hev seen the el'phunt's track !"

A SNIPE-HUNT

A STORY OF JIM-NED CREEK

I

"I AIN'T sayin' nothin' ag'inst the women o'
Jim-Ned Creek *ez women,*" said Mr. Pinson ;
" an' what's more, I'll spit on my hands an' lay
out any man ez 'll dassen to sass 'em. But *ez
wives* the women o' Jim-Ned air the outbeatenes' critters in creation !"

These remarks, uttered in an oracular tone,
were received with grave approbation by the half
a dozen idlers gathered about the mesquite fire
in Bishop's store. Old Bishop himself, sorting
over some trace-chains behind the counter,
nodded grimly, and then smiled, his wintry face
grown suddenly tender.

" You've shore struck it, Newt," assented Joe
Trimble. " You never kin tell how ary one of
'em 'll ack under any succumstances."

Jack Carter and Sid Northcutt, the only
bachelors present, grinned and winked slyly at
each other.

" You boys neenter be so brash," drawled Mr.
Pinson's son-in-law, Sam Leggett, from his perch
on a barrel of pecans ; " jest you wait ontell
Minty Cullum an' Loo Slater gits a tight holt !
Them gals is ez meek ez lambs—now. But so
was Mis' Pinson an' Mis' Trimble in their day an'
time, I reckon. I know Becky Leggett was."

"The studdies'-goin' woman on Jim-Ned,"
continued Mr. Pinson, ignoring these interrup-
tions, " is Mis' Cullum. An' yit, Tobe Cullum
ain't no safeter than anybody else—considerin*
of Sissy Cullum ez a wife !'"

Mr. Trimble opened his lips to speak, but shut
them again hastily, looking a little scared, and
an awkward silence fell on the group.

For the shadow of Mrs. Cullum herself had
advanced through the wide doorway, and lay
athwart the puncheon floor ; and that lady, a
large, comfortable-looking, middle-aged person,
with a motherly face and a kindly smile, after a
momentary survey of the scene before her,
walked briskly in. She shook hands across the
counter with the storekeeper, and passed the
time of day all around.

Bud Hines, the new clerk, shuffled forward
eagerly to wait on her. Bud was a sallow-faced,
thin-chested, gawky youth from the States, who
had wandered into these parts in search of health
and employment. He was not yet used to the
somewhat drastic ways of Jim-Ned, and there
was a homesick look in his watery blue eyes ; he
smiled bashfully at her while he measured off
calico and weighed sugar, and he followed her

out to the horse-block when she had concluded
her lengthy spell of shopping.

"You better put on a thicker coat, Bud,"
she said, pushing back her sun-bonnet and looking down at him from the saddle before she
moved off. "You've got a rackety cough. I
reckon I'll have to make you some mullein
surrup."

"Oh, Mis' Cullum, don't trouble yourself
about me," Mr. Hines cried, gratefully, a lump
rising in his throat as he watched her ride away.

The loungers in the store had strolled out on
the porch. "Mis' Cullum cert'n'y is a sister in
Zion," remarked Mr. Trimble, gazing admiringly
at her retreating figure.

"M - m - m—y - e - e - s," admitted Mr. Pinson.
"But," he added, darkly, after a meditative
pause, "Sissy Cullum is a wife, an' the women
o' Jim-Ned, *ez wives*, air liable to conniptions."

Mrs. Cullum jogged slowly along the brown,
wheel-rifted road which followed the windings
of the creek. It was late in November. A
brisk little norther was blowing, and the nuts
dropping from the pecan-trees in the hollows
filled in the dusky stillness with a continuous
rattling sound. There was a sprinkling of belated cotton bolls on the stubbly fields to the right
of the road ; a few ragged sunflowers were still
abloom in the fence corners, where the poke-
berries were red-ripe on their tall stalks.

"I must lay in some poke root for Tobe's
knee-j'ints," mused Mrs. Cullum, as she turned
into the lane which led to her own door-yard.

" ' YOU BETTER PUT ON A THICKER COAT, BUD ' "

"Pore Tobe! them j'ints o' his'n is mighty oncertain. Why, Tobe!" she exclaimed aloud, as her nag stopped and neighed a friendly greeting to the object of her own solicitude, "where air you bound for?"

Mr. Cullum laid an arm across the horse's neck. He was a big, loose-jointed man, with iron-gray hair, square jaws, and keen, steady, dark eyes. "Well, ma," he said, with a touch of reluctance in his dragging tones, "there's a lodge meetin' at Ebenezer Church to-night, an' I got Minty to give me my supper early, so's I could go. I—"

"All right, Tobe," interrupted his wife, cheerfully: "a passel of men prancin' around with a goat oncet a month ain't much harm, I reckon. You go 'long, honey; I'll set up for you."

"Sissy is that soft an' innercent an' mild," muttered Mr. Cullum, striding away in the gathering twilight, "that a suckin' baby could wrop her aroun' its finger—much lessen me!"

About ten o'clock the same night Granny Carnes, peeping through a chink in the wall beside her bed, saw a squad of men hurring afoot down the road from the direction of Ebezener Church. "Them boys is up to some devil*mint*, Uncle Dick," she remarked, placidly, to her rheumatic old husband.

Uncle Dick laughed a soft, toothless laugh. "I ain't begrudgin' 'em the fun," he sighed, turning on his pillow, "but I wisht to the Lord I was along!"

The "boys" crossed the creek below Bishop's

and entered the shinn-oak prairie on the farther
side.

"Nance ast mighty particular about the lodge
meetin'," observed Newt Pinson to Mr. Cullum,
who headed the nocturnal expedition ; "she
know'd it wa'n't the regular night, an' she suspi-
cioned sompn, Nance did."

"Sissy didn't," laughed Tobe, complacently.
"Sissy is that soft an' innercent an' mild that
a suckin' baby could wrop her aroun' its finger
—much lessen me !"

Bud Hines, in the rear with the others, was in
a quiver of excitement. He stumbled along,
shifting Sid Northcutt's rifle from one shoulder
to the other, and listening open-mouthed to Jack
Carter's directions. " You know, Bud," said
that young gentleman, gravely, " it ain't every
man that gets a chance to go on a snipe-hunt.
And if you've got any grit—"

" I've got plenty of it," interrupted Mr. Hines,
vaingloriously. He was, indeed, inwardly—and
outwardly — bursting with pride. " I thought
they tuk me for a plumb fool," he kept saying
over and over to himself. " They 'ain't never
noticed me before 'cepn to make fun of me ; an'
all at oncet Mr. Tobe Cullum an' Mr. Newt Pinson ups an' asts me to go on a snipe-hunt, an'
even p'oposes to give me the best place in it.
An' I've got Mr. Sid's rifle, an' Mr. Jack is tellin' of me how ! Lord, I wouldn't of believed it
ef I wa'n't right here ! Won't ma be proud when
I write her about it !"

" You've got to whistle all the time," Jack

continued, breaking in upon these blissful reflections ; " if you don't, they won't come."

" Oh, I'll whistle," declared Bud, jauntily.

Sam Leggett's snigger was dexterously turned into a cough by a punch in his ribs from Mr. Trimble's elbow, and they trudged on in silence until they reached Buck Snort Gully, a deep ravine running from the prairie into a stretch of heavy timber beyond, known as The Rough.

Here they stopped, and Sid Northcutt produced a coarse bag, whose mouth was held open by a barrel hoop, and a tallow candle, which he lighted and handed to the elate hunter. " Now, Bud," Mr. Cullum said, when the bag was set on the edge of the gully, with its mouth toward the prairie, " you jest scrooch down behind this here sack an' hold the candle. You kin lay the rifle back of you, in case a wild-cat or a cougar prowls up. An' you whistle jest as hard an' as continual as you can, whilse the balance of us beats aroun' an' drives in the snipe. They'll run fer the candle ever' time. An' the minit that sack is full of snipe, all you've got to do is to pull out the prop, an' they're yourn."

" All right, Mr. Tobe," responded Bud, squatting down and clutching the candle, his face radiant with expectation.

The crowd scattered, and for a few moments made a noisy pretence of beating the shinn-oak thickets for imaginary snipe.

" Keep a-whisslin', Bud !" Mr. Cullum shouted, from the far edge of the prairie.

A prolonged whistle, with trills and flourishes,

was the response; and the conspirators, bursting with restrained laughter, plunged into the ford and separated, making each for his own fireside.

Mrs. Cullum was nodding over the hearth-stone when her husband came in. The six girls, from Minty—Jack Carter's buxom sweetheart—to Little Sis, the baby, were along abed. The hands of the wooden clock on the high mantel-shelf pointed to half-past twelve. "Well, pa," Sissy said, good - humoredly, reaching out for the shovel and beginning to cover up the fire, "you've cavorted pretty late this time! What's the matter?" she added, suspiciously; "you ack like you've been drinkin'!"

For Tobe was rolling about the room in an ecstasy of uproarious mirth.

"I 'ain't teched nary drop, Sissy," Mr. Cullum returned, "but ever' time I think about that fool Bud Hines a-settin' out yander at Buck Snort, holdin' of a candle, and whisslin' fer snipe to run into that coffee-sack, I—oh Lord!"

He stopped to slap his thighs and roar again. Finally, wiping the tears of enjoyment from his eyes, he related the story of the night's adventure.

"Air you tellin' me, Tobe Cullum," his wife said, when she had heard him to the end—"air you p'intedly tellin' me that you've took Bud Hines *snipin'*? An' that you've left that sickly, consumpted young man a-settin' out there by hisse'f to catch his death of cold; or maybe git his blood sucked out by a catamount!"

"Shucks, Sissy! replied Tobe; "nothin' ain't

goin' to hurt him. He's sech a derned fool that a catamount wouldn't tech him with a ten-foot pole! An' him a-whisslin' fer them snipe—oh Lord!"

"Tobe Cullum," said Mrs. Cullum, sternly, "you go saddle Buster this minit and ride out to Buck Snort after Bud Hines."

"Why, honey—" remonstrated Tobe.

"Don't you honey me," she interrupted, wrathfully. "You saddle that horse this minit an' fetch that consumpted boy home."

Tobe ceased to laugh. His big jaws set themselves suddenly square. "I'll do no sech fool thing," he declared, doggedly, "an' have the len'th an' brea'th o' Jim-Ned makin' fun o' me."

"Very well," said his wife, with equal determination, "ef you don't go, I will. But I give you fair warnin', Tobe Cullum, that ef you don't go, I'll never speak to you again whilse my head is hot."

Tobe snorted incredulously; but he sneaked out to the stable after her, and when she had saddled and mounted Buster, he followed her on foot, running noiselessly some distance behind her, keeping her well in sight, and dodging into the deeper shadows when she chanced to look around.

"I didn't know Cissy had so much spunk," he muttered, panting in her wake at last across the shinn-oak prairie. "Lord, how blazin' mad she is! But shucks! she'll git over it by mornin'."

Mr. Hines was shivering with cold. He still whistled mechanically, but the hand that held the sputtering candle shook to the trip-hammer thumping of his heart. "The balance of 'em must of got lost," he thought, listening to the lonesome howl of the wind across the prairie. "It's too c-cold for snipe, I reckon. I wisht I'd stayed at home. I c-can't w-whistle any longer," he whimpered aloud, dropping the candle-end, the last spark of courage oozing out of his nerveless fingers. He stood up, straining his eyes down the black gully and across the dreary waste around him. "Mr. T-o-o-be!" he called, feebly, and the wavering echoes of his voice came back to him mingled with an ominous sound. "Oh, Lordy! what is that?" he stammered. He sank to the ground, grabbing wildly for his gun. "It's a cougar! I hear him trompin' up from the creek! It's a c-cougar! He's c-comin' closter! Oh, Lordy!"

"Hello, Bud!" called Mrs. Cullum, cheerily. She slipped from the saddle as she spoke and caught the half-fainting snipe-hunter in her motherly arms.

"Ain't you 'shamed of yourse'f to let a passel o' no-'count men fool you this-a-way?" she demanded, sternly, when he had somewhat recovered himself. "Get up behind me. I'm goin' to take you to Mis' Bishop's, where you belong. No, don't you dassen to tech any o' that trash!"

Mr. Hines, feeling very humble and abashed, climbed up behind her, and they rode away, leaving the snipe-hunting gear, including Sid Northcutt's valuable rifle, on the edge of the gully.

She left him at Bishop's, charging him to swal-

"'THE BALANCE OF 'EM MUST OF GOT LOST'"

low before going to bed a "dost" of the home-brewed chill medicine from a squat bottle she handed him.

"He cert'n'y is weaker'n stump-water," she murmured, as she turned her horse's head; "but he's sickly an' consumpted, an' he's jest about the age my Bud would of been if he'd lived."

And thinking of her first-born and only son, who died in babyhood, she rode homeward in the dim, chill starlight. Tobe, spent and foot-sore, followed warily, carrying the abandoned rifle.

II

Consternation reigned the "len'th an' brea'th" of Jim-Ned. Mrs. Cullum—placid and easy-going Mrs. Tobe—under the same roof with him, actually had not spoken to her lawful and wedded husband since the snipe-hunt, ten days ago come Monday!

"It's plumb scan'lous!" Mrs. Pinson exclaimed, at her daughter's quilting. "I never would of thought sech a thing of Sissy—never!"

"As ef the boys of Jim-Ned couldn't have a little innercent fun without Mis' Cullum settin' in jedgment on 'em!" sniffed Mrs. Leggett.

"Shet up, Becky Leggett," said her mother, severely. "By time you've put up with a man's capers fer twenty-five years, like Sissy Cullum have, you'll have the right to talk, an' not before."

"They say Tobe is wellnigh out'n his mind," remarked Mrs. Trimble. "Ez fer that soft-

headed Bud Hines, he have fair fattened on that
snipe-hunt. He's gittin' ez sassy an' mischee-
vous ez Jack Carter hisse'f."

This last statement was literally true. The
victim of Tobe Cullum's disastrous practical joke
had become on a sudden case-hardened, as it
were. The consumptive pallor had miraculously
disappeared from his cheeks and the homesick
look from his eyes. He bore the merciless chaf-
fing at Bishop's with devil-may-care good-nature,
and he besought Mrs. Cullom, almost with tears
in his eyes, to "let up on Mr. Tobe."

"I was sech a dern fool, Mis' Cullum," he
candidly confessed, "that I don't blame Mr. Tobe
fer puttin' up a job on me. Besides," he added,
his eyes twinkling shrewdly, "I'm goin' to git
even. I'm laying off to take Jim Belcher, that
biggetty drummer from Waco, a-snipin' out Buck
Snort next Sat'day night. He's a bigger idjit
than ever I was."

"You ten' to your own business, Bud, an' I'll
ten' to mine," Mrs. Cullum returned, not un-
kindly. Which business on her part apparently
was to make Mr. Cullum miserable by taking no
notice of him whatever. The house under her
supervision was, as it had always been, a model
of neatness; the meals were cooked by her own
hands, and served with an especial eye to Tobe's
comfort; his clothes were washed and ironed,
and his white shirt laid out on Sunday mornings,
with the accustomed care and regularity. But
with these details Mrs. Cullum's wifely atten-
tions ended. She remained absolutely deaf to

any remark addressed to her by her husband, looking through and beyond him when he was present with a steady unseeing gaze, which was, to say the least, exasperating. All necessary communication with him was carried on by means of the children. "Minty," she would say at the breakfast-table, "ask your pa if he wants another cup of coffee;" or at night, "Temp'unce, tell your pa that Buster has shed a shoe;" or, "Sue, does your pa know where them well-grabs is?" et cætera, et cætera.

The demoralized household huddled, so to speak, between the opposing camps, frightened and unhappy, and things were altogether in a bad way.

To make matters worse, Miss Minty Cullum, following her mother's example, took high and mighty ground with Jack Carter, dismissing that gentleman with a promptness and coolness which left him wellnigh dumb with amazement.

"Lord, Minty!" he gasped. "Why, I was taken snipe-hunting myself not more'n five years ago. I—"

"I didn't know you were such a fool, Jack Carter," interrupted his sweetheart, with a toss of her pretty head; "that settles it!" and she slammed the door in his face.

Matters were at such a pass finally that Mr. Skaggs, the circuit-rider, when he came to preach, the third Sunday in the month, at Ebenezer Church, deemed it his duty to remonstrate and pray with Sister Cullum at her own house. She listened to his exhortations in grim silence, and knelt without a word when he summoned her to wrestle before the Throne of Grace. "Lord," he concluded, after a long and powerful summing up of the erring sister's misdeeds, "Thou knowest that she is travelling the broad and flowery road to destruction. Show her the evil of her ways. and warn her to flee from the wrath to come."

He arose from his knees with a look of satisfaction on his face, which changed to one of chagrin when he saw Sister Cullum's chair empty, and Sister Cullum herself out in the backyard tranquilly and silently feeding her hens.

"She shore did flee from the wrath to come, Sissy did," chuckled Granny Carnes, when this episode reached her ears.

As for Tobe, he bore himself in the early days of his affliction in a jaunty, debonair fashion, affecting a sprightliness which did not deceive his cronies at Bishop's. In time, however, finding all his attempts at reconciliation with Sissy vain, he became uneasy, and almost as silent as herself, then morose and irritable, and finally black and thunderous.

"He's that wore upon that nobody dassent to go anigh him," said Mr. Pinson, solemnly. "An' no wonder! Fer of all the conniptions that ever struck the women o' Jim - Ned, *ez wives*, Sissy Cullum's conniptions air the outbeatenes'."

But human endurance has its limits. Mr. Cullum's reached his at the supper-table one night about three weeks after the beginning of his dis-

cipline. He had been ploughing all day, and
brooding, presumably, over his tribulations, and
there was a techy look in his dark eyes as he seated himself at the foot of the well-spread table,
presided over by Mrs. Cullum, impassive and
dumb as usual. The six girls were ranged on
either side.

"Well, ma," began Tobe, with assumed gayety, turning up his plate, "what for a day have
you had?"

Sissy looked through and beyond him with
fixed, unresponsive gaze, and said never a
word.

Then, as Mr. Cullum afterwards said, "Ole
Satan swep' an' garnish*eed* him an' tuk possession of him." He seized the heavy teacup in
front of him and hurled it at his unsuspecting
spouse; she gasped, paling slightly, and dodged.
The missile, striking the brick chimney-jamb
behind her, crashed and fell shivering into fragments on the hearth. The saucer followed.
Then, Tobe's spirits rising, plate after plate
hurtled across the table; the air fairly bristled
with flying crockery. Mrs. Cullum, after the
first shock of surprise, continued calmly to eat
her supper, moving her head from right to left
or ducking to avoid an unusually well-aimed
projectile.

Little Sis scrambled down from her high chair
at the first hint of hostilities, and dived, scream-
ing, under the table; the others remained in their
places, half paralyzed with terror.

In less time than it takes to tell it, Mr. Cul-

3

lum, reaching out his long arms, had cleared
half the board of its stone and glass ware. Finally he laid a savage hand upon a small old-
fashioned blue pitcher left standing alone in a
wide waste of table-cloth.

At this Sissy surrendered unconditionally.
"Oh, Tobe, fer Gawd's sake!" she cried, throwing out her hands and quivering from head to
foot. "I give in! I give in! *Don't* break the
little blue china pitcher! You fetched it to me
the day little Bud was born! An' he drunk
out'n it jest afore he died! Fer Gawd's sake,
Tobe, honey! I give in!"

Tobe set down the pitcher as gingerly as if it
had been a soap-bubble. Then, with a whoop
which fairly lifted the roof from the cabin, he
cleared the intervening space between them and
caught his wife in his arms.

Minty, with ready tact, dragged Little Sis
from under the table, and driving the rest of
the flock before her, fled the room and shut the
door behind her. On the dark porch she ran
plump upon Jack Carter.

"Why, Jack!" she cried, with her tear-wet
face tucked before she knew it against his breast,
"what are you doing here?"

"Oh, just hanging around," grinned Mr. Carter.

"Gawd be praised!" roared Tobe, inside the
house.

"Amen!" responded Jack, outside.

"An' Tobe Cullum," announced Joe Trimble

at Bishop's the next day, "have ordered up the fines' set o' chiny in Waco fer Sissy."

"It beats *me*," said Newt Pinson; "but I allers did say that the women o' Jim-Ned, *ez wives,* air the outbeatenes' critters in creation!"

THE GROVELLING OF JINNY TRIMBLE

Mrs. Trimble paused half-way down the cotton row and looked over towards the house, where Joe sat on the rickety porch. He was playing a hymn tune. His blond head was laid lovingly against the neck of his fiddle, his eyes were closed, and a beatific smile hovered about his handsome mouth. He accompanied the droning notes with a steady pat of his foot on the floor, and an occasional mellow burst of song.

"Joe Trimble shore can make the fiddle *talk!*" exclaimed his wife, admiringly. "Git up from there, Lodelia!" she added, with sudden sharpness, to a tow-headed little girl in the adjacent row, who had slipped the half-filled cotton-sack from her neck and was squatted upon it. "Git up from there this minit! An' don't you, ner Little Joe, dassen to stop tell them las' rows is picked—ner Randy nuther! It's nigh about sundown, an' yo' pappy 'll be plumb outdone waitin' fer his supper."

Thus admonished, the children went sullenly

to work, the four-year-old Randy snuffling audibly, and she herself with an involuntary sigh of weariness stooped again over the stunted stalks.

The straggling cotton-patch was all but clean— a few down-hanging bolls only showing here and there along the outer rows. The year's crop— flocculent, snow-white—was heaped in a couple of big rail-pens behind the smoke-house, protected by a few planks from the heavy night dews and the rare October rains.

When Mrs. Trimble, with the last bulging sackful on her shoulder, hurried past the porch, Mr. Trimble looked up. "Hi, oh, Jinny!" he cried, affectionately. "I knowed in reason you'd git done ter-day. I'll haul ter the gin fust thing ter-morrer. By jing! th' ain't no sech crap this year up *ner* down Jim-Ned. Fo' bales ef it's a poun'!" And with an air of triumph he struck anew into "Amazing grace."

Mrs. Trimble fetched in wood, made a fire in the open fireplace, and set about getting supper, while Lodelia milked the cow, with Little Joe to hold off the calf.

"Triflin'," his neighbors along Jim-Ned Creek were used without scruple to call Joe Trimble. The air of dilapidation about his small farm more than justified the epithet. The rail fences were rotting visibly; the lop-sided shed, which served at once as barn and stable, threatened to succumb to the breath of the first genuine norther; the cow-pen gate was propped upon a broken hoe-handle; the one-roomed cabin itself, with its ill-built chimney and sagging roof, was, as Mrs.

Newt Pinson said over her snuff-bottle to Granny Carnes : "A plumb sight. An' Jinny Trimble is fair druv to keep Joe hissef fum drappin'
ter pieces. Cert'n'y ef she wa'n't so po'-sperrit-
ed she wouldn't stand it—*ner* him."

But Jinny had stood both with apparent equa-
nimity for a matter of ten years or thereabouts.
She might, indeed, be said to share in the general demoralization going on around her. Time
was when the pretty, saucy, jimp coquette, Jinny
Leggett had, in Jim-Ned vernacular, "kicked"
every marriageable young man in the county
for—the sake of Joe Trimble's blue eyes and
wheedling ways, be it understood. Now the
wifely drudge—thin, sallow-faced, hollow-eyed—
had hardly spunk enough left to borrow a pair
of quilting-frames. As to the cooking, washing,
and ironing, the wood-chopping and water-draw-
ing, tending the ash-hopper and the cattle, grind-
ing the coffee and the axe—all this was as much
a matter of course as taking care of the successive babies and making soft soap. So, for aught
known to the contrary, was the rougher farm-
work, which yearly fell more and more to her
hand, while her lazy, good-looking lord rode
about the country swapping stories and drinks
across his neighbors' gates, or sat on his own
porch playing the fiddle.

"It's *ez* much," said Mrs. Pinson, in a mighty
pucker about Jinny, "ef Joe Trimble hez picked
fo' poun's out'n them fo' bales he's braggin' 'bout.
It's scan'lous! But Jinny hez lost her back-
bone !"

Mrs. Trimble at that moment was putting the supper on the table, and as the aromatic smell of coffee and bacon greeted her husband's nostrils, he hastened to hang up his fiddle and fall to.

"Jinny, honey," he said, leaning back in his chair when he had finished, "I wisht you'd go out ter the lot an' shake down some feed for them steers."

On a crisp November morning ten days later Mr. Trimble took a boisterously affectionate leave of his family and started with his cotton, ginned and baled, for the nearest market-town, something like a hundred miles distant.

"Don't werry concernin' the childern's Chris'-mus, Jinny," he called, gayly, over his shoulder, as he tucked his fiddle into the feed-trough and picked up the long whip; "I'm goin' ter fetch back truck fum Waco ez 'll make yo' eyes bug out'n yo' head — loaf-sugar an' bear-grease an' pep'mint, an' sech. I ain't fergittin' yo' silk dress nuther, honey, ner yo' side-combs."

The children raced after him down the hard road. Mrs. Trimble with reddened eyes watched the brand-new unpaid-for wagon until it disappeared in a mesquite thicket beyond the field. It was drawn by two fine yoke of oxen—great, wide-horned brutes that she had herself raised from calves; the four trim, compact bales were piled upon it; a skillet and coffee-pot swung beneath the hinder axle. Mr. Trimble walked beside the team cracking his whip. Spot, the lean old hound, trotted at his master's heels.

" Th' ain't a laklier man ner a better fiddler
on Jim-Ned," murmured the little woman ; "ner
a studdier church-member — ef he *do* sometime
take a leetle drap too much !"

Anticipation ran high in the Trimble household as the days drifted by and the time drew
near for the return of its lawful head. Marvel-
lous stories of past Christmases kept little Joe
and Randy awake o' nights; up betimes o' mornings, they perched the livelong day on the fence,
their bare red feet tucked under them, their
eyes fixed eagerly on the turn of the road, impatient for the first glimpse of Morg's and
Mike's well-known, wide-spread, shining horns.
Lodelia ran back and forth frantically, her
small soul fairly rent in twain betwixt continual false alarms without-doors and maternal rep-
rimand within. Mrs. Trimble's own excitement
was overlaid by a flustered pretence of indifference.

A sort of incredulous consternation succeeded
this expectant rapture when Christmas came and
went without any sign of the absent husband
and father. The lank, empty stockings depended unnoticed from the chimney, while the frightened children huddled in the falling dusk about
their mother's knees. " Somp'n must ha' happened to Joe ! Oh, I know somp'n turrible has
happened !" she moaned, visions of Joe's blond
curls all dabbled in blood swimming before her
eyes.

But, a little later, Mr. Pinson dropped in to
allay his neighbor's probable fears. He said,

squirming awkwardly in his chair, and with his
eyes on the floor, that he had seen Joe a few days
before in Waco, whither he had hauled his own
cotton.   Ye-es, Joe were well.   Joe had sold his
cotton.   Joe talked like he mought stay awhile
down ther.   "An', an', don't you be oneasy,
Mis' Trimble, Joe's all right.   In fac', Joe was
fiddlin' like a cherry-bin at the wagin-yard the
night afore I lef'."

"It's scan'lous!" cried Mrs. Pinson, when Newt
reported at home how Mrs. Trimble "took" the
news.   "She orter up an' part fum sech a out-
beaten, triflin' houn'—stidder thankin' the Lord
that he ain't on the road som'er's, dead!   Jinny
shore is a po'-sperrited creeter!"

Vague rumors of Joe's gay cuttings-up in the
far-away town floated out to Jim-Ned during the
next few months.   If they reached his wife's ears
she made no sign.   She sat on Sundays, more
forlorn-looking and hollow-eyed than ever, in her
accustomed place in Ebenezer Church, and passed
the time of day meekly with the neighbors on
coming out.   But she shrank from their well-
meant attempts at consolation.   And divining
with innate courtesy that she wished to be alone,
even Mrs. Pinson presently forbore to intrude
upon her.   The front door of the Trimble cabin
was rarely opened, save when its mistress appeared there for a moment, shading her eyes
with her hand and gazing wistfully down the
road.   Randy and little Joe had long abandoned
their lookout on the fence.   A pitiful air of
desolation brooded over the place, the farm and

its belongings running, if possible, still further down at the heel.

Suddenly one morning—it was when the short, sharp winter had fairly broken, the first spring rains had softened the ground, and the pink of peach blossoms was making splashes of color everywhere—Mrs. Trimble appeared in her field walking behind a plough and driving Joe's old sorrel horse, Baldy. She seemed at first to be rather dragged by the plough-handles than to guide them. But she held on with grim determination ; and by the time the garden-patch was turned under, the passers-by admitted that the rows were run ding straight, for a woman.

" Yes," she said, slowly, with her eyes turned away from the questioner's face and a faint flush on her cheek, " me an' the childern has concluded to make the crop 'gins' the time Joe comes back."

Upon this, offers of help poured in upon her. Jim - Ned to a man—and woman — stood by her until her crop was planted. Thereafter, early and late, through the showery spring and the long hot summer, her slight, spare form could be seen, hoe in hand, moving up and down corn or cotton row, accompanied by Lodelia and the two little boys—all patiently and manfully heaping or levelling the brown soil, digging, ditching, fighting grass and tie - vine. There were such tinkerings, too, between times, at fences and gates and pens that towards the end of September it is doubtful whether Joe, had he presented himself, would have recognized his own freehold. The

corn was gathered and cribbed, and the fodder
stacked ; the cotton - patch, green and healthy
under a favoring sky, was dotted with blooms,
amid which the bolls were bursting, white and
thick as pop-corn.

And Joe all this time?   Fiddling in the Waco
wagon-yards at night by the freighters' camp-
fires—fiddling, and swapping stories, and taking
blithely, in season and out of season, that leetle drap too much which, away from home in
particular, was one of his besetting sins ; selling
his cotton for a sum far beyond his expectation ;
laying in groceries and dry-goods enough to run
a sto', by jing ! bragging and swaggering about
the streets one day, and waking out of a drunk-
en sleep the next, to find his wagon rifled of its
contents and his money gone.   An epic, indeed,
might be written concerning Mr. Trimble's three-
quarters of a year "in town."   One goodly steer
after another passed from his possession into the
hands of the unscrupulous sharpers who were
fattening upon him ; and then the brand-new,
unpaid - for wagon, with its bows and sheets ;
even the old gun, belt, and cartridge-box—everything except the beloved fiddle, with which he
continued to make merry, and old Spot, who followed his disreputable master from one drinking-
shop and gambling - hell to another, regarding
him with eyes which had in them something of
the wistfulness that dwelt in Jinny's own.
But all things sooner or later come to an end,
and at last, one day, this lazy, rollicking, good-

humored prodigal bethought himself of Mis'
Trimble and the childern.

The Ebenezer School had just been dismissed.
Mr. Tolliver, the old teacher, was standing on
the door-step in the sunset glow, brooding with
habitual depression over the scant desire for
learning exhibited by the freckled, sunburned,
whooping urchins of both sexes at that moment
scurrying gayly homeward. "Truly," he sighed,
"the fruit of knowledge does not tempt the
youth of James-Edward"—for the old peda-
gogue's classic tongue repudiated the common-
ly accepted name of the district in which he labored. He turned to fasten the door. But a
tumultuous and prolonged burst of laughter drew
his attention to the high-road which ran across
a shinn-oak prairie in front, and curved around
the corner of the school-house. A noisy rabble
of men and boys, some mounted, some on foot,
surged forward in pell-mell disorder. A nearer
approach disclosed the cause of their mirth.
"Bless my soul!" said Mr. Tolliver, from his
post of observation on the school-house steps.
"I believe that is Joseph Trimble!"
It was in truth that home-returning hero. An
axle and a single pair of cart-wheels, dragged by
a small, gaunt, slab-sided ox, served as a support
for a barrel lying upon its side, and braced by a
couple of stanchions. Astride of the barrel, clad
in mud - bespattered rags, and hatless, sat Joe
himself—enthroned as it were—fiddle in hand.
It was not a hymn tune whose notes rang out

on the still afternoon. A tipsy smile illuminated
the player's red face as the bow frisked and
capered over the strings, and his bare heels
against the sides of the barrel kept time to the
profane strains of "Granny, will yo' dog bite?"
A tin cup swung from the spigot in the bung,
and an unmistakable smell of whiskey pervaded
the air around.

"Bless my soul!" ejaculated Mr. Tolliver again,
as the cavalcade swept by, "this is a survival of
the ancient Bacchic festival!"

"How 'bout Mis' Trimble, Joe?" demanded
Mr. Pinson, during one of their frequent con-
vivial halts, and he winked slyly at the crowd as
he took a pull at the tin cup.

"Mis' Trimble? Jinny?" shouted Joe, looking
down with a fatuous smile. "Don't you fret yo'
gizzard 'bout Jinny Trimble! Jinny's goin' ter
be so ding glad ter see me thet she'll fair grub-
ble at my feet!"

And the train, augmented at every cross-road
by some laughter-loving crony, moved noisily
on.

At the moment they emerged from the mesquite thicket, and came in sight of Joe's recon-
structed estate, Mrs. Trimble was at the wood-
pile cutting wood for the supper fire; Randy was
picking up chips in his blue cotton apron; Lodelia and Little Joe were tending the ash-hopper.
The sound of horses' feet, mingled with the hilarious uproar, borne on the mild wind, came floating across the level fields. She lifted her head,
pushing back her sun-bonnet, and stared with

out-starting eyes. Her arm dropped nerveless at her side ; her lips quivered ; her knees shook beneath her. She moved mechanically towards the front gate, followed by her three children.

The procession had halted in the road there. A sudden shamed silence fell upon the crowd—hurried on thus far partly by a spirit of fun, partly by sincere rejoicing in the return of their jovial gossip—at sight of the patient and courageous though poor-spirited little woman coming across the field, her head drooped upon her breast, the heavy axe grasped unconsciously in her hand.

" Hello, Jinny !" called Mr. Trimble, with jaunty assurance, from his perch on the whiskey barrel. " Here I am onct mo' ! Safe *an'* soun'. Pervided with a bar'l o' ginooine rye ! Onloose the latch-string, honey, an' look out fer a rip-roarin' celerbation of these here joyful perce-dences—"

His maudlin laugh was suddenly checked ; his jaws dropped ; he gazed at his wife with dilating eyes. She stood in the open gateway confronting him : her dark eyes, fixed full upon his, were blazing ; her lips were firmly set ; a scarlet spot burned in either sunken cheek ; she looked dangerously like the imperious, high-spirited Jinny Leggett, of whom Joe in his courting days had been mortally afraid.

" Joe Trimble," she said, with terrifying calmness. " shet yo' mouth and git off'n that whiskey barrel !"

Mr. Trimble meekly obeyed, scrambling down

with what grace he could muster, and casting sheepish glances at his followers, huddled breathless and abashed on the farther side of the road.

"Stand out'n the way with yo' onchristian, hell-temptin' fiddle," Mrs. Trimble added, stepping forward.

Joe slunk to one side like a whipped hound; old Spot, after an uncertain, appealing glance around, crept after him.

She lifted the axe.

It was not for naught that the down-trodden wife had chopped wood—aye, and split rails into the bargain, during all these years. The muscles stood out like thongs on the skinny little arm; the wrist was as firm and hard as iron. The axe, poised an instant in the air, caught on its keen edge a gleam of sunlight, then it descended with a sidewise telling blow on the head of the barrel; it rose and fell again, and the seasoned wood splintered and crashed inward : a small deluge of amber-colored liquor gushed over the axle, and ran in a foamy, ambrosial rivulet across the road.

The lean ox turned his head to gaze with mild, surprised eyes at the wrack behind him, then whisked his tail, and resumed his abstracted ruminations.

An involuntary murmur of applause ran through the spectators; every man and boy of them took off his hat. Regret over the waste of so much ginooine rye was lost for the moment in admiration of Mis' Trimble's spunk.

Mrs. Trimble did not acknowledge their pres-

ence by so much as a look. "Lodelia," she ordered, "kiss yo' poppy, an' onhitch that pore
creeter from them wheels, an' give it some feed.
Come erlong, Joe, an' min' you fasten the gate
a'ter you."

Mr. Trimble, completely sobered, mute, and
dumfounded, lifted Randy in his arms, and
walked after his wife towards the cabin, with
little Joe and Spot tagging at his heels.

"Ding my hide, this beats *me!*" exclaimed
Newt Pinson. And clapping spurs to his horse,
he galloped down the road, the demoralized
squad clattering and padding behind him.
"This *beats* me!" he cried again, turning in his
saddle to look back.

Mrs. Trimble was nowhere visible.

Joe was at the wood-pile chopping wood.

The next day, and for many a long day thereafter, Mr. Trimble, with a cotton-sack hung about
his neck, dragged on his knees through the cotton-patch, reaping, as Mrs. Pinson sarcastically
observed, where he had not sowed. His was
now the hand that shook down feed for Baldy
and the solitary steer. He it was who turned
the windlass at the deep well and packed in the
wood; he tended the ash-hopper and set the
clothes-lines; he even went so far as to get up
of mornings and make the fire.

He seemed, moreover, pitiably anxious lest he
should by accident leave some of these unaccus-
tomed tasks undone. Jim-Ned looked on, shaking its head, not knowing what to make of this
extraordinary transformation, and momentarily

expecting, if the truth were told, a fall from grace.

Joe's old exuberance of spirit, too, had given place to a kind of timid humility; his merry eyes were downcast and dull; his contagious laugh was hushed; his fiddle hung unused on the cabin wall, gathering cobwebs on its crooked neck.

Mrs. Trimble, though outwardly calm, was inwardly exultant. "It's good fer so' eyes," she said to herself, watching Joe pass the porch with the cotton slung over his shoulder, and remembering all her own pains and mortifications. The men made way for her with marked deference when she took her place in the Amen corner of Ebenezer Church, with Mr. Trimble, dashed and browbeaten, at her elbow. The women gazed at her in hushed wonder. "Yes, it's good fer so' eyes!" she repeated again and again in the first transport of her freedom.

But, as time passed, a vague feeling of discomfort crept into her secret soul. Something was missing. What was it? Was it the old-time, half-contemptuous, wholly cordial regard of her neighbors, who now held respectfully aloof, eyeing her askance as if afraid of her? Was it the strange silence around her own fireside at night, where Joe sat with his head hanging and his eyes fixed vacantly on the flames, and the children cowered in the corner, dumbly questioning, first his dull face and then her own?

One night Mr. Trimble, coming in with an armful of firewood, found his wife sitting alone by the hearth. The children were abed. She

4

had her apron to her eyes and was crying silently.

"Gawd-a-mighty, Jinny!" he cried, throwing
down the wood and running to her in alarm,
"what hev I done? Ain't the wood chopped
ter suit ye? Ain't the wash - kittle filled? I
b'leeve in my soul I've fergot them clo's-lines.
I'll go an' prop 'em this minit!"

"'T-t'ain't the lines," whimpered Jinny.

"Ain't the ash-hopper sot? Ain't—"

"Oh-h, Joe!" sobbed his wife, "I don't keer
nothin' 'bout the ash-hopper! I want to hear
you laugh onct mo'! I want to see you cavort
roun' Jim-Ned like you used to! I'm plumb
tired o' havin' them fool men look at me like
I wuz wearin' the britches! I'm sick o' hearin'
Mis' Pinson an' Granny Carnes talk like you
didn't have spunk enough to spank Randy! I
wisht ter the Lord I hadn't of made no crop!
I'm so lonesome! Oh, *Joe!*"

And she jumped up and hid her face on his
breast.

"Lord, Jinny!" he exclaimed, blushing red
with delight, and as bashful as ever he was in
his courting days. "Lord, honey, them women
folks ain't wuth shucks, nohow. I don't keer
nothin' 'bout Mis' Pinson an' Granny Carnes!
But ef Newt Pinson er any of that gang hez dast
ter look cross-eyed at you, I'll tek the hair off'n
the'r hide afore mornin'." And his eyes grew
suddenly sombre.

"Oh no, no!" she cried, clinging to him.
"Not that-a-way! Not that-a-way!"

The result of their long conference was that
Joe, the next morning, leaving the few scattering
unpicked bolls in the field to Lodelia and Little
Joe, mounted Baldy, and rode the length and
breadth of Jim - Ned, inviting his neighbors to
a play-party at his house the following night.
And the neighbors came, bubbling over with
good-humor and curiosity.

And so it was that in the presence of the Ebenezer congregation Jinny Trimble "grubbled"
at her husband's feet! She took the fiddle from
the wall with her own hands and gave it to him.
She consulted him audibly, and in a tone of
deep humility, concerning the disputed steps of
"Peeping at Susan"; she fetched him his pipe,
and hovered over him, radiant, while he lighted
it; she ran out when the fire in the big fireplace
burned low, and came in, ostentatiously carrying
a heavy back-log, her head lifted defiantly and
her dark eyes dancing.

Joe's blue eyes shone back at her. He fid-
dled like one inspired ; his gay laugh rang out
above the shuffling feet of the young men and
women winding the mazes of "Weev'ly Wheat."

Never had Mr. Trimble been so hilarious or so
masterful.

Never was Mrs. Trimble so abject.

"Verily," observed old Mr. Tolliver to Mr.
Pinson, "the Prodigal of James - Edward hath
the fatted calf, and a ring upon his finger!"

"Jinny hev drapped back," said Mrs. Pinson
to Granny Carnes out in the brush-arbor, where
they were overseeing the supper. "Her spunk

hev died a natch'l death.   She cert'n'y hev grubbled !"

All the same, the next day, when Mr. Trimble hinted that he shore orter haul them five
bales of cotton o' his'n to Waco, Jinny put her
foot down.

II

FLYING THREADS

THE SONG OF THE OPAL

JOHN DENE stood for a moment in the squat doorway of his rock hut, his slouch hat brushing the heavy lintel, and his square shoulders almost touching the rough framework on either side; then, mounting the short outer flight of steps that led to the flat roof above, he seated himself on the rude parapet and bared his forehead to the crisp October night wind. He breathed into his lungs with conscious delight the aromatic perfume of the "rosum" weed, whose yellow blossoms, faintly visible in the starlight, overlaid the abrupt slopes and wide levels of the prairie stretching away to his right. On his left, the mountains, a mile or so away, were banked like a semicircle of soft dark cloud against the clear sky. There was a fire-fly or two astir among the late-blooming flowers, whose faint odor came up to him in little balmy puffs from the garden patch about the cabin door; and a night bird now and then flitted on stealthy wing from one clump of trees in the hollow below to another. But it was very still, so still that he could hear the musical drip-drop of the water falling from the spring into the reedy pool at the head of the hollow; the howl of a coyote somewhere on Quarry Mountain rang so distinctly on his ear that he clutched his rifle and threw it instinctively to his shoulder. But he smiled and laid it on his knee again as the echo of a burst of laughter, familiar, cheery, prolonged, came floating across the valley from the store over in Logan's Gap.

They were in truth talking about him there. Or, to be more accurate, old Uncle Dicky Crawls, tilted back against the chimney jamb, in a rawhide-bottomed chair, with a cob pipe between his toothless gums, was talking, and "the boys" were listening respectfully. A handful of gnarled and knotted mesquite roots blazed in the wide fireplace by way of a light, the dingy kerosene-lamp on one end of the counter barely illuminating with its dim circle the greasy pages of the ledger wherein Joe Matthews, the store-keeper, was perfunctorily recording the business of the day. The boys, long, lank, and middle-aged for the most part, with grave faces and keen, humorous eyes, sat in an irregular semi-circle about the hearth. The store door was open: the flat-topped mountain on the farther side of the Gap seemed to stand squarely across it in the luminous darkness; the wire fence, zig-zagging along the hard, smooth road, gleamed like a strand of silver thread where the out-streaming firelight found and touched it. Half a dozen horses, whose high-pommelled saddles were adorned with hairy, many-coiled lariats,

were hitched to the saplings on the wind-shel-
tered side of the store, and as many dogs lounged
on the steps or dozed under their owners' chairs
within.

"When I seen him come a - ridin' up to the
Gap las' Crismus a year," Uncle Dicky was saying, "I knowed lak a shot thet he wuz a-hidin'
out. Some o' you boys 'lowed ez how he looked
mighty biggaty ; an' thet this here pre-cink wa'n't
a-goin' to hol' him mo'n a week 'thout a inter-
view with a rope an' a lim'. But yo' unk Dicky
ain't off'n mistakened, an' yo' unk Dicky tuk him
by the han' at oncet. An' now they ain't no man
nowher's roun' the Gap who hez mo' the respeck
of his feller-citizens than Jack Dene. Naw, sir !
I hain't no doubt whatsomedever thet he hez
killed his man wher' he come fum. An' I don't
no mo' b'leeve his name air Jack Dene than I
b'leeve Billy Pitt thar hed that wrastle with a
catamount t'other day over on Jim-Ned."

Billy Pitt drew a playful bead on Uncle Dicky
with his stubby but unerring rifle, and joined
in the good-natured laugh at his own expense—
that resonant laugh which, echoing across the
still valley, found John Dene a-dreaming on his
house-top.

"I ain't keerin' what his name mought be,"
he said, when the laugh subsided ; "he's mighty
fa'r an' squar', Jack is."

"Thet's so," assented Matthews, looking up
from his ledger, but keeping an inky finger on
his column of figures ; "an' he's nigh 'bout the
contrivinest pusson I ever seen. Thet thar rock

house o' his'n, which he hev quayried the rock
an' put up hisse'f, I 'low it's the beatenes' house
in creation. Made out'n rock, ever' bif, sir,
chimbly an' all, an' a reg'lar chimbly-she'f over
the fireplace! It's 'stonishin' how thet rock do
cut, anyhow," he concluded, meditatively.

"He 'ain't teched the ole quayry, hez he?"
asked Red Nabers from his corner of the fireplace.

"God-a-mighty. naw!" cried Uncle Dicky,
bringing his chair down to the floor with a jerk.
"Thet ole quayry were here when I come to
Comanche County; an' thet wuz befo' the Injuns
lef'. I heered the tales 'bout them Digger people fum a chief hisse'f. An' thet ole quayry ain't
a-goin' to be teched—not to git rock out'n—
whilse my head air hot."

"Co'se not, Unk Dicky, co'se not," said Matthews, to whom the old quarry really belonged,
in a soothing tone. "Jack Dene 'ain't teched
the ole quayry. Didn't I he'p him haul ever'
las' one o' them slabs thet his cabin air made
out'n? Howsomedever, he does bogue roun'
thar mighty studdy a-s'archin' for them turkles
Uncle Dicky's been a-noratin' 'bout ever sence I
were born."

"Thet's all fa'r an' squar'," said the old man,
tilting his chair back and resuming his pipe.
"He air welcome to dig fer them leetle turkles
ez much ez he pleases. I don't keer. I wisht
to the Lord he could mek out what them Digger
people wuz a'ter."

"Is it p'intedly yo' 'pinion, Unk Dicky," inquired Green Nabers, the stalwart twin of Red, "thet the ole quayry hes been dug fer di'mon's?"

"Waal, ez to *di'mon's*," replied Uncle Dicky, deliberately, "I ain't sho in my min'. But what *air* sho air thet oodles o' time ago thet ole quayry wuz dug by somebody *fer* somepn. An' thet somepn wa'n't buildin' rock, nuther. Thar's the quayry, an' thar's them turkle-shape rocks all scattered roun' the aidge o' the pit; an' ever' las' one o' them turkles hev been busted open. 'Tain't one in a bushel, 'cordin' to my calkilation, ez hed anything inside. But I hev foun' 'em myse'f with a holler in the middle, an' I hain't no doubt whatsomedever thet in thet holler them Digger people foun'—min' yer, I don't edzackly say *di'mon's*, but somepn of nigh 'bout ekal vally. I 'ain't nuver come 'crost a whole turkle yit, an' ef Jack Dene kin fine one whilse he air a-hidin' out an' a-puttin' in o' his time, I'll be pow'ful rej'iced."

John Dene, sitting alone on the roof of his odd little hut, would have laughed outright had he known that the chief reason for his popularity in Logan Gap Precinct was due to a belief that he was in hiding for a crime—a murder, perhaps—committed "wher' he come fum." Yet his neighbors would have sympathized in a hardly less degree with the real cause of his presence among them. Restless themselves, nomads by instinct, wrought of the stuff from which pioneers are moulded, they at least would have understood that nameless feeling, so inexplicable to

the conservatism of his family, which had made
of him—John Dene, of Dene Place—a wanderer.
and, the more pious among his kindred did not
scruple to add, a vagabond on the face of the
earth. He had it, perhaps—who knows?—this
strain of lawlessness—from the beautiful savage
woman whom his far-away ancestor had married
somewhere over seas, and brought to his stately
home in England to die. She had sent down to
him too, they said, glancing at her portrait, her
bright tawny hair, and the soft, yellowish brown
eyes with their curious-shifting lights, and her
firm, slim hands, and lithe, straight body. Any-
way, concluded the prim, angular Denes, with
a touch of scorn in their dry voices, it was
not the Dene blood that had sent him when a
mere lad gypsying about green English lanes;
and later, when the vast estate came into his
own hands, drove him irresistibly from its power
and responsibility into barbarous and unknown
countries.

He sighed a little in the darkness now, as a
memory of that fair, far-away home of his boyhood came to him with a breath of the English
flowers abloom in his garden patch. But he laid
his hand, palm downward, upon the giant slab
that roofed his hut, and at the touch a curious
sense of freedom and content seemed to thrill
along his arm and expand his heart.

"They manage well enough without me
there," he said to himself; and a smile, which
was not in the least cynical, curled the lip under his long, brown mustache, as he thought

of the upright and respectable Dene who managed Dene Place, while its owner, the vagabond Jack, loafed away his existence on the frontier of Texas.

He gathered his rifle into the hollow of his arm and stood up, casting, as was his wont, a last look over the valley before going down into his cabin. He uttered a sudden exclamation, startled by the glimmer of a light over the crest of Quarry Mountain. It seemed to be moving along the upper edge of the old quarry, now dipping out of sight, now twinkling like a star against the dark blue of the sky, as if the hand that held it were lifted high above the owner's head. Jack frowned; he was almost as jealous of the old quarry as Uncle Dicky himself. "Who can be prowling around there this time of night, I wonder?" he muttered.

He followed the movements of the flickering torch until it vanished suddenly in the neighborhood of the burned thicket. "Some of Crawls's boys hunting wild-cat," he decided, finally, as he turned to descend the stone stairway.

It was not yet sunrise the next morning when he started across the valley for his daily walk to the mountains. The pale disk of the harvest-moon hung yet in the vaporous sky, with one slowly fading star at its side. But a rosy light was shimmering along the edges of the eastern horizon, and a brisk west wind was lifting the misty shadows from the hollows. His own step was as elastic and springy as the brown turf beneath his feet. A dispassionate observer watch-

ing him as he made his way between the ragged
cotton-rows, with the shaggy retriever at his
heels, might have conceded that the Denes did
well to be angry. This tall figure, supple and
erect, which appeared to such advantage in the
simple frontier dress; this manly, handsome face,
with its careless air of independence and content
—what credit would not these have reflected upon
the family in general had their owner but seen fit
to follow the traditions of the family!

He dipped a wooden bucket in the reed-fringed
pool below the spring, and carried it brimming
to Roland his horse, stabled in a rude shed on the
farther side of the field, then strode whistling on
his way. He followed the little trail which he had
himself made up the steep face of the mountain.
On the level top he paused and looked back. The
valley below was steeped in a soft grayish shadow,
but the outlying prairie in its yellow mantle was
already agleam with the morning sun. Beyond
stretched a chain of pyramidal, flat-topped hills,
cut at almost regular intervals by clean gaps,
through which glowed purple inner distances.
From the cabins dotted about the prairie thin
spirals of blue smoke were rising; and in the
fields about them, white with bursting cotton-
bolls, he could see the figures of women and
children moving to and fro. A few horses were
hitched already to the saplings around the store
in the Gap, and a mover's wagon, with dingy
cover, was creeping slowly townward along the
white road.

He gazed a moment at the familiar picture

spread out beneath him, and went leisurely on
across the rock-strewn ridge. The wild thyme
crushed by his feet filled all the air with heart-
some fragrance; the thickets of prickly-pear
were ablaze with the red and gold of ripening
fruit; the dwarf shinn-oaks, loaded with clusters
of dark, shining acorns, were overlaid here and
there with a fine, filmy net-work of love-vine,
which was radiant with dew-drops; a mocking-
bird sang in the red-haw tree near the mouth of
the new quarry; a squirrel, with bushy tail curled
over his back, ran slowly across an open space
beyond, defying the weaponless hunter. When
he came around the point of burned thicket so
plainly visible from his own house-top he stopped
abruptly; the dog uttered a low growl, instantly
hushed at an imperious gesture from his master. A woman was sitting on the edge of the old
quarry. Her face was turned away from him,
but the outlines of her form were young and gracious in the close-fitting black gown she wore;
her throat arose full and white from the kerchief
knotted loosely about it; her bare head, crowned
with a wavy coil of golden-bronze hair, was small
and shapely. Her hands were lying idly in her
lap, and he saw, as he drew nearer, that in one
of them she held a short, thick, almost grotesque-
looking hammer. A little pile of stones lay in a
heap by her side. He continued to advance noiselessly while noting these details, and he stood
quite near her on the ledge of gray rock before
she seemed aware of his presence. When she
turned her head with a faint, startled cry, he was

not surprised to find her beautiful and young. He
had expected, somehow, just this delicate, oval
face, with its velvety, magnolia-leaf pallor; these
golden - brown eyes, with their phosphorescent
depths, the long curling lashes, the slender dark
brows, the scarlet lips, and round girlish chin.
Speech failed him utterly for the second during
which they gazed into each other's eyes; she
with her first look of surprise changing visibly
from frowning inquiry to a kind of troubled delight; he with a strange, confused stopping and
starting of his pulses that thrilled him from head
to foot.

"Pray, do not let me disturb you," he stammered at length. "I—I was only passing by."

"Are you come from far?" was her unexpected response. Her voice was singularly low
and musical; the flavor of her speech was
distinctly foreign, though the words were pronounced correctly and with a kind of quaint
precision.

He had taken off his hat, and he made a gesture with it towards his cabin, whose flat roof
gleamed whitely in the valley below. "There is
my home," he said; then catching, as if by in-
spiration, her real meaning, he added: "Yes. I
come from England."

"From England." She repeated the words
after him slowly; and another question rose into
her eyes and trembled perceptibly on her lips;
but she lowered her eyelids suddenly and remained silent.

"Are you searching for the jewel?" he asked,

with a smile and a significant glance at the hammer in her lap.

Her colorless face grew a shade paler; her fingers tightened their grasp about the clumsy handle of the hammer. "Yes," she replied, gravely, after a momentary pause. But, springing to her feet, she shook the fragments of stone and moss from her skirts, and went on, in a lighter tone, "It is a foolish old legend; but I suppose everybody who hears it comes up and tries to find the opal—and so I come too."

She drew a black woollen scarf over her head as she spoke, and gathered its folds under her chin; then, with a slight formal gesture of adieu, she stepped into the path and went rapidly down the mountain-side, bounding from ledge to ledge with the grace and fleetness of a young fawn. When she had at last disappeared from his sight, Dene walked deliberately to a rocky recess near by, and drew from its hiding-place his own hammer. He looked at it curiously a moment, turning it over and over in his hand; then, with a quick upward jerk of his elbow, he sent it spinning into the air, and watched its downward course as it leaped clanging from point to point, and dropped heavily into a brier-grown ravine below. "I will never use it again," he said, with a whimsical laugh. "I have found the jewel of the old quarry. Who can she be?" he went on. "Where did she come from? Not from Logan Gap Pre-cinct, surely. Ah! I will ask Uncle Dicky. *Are you come from far?* Now. why should she have asked me that? Have I

5

ever heard before that the jewel of the old quarry is an opal ?"

He threw himself at full length upon the ground, and took from the pocket of his blue flannel overshirt a little volume of *Border Ballads*. But the morning's adventure had gone to his head. With his eyes fixed steadily upon the printed page, he caught himself repeating mechanically, *Are you come from far? Are you come from far?*

He closed the book with a snap, and got up. "I think I'll go down to the store and get my mail," he declared, aloud.

The sunlight lay warm and quivering on the reaches of yellow flowers and the clumps of purple thistle abloom on the wind-swept ridges of the prairies. There was a twitter of nonpareils in among the feathery branches of the scattering mesquite bushes ; and at almost every turn of the winding path a whir of wings sounded beneath his feet, and a covey of young partridges arose with shrill cries, and dropped and disappeared again under the warm shelter of the weeds. As he approached the store a horseman came riding swiftly down the Gap from the west. The silver ornaments of his bridle shone through the cloud of gray dust which enveloped him. A second horse, without saddle or bridle, followed a few paces behind him. He halted in front of the store, and was courteously asking of Matthews, as Dene came up, directions to Ranger's Spring, some two or three miles distant. The horse he bestrode was a fine, powerfully built iron-gray, with black flowing mane and tail; the other, which had stopped in the shadow of the mountain, and was daintily cropping the short mesquite grass, was a small, beautifully formed bay mare, whose skin had the gloss and smoothness of satin. A genuine feeling of admiration stirred Dene at the sight of these two handsome animals, and he glanced up at their owner with the ready compliment of the frontiersman on his lips. But the greeting died in his throat, and he involuntarily fell back a step or two. The new-comer was a man long past middle-age—old in years, perhaps, though a look of almost brutal strength pervaded his whole person. His wrinkled face, half hidden by a bushy white beard which descended almost to his knees, was brown as time-stained parchment; his dark, deeply sunken eyes glowed like carbuncles beneath thick, bristly brows; his long, hooked nose was thin, with narrow nostrils that closed curiously with each indrawn breath. His legs, as he sat erect upon the tall horse, seemed much too short for his thick square body, and his powerful-looking arms much too long; his brown, vein-knotted hands were misshapen and large, the finger-nails claw-like in their length and sharpness. Altogether he was a sinister-looking personage, and Dene was sensible of something like a feeling of relief when he replaced his wide-brimmed hat upon his head and rode away. The mare threw up her pretty head in response to a low whistle, and galloped lightly after him.

"What the d—l is he doin' roun' yer agin?" It was Uncle Dicky who spoke. He was stand-

ing on the door-step, gazing after the stranger,
his wrinkled old face expressing as much dislike
as its genial outlines would permit. "He ain't
a'ter no good, I'll lay. What the d—l does he
want?"

"A rope and a limb, I reckon," said Dene,
good-naturedly, quoting one of Uncle Dicky's
familiar sayings. "Who is he, anyhow, Uncle
Dicky?"

"Hello, Jack! howdy? He's a durn Mexican—thet's what he is. He uscter call hisse'f
Don Hosy. I d' know what he mought call hisse'f now. I 'ain't seen him sence '67, an' thet's
nigh twenty year ago, jis a'ter I come home fum
the wah. They wa'n't scarcely no white folks
out yer then. Me an' Jim Crump wuz campin'
down yunder at Ranger's Spring, an' this yer Don
Hosy wuz layin' roun' yer a-doin' of the Lord
knows what. He hed a gal long o' him which he
purtended wuz his own chile. An' I don't no
mo' b'leeve thet gal wuz Don Hosy's chile than I
b'leeve—" . The speaker's eyes wandered vaguely
around the group of listeners.

"No yer don't, Unk Dicky!"

"I ain't a-honin ter be a eggsample."

"'Light on Joe Crump; he's been a-braggin'."

Uncle Dicky grinned. "Waal," he continued,
"thet gal wuz here 'long o' the Mexican one day,
an' the nex' day she wa'n't nowher's to be seen.
An' ef I'd of had my way, Don Hosy'd of had a
rope an' a lim' *then*. Durn his yaller hide! what's
he purtendin' he don't know whar Ranger's
Spring is fer?"

"Mighty fine hosses he's got," ventured one of the boys.

"An' I'd swear on a stack o' Bibles high ez this sto' thet he stole 'em," retorted the old man, angrily.

Dene followed Matthews into the store, and asked if there were any letters for him. Matthews went behind the counter, and took from under it the candle-box that served as a post-office, and grabbled among the miscellaneous contents. He handed out a package or two, a bundle of newspapers, and a thick square envelope bearing a foreign post-mark.

"Hasn't that fishing-tackle of mine—" Dene began; he stopped abruptly. Uncle Dicky had returned to his seat by the fireplace, and Matthews was addressing him across the counter:

"Hez that furrin gal got her school, Unk Dicky?"

"Sech a fool time o' year ter git up a school," put in Red Nabers, from the doorway, "an' all the childern in the cotton-patch, an' the Lord knows when the crap 'll be in. 'Sides, who's knowin' ef the gal air fitten to teach?"

"Shet yo' mouth, Red," said Uncle Dicky, shortly. "She hev been tried by the school boa'd in the town o' Comanche—"

"Eggsamined ye mean, Unk Dicky," corrected Billy Pitt.

"She hev been tried by the school boa'd in the town o' Comanche," repeated the old man, ignoring the abashed young Billy, "an' Doc Hamilton hev giv' her her papers, an' I don't keer if ever'

blame chile in the pre-cink air in the cotton-
patch. I nuver seen my ole woman an' Polly's
gal childern tek sech a streak to anybody befo'
in all my born days, an' thar in my house thet
gal air goin' to stay, school er no school, long's
we kin keep her."

"She's kind o' furrin lak, ain't she?" asked
Matthews, timidly.

"I d' knaw, an' I don't keer. She kin speak
United States, an' she kin keep Polly's gal childern out'n mis-cheef; an' I'll lay she air caperbul
o' teachen ary voter in this here doggon settlement, much less the childern."

"Co'se, Unk Dicky, co'se," admitted Matthews. "Hello, Jack! ye goin'? Ye mus' of
come to git a chunk o' fire."

Jack heard neither this nor the other friendly
sarcasms which were flung after him as he quitted the store. *She* had come to stay, then. She
felt evidently the same romantic interest in the
legend of the old quarry that had stirred himself
from the moment he had set foot in this remote
little valley. She would be often there, no doubt;
she would— He pulled himself together, with
a short laugh, and set resolutely to work in his
little field.

"I cannot get that girl out of my head, and I
am not going to try," he murmured that night,
in a half-aggrieved tone; "and, by Jove! I'll
take her some flowers to-morrow."

He was walking impatiently up and down the
narrow garden path in the odorous dusk. The
few hardy roses glimmered palely on the over-

grown bushes; they were almost scentless. But there was a pungent perfume from the marigolds in the heart of the asparagus bed; by daylight these were a blaze of vivid orange. A straggling array of blue and white larkspur filled all one corner of the patch; a mass of brown gold-dusted nasturtiums shone against the sombre wall of the cabin, and the ragged mignonette clustered about the door-step was still in bloom. "Yes," he repeated, "to-morrow I will take her some flowers."

He saw her the next morning long before he reached the foot of the mountain. She was coming down the winding path; her shawled head was bent upon her breast. He could see her slender form now clearly defined against the blue sky, now moving between gray masses of rock. Once she stopped and stooped; he felt sure that she was hiding her hammer in some fern-hung cleft.

He waited for her by a lichen-covered bowlder jutting out from the abrupt curve of the mountain. He thought that a faint look of pleasure came into her eyes when she caught sight of him: and as she drew near he greeted her silently, holding out the flowers, a great awkward dewy posy. "I thank you, señor," she said, simply, taking them, and looking at him over them with wonderful shining eyes, golden-brown as the nasturtiums themselves.

He had meant to tell her of the garden-patch about his cabin door, and of the homely mother flowers he had planted there, but before he could bring himself to speak she was gone.

The next day he was up betimes. A monotonous, windless rain was falling, the sort of rain
through which the bob-whites call, and which
seems to hush every other living thing on the
prairie into silence. In spite of it he went up
to the quarry, telling himself persistently that
she could not possibly be there, yet wholly taken
aback when he did not find her there.

Twenty-four hours later the rain was over, and
the October sun warmer and more golden still on
the clean-washed bowlders. She was there. He
heard the little clicking sound of her hammer as
he came up the trail. She received his flowers
as before, with a kind of gentle gravity. And
this time he found it easy enough to say: "They
are all English flowers. I planted them around
my cabin yonder when I first came. And you've
no idea how they bloom. If the gardener—if
some of the people at home who grow flowers
could see them, they would turn green with
envy."

"Why did you come?" she demanded, abruptly.

Again he divined the undercurrent of her
thought. "Oh," he replied, a trifle embarrassed, "I can hardly say. I had a restless sort
of feeling that seemed to drive me, and I drifted
about the world until I found myself here. The
place suited me, and so I have stayed on. I suppose I shall have to go back some day."

"When you have found the opal?" Her tone
was light, but a frown contracted her smooth forehead as she spoke.

"Yes, when I have found the opal," he said, flushing at a sudden mental vision of his hammer flying out into space and dropping downward.

"Do you know the tradition?" she asked. Her eyes were fixed on the little rock hut in the valley.

"I know Uncle Dicky's version of it," he replied, smiling.

"There is a beautiful and wonderful jewel—an opal—which may be found here—" she began, in measured monotone.

"In a turtle-shaped stone. I know," he interrupted, gayly.

"But it is not a jewel only," she went on, unheeding; "it is a talisman that brings to its possessor riches and power and—oh, I know not what beside." Surely a cold pallor was creeping over her lovely face. "They are very rare, those jewels. And they say that only a man or a woman of the slave people can find them."

"Slave people!" he echoed, inquiringly.

"I forgot that you do not know," she answered, turning her large eyes upon him and smiling wistfully. "A long, oh, a very long time ago, a people, a dark and terrible people, used to come here from—from another country to seek for those jewels. But they had not the power themselves to find them. And they brought with them the strange, beautiful white people whom they had conquered and made to be their slaves. And it was that of all the people in the whole world those slaves only might

find those jewels. So the masters sat and
watched with eyes like coals of fire while the
white slaves digged and brought up the little
turtle-shaped stones from the quarry. And it
was only once in a great while that an opal was
found in the little stones; and then there was
strife and bloodshed among the masters. And
many slaves died to find one opal. Oh yes, the
masters were dark and terrible, but the slaves
were white and lovely. The men were tall and
strong and beautiful "—she lifted her eyes that
said *like you* to his, and then dropped them so
that the long, silken lashes rested on her white
cheek—"and the women were lithe and graceful—"

"Like you," he breathed involuntarily.

A faint flush passed over her face and died
away along her full throat. "They say," she
presently added, looking up suddenly, "that
some of those slave people still live in that far
country and elsewhere, and that if they came
they might find the opal for their masters."

"If they found it they would most likely
keep it for themselves. I should," he declared,
lightly.

"Oh, you would not dare!" she cried, her
voice sharpened by some inexplicable feeling;
it sounded like terror. "But it is a foolish tale,"
she resumed, more naturally, rising and stepping
down into the trail.

He followed her hastily as she began the descent. She heard his footsteps behind her and
paused, looking back at him over her shoulder.

"Do you know," he found himself saying before he knew it—"do you know that I do not even know your name?"

"My name is Atla," she replied, after a momentary hesitation. And she sped rapidly on her way.

He returned to the quarry. *Atla!* It seemed to him as if he ought to have known it without the telling, that soft-syllabled name—the only name that could ever have been hers. He did not find it strange that she should not have told him her surname. Let that be for the outside world. He did not wish to know it. He would be glad for her to have no other for him until she should be called Atla Dene! "And why not?" he reasoned, as if in answer to the inevitable arguments of all the Denes. "Why should she not be my wife? I have never looked at a woman in all my life before. I will never look at any other after her. I am my own master, and if I can win her, why—so much for the Denes!"

After that there were many meetings on the mountain-top in the hazy dawn of the sweet Indian-summer mornings. Sometimes she did not come, and then the day was a blank to him, though he busied himself as usual about his field and cabin, and hunted with ardor betweenwhiles over the browning prairies and up the leaf-strewn mountain ravines. He rarely saw any of the Gap folks nowadays. He kept purposely away from the store, where, had he but known it, his "keepin' comp'ny" with the new school-teacher was a topic of friendly interest.

"I seen 'em a-settin' on the aidge o' the ole quayry," Uncle Dicky told the boys, "when I wuz boguein' roun' thar 'mongst the rocks. An' I 'lowed innardly ez how they mus' be gittin' ready to jine. Lord! it air plumb natchl fer young folks ter jine. Yo' unk Dicky hev been thar."

To this simple-minded people there was nothing strange or unconventional in these early morning meetings on Quarry Mountain. Jack Dene was "courtin'," that was all. And by-and-by there would come the wedding, and an infair, perhaps, at Uncle Dicky's, at which all the girls and boys about the Gap would dance. This love affair between the man who was "hidin' out" and the soft-voiced "furrin" young teacher who came down from the mountain of mornings to marshal her tow-headed flock into the log school-house, and the unexplained stay of Don José, who rarely showed himself at the Gap, however, were the subjects mostly discussed by the circle around Matthews's mesquite fire.

Dene, who had never seen Don José since the day of his arrival, had long ago forgotten the evil-favored old Mexican.

One morning, when he seated himself as usual beside the young girl on the edge of the quarry, he was conscious of some change in her appearance. It puzzled him for a moment, and then he made it out to be her dress. She wore white— she whom he had always seen robed in sombre black. A curious sort of rapture possessed him as he looked at the slight figure in its girlish

gown of clinging wool. He bent towards her,
his lips almost touching her hair, and murmured
some words inarticulate even to himself. But he
started back in dismay when she raised her eyes
to his. She had been weeping. Her cheeks,
usually so pale, were flushed, and her eyelids
were swollen and heavy. He turned away troubled and embarrassed, and began pulling nervously at a tuft of thyme which grew in a fissure
of the ledge beside him. The loose root gave
way suddenly, and a stone detached itself from
the crevice and dropped out. He caught it as it
fell. A thrill of excitement stirred him as he
turned it over in his palm. Here was at last one
of Uncle Dicky's "turkles"—a small oval of dark,
corrugated rock. He laid it on the ledge and
seized the hammer lying in Atla's lap. An exclamation broke from her which he neither heard
nor heeded. He struck a vigorous blow, and the
two halves of the sphere flew apart.

Was it a bit of glowing red-hot coal which fell
from the pink, almond-shaped cavity and lay
throbbing and quivering upon the gray ledge?
Was it a great drop of shining, transparent dew
with a heart of greenish flame? Was it a living,
leaping, azure-tipped blaze? A sheaf of ardent,
purple-shotted rays? He uttered a cry of admiration as he picked it up.

"See, Atla, the opal!"

But her face was buried in her hands. She
was rocking herself to and fro, and moaning in
unmistakable anguish. He looked at her wonderingly; then thrusting the gem into the breast-

pocket of his shirt, he leaned over and touched her gently on the arm. "What is it? What is it, Atla?"

"Oh," she moaned, "I knew it from the first that you were one of us. Do you not see," she cried, facing him suddenly, "have you not understood, that I am one of that race which possesses the power to find the talismanic jewel? Do you not see that you, too, are of that fated slave people? My mother died—here—on this very edge of this accursed quarry"—she looked around shudderingly. "*He* brought her here when she, too, was young, hardly older than I am now, to search for the opal. She laid me in the arms of my old nurse when he took her away, and she never came back. And it was that only I was left who might find it for him. It was for this that he had me taught to speak the tongue of the dear good people who live here. It was for this that he brought masters to show me music and singing, and the way to gather little children about my knee and teach them to read from pictured books. It was that he might bring me here and set me to the task without exciting suspicion. He brought me here — *himself* — at night, and explained to me in his cold and terrible way how I must search for the little round stones and break them with the hammer. He comes nightly to see whether I have been truly at work. Last night he called me with the strange, awful call. I heard him in the cabin, where I sat with the children, and I came. Ah!" a long, quivering cry escaped her, and she buried her face again in her hands.

He had hardly heard her frantic outburst of words. He had made no effort to understand her, conscious only of an overwhelming desire to take her in his arms and soothe her out of the superstitious delusion, whatever it might be, into which she had fallen.

"There is a song of the opal," she went on, lifting her head and regarding him with wild eyes; "it was sad when my mother sang it, sad as life and death even to my baby ears; it is weird and strange when my nurse croons it yonder—yonder in the far land where she waits for me in the shadows of the passion-vine; it is terrible when the *master* chants it." She broke abruptly into a kind of rude rhythmic strain, her voice scarcely reaching farther than the half-heedless ears of her companion :

"*Fateful and wondrous art thou, O far-shining Opal, compeller of stars in their courses; of red gold in the rock-hidden chambers; of woman, yea, woman, white-bosomed, with long-lidded eyes that speak passion.*

"*Alas, thou art sealed in the womb of the mountain! Hidden in roseate flint is the joy of thy shining. Who forth can compel thee? who master thy secret?*

"*Nay, before me I drive the white slave-gang, tawny-haired, and with cheeks that are pallid. Deep in the womb of the earth let them burrow; they alone have the power to conjure thee!*

"*Leap from the matrix, my Beauty! The white slave from the depth of the quarry hath fetched thee. Mine enemy, now in my hand lies thy heart-beat. Red gold, thou art mine; and woman, yea, woman, white-bosomed, with long-lidded eyes that speak passion!"*

She paused. "There is yet a stanza," she said, "but I—I—" She faltered, and a rain of tears gushed from beneath her down-drooped eyelids.

He was almost beside himself with love and compassion. He leaned towards her, drawing her hands from her face, and compelling her eyes to meet his. "Atla," he whispered, "look at me. I love you—I love you!"

As she drooped against his breast with a long-drawn, sobbing sigh, the hammer lying on the moss-grown ledge dropped over into the pit, slipped down between the weather-worn rocks, and rested out of sight in the bottom of the quarry.

When the hour came for the gathering of her little flock, he descended the mountain with her. It was the first time. It was the beginning of their life-journey together, he told her, gayly, helping her with all a lover's carefulness along the path she had so often traversed alone. They stopped by the bowlder where he had once watched her coming down with the dew-wet posy in his hand.

"How I hate Polly Crawls's tow-headed brats!" he exclaimed, playfully, when she turned at last to leave him.

"They are not tow-headed at all," she remonstrated, seriously. "They are dear little girls, and I love them—Jack." How sweet and strange the familiar name sounded on her lips!

"Do you? Well, then, I will come over to Uncle Dicky's this very night to see them—and you," he laughed. Then, as a sudden recollection struck him, "A slave!" he cried—"a slave did you call me, Atla?" He caught her hands in his and drew her towards him. "A slave! Why, I am a king!"

He felt her long, firm fingers grow cold and tighten like manacles upon his wrists as he spoke. Her eyes dilated, and a gray pallor swept over her face. He followed the direction of her gaze. The old Mexican, Don José, was coming slowly along the narrow pathway from around the spur of the mountain. His shaggy head was bent; his bushy brows knit together; his lips were moving silently; his long arms swung loosely at his side. He looked impassively at the girl as he passed, and turned his deeply set eyes for a second upon her companion. A flame leaped into them like a sudden flash of lightning. A curious numbness crept over John Dene, and a sensation which in all his life he had never felt before—a sensation of abject, unreasoning, unreasonable terror—possessed him. It was gone before he could define it, and Don José with lowered eyelids went slowly on his way, and disappeared behind a thick-set *motte* of live-oak.

"He knows!" gasped Atla, the ashen gray in her cheeks fading to a ghastly white.

"Knows what? Who?" Dene asked, bewildered. Then, a vague light struggling into his brain, he exclaimed, "Is he—is Don José—"

"Don José is my master," she whispered,

6

hoarsely, glancing fearfully over her shoulder.
"Oh, he knows!" she sobbed, wildly. "*Madre
de Dios*, he knows!"

He clasped her to his breast, soothing her with
caresses and incoherent words. "But listen,
Atla," he insisted at length; "listen, you absurd
child. Are you really afraid of Don José? Is it
because of the opal? If you feel like this, why,
let him have it. I—"

At this she clung only the more frantically to
him. "Never! never!" she almost shrieked.
"Oh! promise me that you will hide it from
him. Promise! promise!"

"I will promise anything you like, my darling,"
he replied; "but surely you know that in this
country at least no one is a slave; that you can
leave Don José if he is your guardian—whatever
he is—at any moment you wish. I will take you
away myself. Ah, when you are my wife he will
not dare to come near you."

She lifted her face from his breast and gave
him an eager, searching look. "You will take
me away?" she asked, breathlessly.

He gathered her more closely in his arms. "So
far away, Atla, that he can never find you again."

"When?" she demanded, almost sharply.

"Now — this very moment," he responded,
laughingly, sweeping her a step or two forward.

But she repeated her question yet more gravely: "When? Will it be to-night?"

He looked at her, doubtful whether he had
heard aright.

"Listen," she continued, hurriedly, clasping

her hands about his arm: "if you will take me away, let it be to-night. I am afraid of him—Mother of God, how I am afraid! To-night, Jack, if you will—let it be to-night. I will wait for you around the mountain in the edge of the Gap, by the big rock in the shadow. I will have Huayric there. Oh, she is mine, the beautiful creature! She will come to me if I but call her ever so lightly. I know where he hides her when he comes at night to the Gap, and waits beyond the west ridge for the midnight, to creep up to the quarry. I will wait for you with Huayric, and when it is night—as soon as it is well night—you will come for me, and you will take me away."

He covered her feverish lips with kisses. Would he come? Oh, love and life! All the blood in his heart leaped and throbbed at the thought. "Do you understand, Atla?" he said at last. "By this time to-morrow you will be my wife, and we will be setting our faces towards England."

"You will come?" she repeated, a tender color dawning upon her tear-wet cheeks.

"Yes, I will come."

"But you will not go to your cabin, Jack! You must not go to your cabin. Promise me that too!" she exclaimed, as if struck by some new and terrifying thought.

He smiled indulgently. His mind was already busied with plans for their flight, and he murmured some sort of assent, with his lips upon hers. And then she left him. He watched her out of sight. At the last turn of the path she

paused and smiled back at him, waving a light
adieu with her slender hand.

He turned mechanically in the direction of his
cabin, but halted perplexed, smiling at the recollection of the half-promise he had given. "But
I will keep it," he said to himself, tenderly—
"the first promise made to my sweetheart. Oh
yes, I will keep it. I can send a line to Uncle
Dicky from town; that will do just as well."
And he struck once more into the trail and went
up the mountain.

Towards nightfall he came out upon the point
overlooking the valley. The world below was suffused with the serene radiance of sunset. Miles
away the straggling little town shone like an
enchanted city, its spires tipped with gold, its
windows gleaming like many-colored jewels.
A young moon hung tenderly luminous in the
western sky; above it a bank of fleecy cloud was
gathering; a flock of wild-geese shaped their
arrowy flight southward with sharp cries across
the slowly coming twilight.

"There's a norther behind that flock of geese,
and plenty of Uncle Dicky's rain-seed in that
bank of cloud," commented the lonely watcher.

Lights appeared at the store and twinkled
here and there in the scattered cabins. It was
night in the valley. His heart gave a great
bound. He cast one last long look around, and
began the descent.

When he reached the foot of the mountain he
made his way quietly to the shed where Roland
was stabled. He threw the high-pommelled sad-

dle on the horse's back, and buckled the girth
rapidly and deftly. She was there by this time
waiting for him. He put a foot in the stirrup,
and laid his hand on Roland's arched neck. All
at once there flashed across his mind a thought
of his mother's picture, lying in its tiny oval case
on his mantel. Could he leave behind him that
dear shadow of a face which in all his life had
never worn a frown for him? After all it was
not really a promise. She was half crazed by
some superstitious fear, poor child. He smiled,
and touched the hilt of his knife, and felt the
handle of the pistol in his belt. He walked rapidly across the field, hard beset not to shout
aloud the exultation that possessed him. In the
little garden-patch he paused a moment. The
sweet familiar perfume of the night-hidden
flowers moved him strangely. He stooped and
plucked a lavender leaf in the darkness. Its
dewy fragrance brought before him a swift vision
of his waiting bride. He thrust it in his bosom
and went into the cabin. The dog, lying across
the threshold, leaped up against him, barking
joyously. He found the miniature without striking a light, and came out, shutting the heavy
door behind him. As he stepped again into the
garden-path a misshapen form rose up from behind the tangled morning-glory and cypress vines.
The dog sprang forward with a growl, which
changed into a frightened whine. There was
no other outcry, scarcely a struggle; a long keen
blade flashed in the starlight, once, twice, thrice;
and borne backward by powerful, sinewy arms,

John Dene sank heavily to the ground, crushing the late-blooming roses and the mignonette in his fall. Don José drew the knife out of his victim's breast with some difficulty, kneeling upon the body. Then, with unerring instinct, he plunged his hand in the breast-pocket of the hunting-shirt, and drew forth the opal. It flashed like a meteor in the darkness as he opened his palm for a second to gloat upon it. Stooping still lower then, he fumbled about the wound whence gushed a palpitating stream of blood. Once, twice, thrice he buried his clinched hand in the warm red rivulet, letting it trickle slowly through his knotty fingers.

A kind of exultant sigh escaped his lips as he stood erect. Then he glided stealthily across the uneven field to the shed where Roland stood awaiting his master.

The upturned face of the master grew whiter and whiter; his limbs stiffened; a warm reeking odor of blood mingled with the breath of the English flowers. The dog watching beside him shivered and moaned like a thing possessed.

Around the spur of the mountain Atla was waiting: she held the jewelled bridle in her hand, standing close beside Huayric. Now and again she laid her soft cheek against the satin shoulder of her playmate, and caressed her with syllables of an unknown and musical language. She laughed joyously when the mare responded with a half-breathed whinny of delight. "Oh, my Huayric," she whispered, "he is coming!"

She had forgotten all her fears. Down at the

Crawlses' cabin awhile ago, as she stepped towards the open door, old Granny Crawls, sitting in the chimney-corner, had said, "Lord, chile, ye air thet peart and rosy thet it air a plumb pleasure to look at ye!"

"Oh, my Haayrie," she breathed once more, "he is coming!"

The sound of a horse's feet treading softly as only Roland could tread, trained to a hunter's need, was on the still air. Nearer it came and nearer; swifter too, and in that she read her lover's impatience. A second more and the horse and his rider had turned the shadow of the rock and had paused. A long arm, down-stretched, caught her lithe, light form in its grip of steel, and swung her to the saddle. A terrible voice hissed in her ear a single sentence in a strange, uncouth tongue. Her head drooped forward on her breast. Don José seized the mare's bridle-rein, and a moment later the clatter of horses' hoofs flying westward came echoing down the Gap on the first long shuddering wail of the coming norther.

Now this was that strain of the Song of the Opal which Atla wist not how to sing to her lover that morning on the crest of Quarry Mountain:

"*Yea, thou art loosed from the womb of thy mother, rejoicing and lovely and proud, but not yet, not yet hast thou put on thy strength as a garment. Far shining but impotent art thou till thou comest from the blood bath!*

"Thrice in the blood of thy Finder—his heart's blood—thrice must I bathe thee, my Opal, my Mistress, compeller of stars in their courses; of red gold in rock-hidden chambers; of woman, yea, woman, white-bosomed, with long-lidded eyes that speak passion!

"Drink deep of the blood of the White Slave, my Beauty; drink deep, and so clothe thee with power as a garment!"

MADAME RAYMONDE-ARNAULT

AT LA GLORIEUSE

MADAME RAYMONDE-ARNAULT leaned her head against the back of her garden-chair, and watched the young people furtively from beneath her half-closed eyelids. "He is about to speak," she murmured under her breath ; "she, at least, will be happy!" and her heart fluttered violently, as if it had been her own thin, bloodless hand which Richard Keith was holding in his; her dark, sunken eyes, instead of Félice's brown ones, which drooped beneath his tender gaze.

Marcelite, the old *bonne,* who stood erect and stately behind her mistress, permitted herself also to regard them for a moment with something like a smile relaxing her sombre, yellow face ; then she too turned her turbaned head discreetly in another direction.

The plantation house at La Glorieuse is built in a shining loop of Bayou L'Éperon. A level grassy lawn, shaded by enormous live-oaks, stretches across from the broad stone steps to the sodded levee, where a flotilla of small boats, drawn up among the flags and lily-pads, rise and fall with the lapping waves. On the left of the house the white cabins of the quarter show their low roofs above the shrubbery; to the right the plantations of cane, following the inward curve of the bayou, sweep southward field after field, their billowy, blue-green reaches blending far in the rear with the indistinct purple haze of the swamp. The great square house, raised high on massive stone pillars, dates back to the first quarter of the century; its sloping roof is set with rows of dormer-windows, the big red double chimneys rising oddly from their midst; wide galleries with fluted columns enclose it on three sides; from the fourth is projected a long, narrow wing, two stories in height, which stands somewhat apart from the main building, but is connected with it by a roofed and latticed passageway. The lower rooms of this wing open upon small porticos, with balustrades of wrought iron-work rarely fanciful and delicate. From these you may step into the rose-garden—a tangled pleasance which rambles away through alleys of wild-peach and magnolia to an orange-grove, whose trees are gnarled and knotted with the growth of half a century.

The early shadows were cool and dewy there that morning; the breath of damask-roses was sweet on the air; brown, gold-dusted butterflies were hovering over the sweet-peas abloom in sunny corners; birds shot up now and then from the leafy aisles, singing, into the clear blue sky above; the chorus of the negroes at work among the young cane floated in, mellow and resonant. from the fields. The old mistress of La Glori-

euse saw it all behind her drooped eyelids. Was
it not April, too, that long - gone, unforgotten
morning ? And were not the bees busy in the
hearts of the roses, and the birds singing, when
Richard Keith, the first of the name who came
to La Glorieuse, held her hand in his, and whispered his love-story yonder by the ragged thicket
of crêpe-myrtle ? Ah, Félice, my child, thou art
young, but I too have had my sixteen years; and
yellow as are the curls on the head bent over
thine, those of the first Richard were more gold-
en still. And the second Richard, he who—

Marcelite's hand fell heavily on her mistress's
shoulder. Madame Arnault opened her eyes and
sat up, grasping the arms of her chair. A harsh,
grating sound had fallen suddenly into the stillness, and the shutters of one of the upper windows of the wing which overlooked the garden
were swinging slowly outward. A ripple of laughter, musical and mocking, rang clearly on the
air ; at the same moment a woman appeared,
framed like a portrait in the narrow casement.
She crossed her arms on the iron window - bar
and gazed silently down on the startled group
below. She was strangely beautiful and young,
though an air of soft and subtle maturity pervaded her graceful figure. A glory of yellow hair
encircled her pale, oval face, and waved away in
fluffy masses to her waist ; her full lips were scarlet ; her eyes, beneath their straight, dark brows,
were gray, with emerald shadows in their luminous depths. Her low-cut gown, of some thin,
yellowish-white material, exposed her exquisitely

rounded throat and perfect neck ; long, flowing sleeves of spidery lace fell away from her shapely arms, leaving them bare to the shoulder ; loose strings of pearls were wound around her small wrists, and about her throat was clasped a strand of blood-red coral, from which hung to the hollow of her bosom a single translucent drop of amber. A smile at once daring and derisive parted her lips ; an elusive light came and went in her eyes.

Keith had started impatiently from his seat at the unwelcome interruption. He stood regarding the intruder with mute, half-frowning inquiry.

Félice turned a bewildered face to her grandmother. "Who is it, Mère?" she whispered. "Did—did you give her leave ?"

Madame Arnault had sunk back in her chair. Her hands trembled convulsively still, and the lace on her bosom rose and fell with the hurried beating of her heart. But she spoke in her ordinary measured, almost formal tones, as she put out a hand and drew the girl to her side. "I do not know, my child. Perhaps Suzette Beauvais has come over with her guests from Grandchamp. I thought I heard but now the sound of boats on the bayou. Suzette is ever ready with her pranks. Or perhaps—"

She stopped abruptly. The stranger was drawing the batten blinds together. Her ivory-white arms gleamed in the sun. For a moment they could see her face shining like a star against the dusky glooms within ; then the bolt was shot sharply to its place.

"SHE FLUSHED AND HER BROWN EYES DROOPED"

Old Marcelite drew a long breath of relief as she disappeared. A smothered ejaculation had escaped her lips, under the girl's intent gaze; an ashen gray had overspread her dark face. "Mam'selle Suzette, she been an' dress up one o' her young ladies jes fer er trick," she said, slowly, wiping the great drops of perspiration from her wrinkled forehead.

"Suzette?" echoed Félice, incredulously. "She would never dare! Who *can* it be?"

"It is easy enough to find out," laughed Keith. "Let us go and see for ourselves who is masquerading in my quarters."

He drew her with him as he spoke along the winding violet-bordered walks which led to the house. She looked anxiously back over her shoulder at her grandmother. Madame Arnault half arose, and made an imperious gesture of dissent; but Marcelite forced her gently into her seat, and, leaning forward, whispered a few words rapidly in her ear.

"Thou art right, Marcelite," she acquiesced, with a heavy sigh. "'Tis better so."

They spoke in *nègre*, that mysterious patois which is so uncouth in itself, so soft and caressing on the lips of women. Madame Arnault signed to the girl to go on. She shivered a little, watching their retreating figures. The old *bonne* threw a light shawl about her shoulders, and crouched affectionately at her feet. The murmur of their voices as they talked long and earnestly together hardly reached beyond the shadows of the wild-peach tree beneath which they sat.

"How beautiful she was!" Félice said, musingly, as they approached the latticed passageway.

"Well, yes," her companion returned, carelessly. "I confess I do not greatly fancy that style
of beauty myself." And he glanced significantly down at her own flower-like face.

She flushed, and her brown eyes drooped, but
a bright little smile played about her sensitive
mouth. "I cannot see," she declared, "how Suzette could have dared to take her friends into
the ball-room!"

"Why?" he asked, smiling at her vehemence.

She stopped short in her surprise. "Do you
not know, then?" She sank her voice to a whisper. "The ball-room has never been opened since
the night my mother died. I was but a baby
then, though sometimes I imagine that I remember it all. There was a grand ball there that
night. La Glorieuse was full of guests, and
everybody from all the plantations around was
here. Mère has never told me how it was, nor
Marcelite; but the other servants used to talk
to me about my beautiful young mother, and tell
me how she died suddenly in her ball dress,
while the ball was going on. My father had the
whole wing closed at once, and no one was ever
allowed to enter it. I used to be afraid to play
in its shadow, and if I did stray anywhere near
it, my father would always call me away. Her
death must have broken his heart. He rarely
spoke; I never saw him smile; and his eyes were
so sad that I could weep now at remembering

them. Then he too died while I was still a little girl, and now I have no one in the world but dear old Mère." Her voice trembled a little, but she flushed, and smiled again beneath his meaning look. "It was many years before even the lower floor was reopened, and I am almost sure that yours is the only room there which has ever been used."

They stepped, as she concluded, into the hall.

"I have never been in here before," she said, looking about her with shy curiosity. A flood of sunlight poured through the wide arched window at the foot of the stair. The door of the room nearest the entrance stood open; the others, ranging along the narrow hall, were all closed.

"This is my room," he said, nodding towards the open door.

She turned her head quickly away, with an impulse of girlish modesty, and ran lightly up the stair. He glanced downward as he followed, and paused, surprised to see the flutter of white garments in a shaded corner of his room. Looking more closely, he saw that it was a glimmer of light from an open window on the dark, polished floor.

The upper hall was filled with sombre shadows; the motionless air was heavy with a musky, choking odor. In the dimness a few tattered hangings were visible on the walls; a rope, with bits of crumbling evergreen clinging to it, trailed from above one of the low windows. The panelled double door of the ball-room was shut; no sound came from behind it.

"The girls have seen us coming," said Félice, picking her way daintily across the dust-covered floor, "and they have hidden themselves inside."

Keith pushed open the heavy valves, which creaked noisily on their rusty hinges. The gloom within was murkier still ; the chill dampness, with its smell of mildew and mould, was like that of a funeral vault.

The large, low-ceilinged room ran the entire length of the house. A raised dais, whose faded carpet had half rotted away, occupied an alcove at one end ; upon it four or five wooden stools were placed ; one of these was overturned ; on another a violin in its baggy green-baize cover was lying. Straight high-backed chairs were pushed against the walls on either side ; in front of an open fireplace with a low wooden mantel two small cushioned divans were drawn up, with a claw-footed table between them. A silver salver filled with tall glasses was set carelessly on one edge of the table ; a half-open fan of sandalwood lay beside it ; a man's glove had fallen on the hearth just within the tarnished brass fender. Cobwebs depended from the ceiling, and hung in loose threads from the mantel ; dust was upon everything, thick and motionless ; a single ghostly ray of light that filtered in through a crevice in one of the shutters was weighted with gray, lustreless motes. The room was empty and silent. The visitors, who had come so stealthily, had as stealthily departed, leaving no trace behind them.

"They have played us a pretty trick," said Keith, gayly. "They must have fled as soon as they saw us start towards the house." He went over to the window from which the girl had looked down into the rose garden, and gave it a shake. The dust flew up in a suffocating cloud, and the spiked nails which secured the upper sash rattled in their places.

"That is like Suzette Beauvais," Félice replied, absently. She was not thinking of Suzette. She had forgotten even the stranger, whose disdainful eyes, fixed upon herself, had moved her sweet nature to something like a rebellious anger. Her thoughts were on the beautiful young mother of alien race, whose name, for some reason, she was forbidden to speak. She saw her glide, gracious and smiling, along the smooth floor; she heard her voice above the call and response of the violins; she breathed the perfume of her laces, backward blown by the swift motion of the dance!

She strayed dreamily about, touching with an almost reverent finger first one worm-eaten object and then another, as if by so doing she could make the imagined scene more real. Her eyes were downcast; the blood beneath her rich dark skin came and went in brilliant flushes on her cheeks; the bronze hair, piled in heavy coils on her small, well-poised head, fell in loose rings on her low forehead and against her white neck; her soft gray gown, following the harmonious lines of her slender figure, seemed to envelop her like a twilight cloud.

"She is adorable," said Richard Keith to himself.

It was the first time that he had been really alone with her, though this was the third week of his stay in the hospitable old mansion where his father and his grandfather before him had been welcome guests. Now that he came to think of it, in that bundle of yellow, time-worn letters from Félix Arnault to Richard Keith, which he had found among his father's papers, was one which described at length a ball in this very ball-room. Was it in celebration of his marriage, or of his home-coming after a tour abroad? Richard could not remember. But he idly recalled portions of other letters, as he stood with his elbow on the mantel watching Félix Arnault's daughter.

"*Your son and my daughter*," the phrase which had made him smile when he read it yonder in his Maryland home, brought now a warm glow to his heart. The half-spoken avowal, the question that had trembled on his lips a few moments ago in the rose-garden, stirred impetuously within him.

Félice stepped down from the dais where she had been standing, and came swiftly across the room, as if his unspoken thought had called her to him. A tender rapture possessed him to see her thus drawing towards him; he longed to stretch out his arms and fold her to his breast. He moved, and his hand came in contact with a small object on the mantel. He picked it up. It was a ring, a band of dull, worn gold, with a

confused tracery graven upon it. He merely
glanced at it, slipping it mechanically on his finger. His eyes were full upon hers, which were
suffused and shining.

"Did you speak?" she asked, timidly. She
had stopped abruptly, and was looking at him
with a hesitating, half-bewildered expression.

"No," he replied. His mood had changed.
He walked again to the window and examined
the clumsy bolt. "Strange!" he muttered. "I
have never seen a face like hers," he sighed,
dreamily.

"She was very beautiful," Félice returned,
quietly. "I think we must be going," she added.
"Mère will be growing impatient." The flush
had died out of her cheek, her arms hung listless-
ly at her side. She shuddered as she gave a last
look around the desolate room. "They were
dancing here when my mother died," she said to
herself.

He preceded her slowly down the stair. The
remembrance of the woman began vaguely to stir
his senses. He had hardly remarked her then,
absorbed as he had been in another idea. Now
she seemed to swim voluptuously before his vision; her tantalizing laugh rang in his ears; her
pale, perfumed hair was blown across his face; he
felt its filmy strands upon his lips and eyelids.
"Do you think," he asked, turning eagerly on
the bottom step, "that they could have gone
into any of these rooms?"

She shrank unaccountably from him.

"Oh no!" she cried. "They are in the rose-garden with Mère, or they have gone around to the lawn. Come ;" and she hurried out before him.

Madame Arnault looked at them sharply as they came up to where she was sitting. "No one !" she echoed, in response to Keith's report. "Then they really have gone back ?"

"Madame knows dat we has hear de boats pass up de bayou whilse m'sieu' an' mam'selle was inside," interposed Marcelite, stooping to pick up her mistress's cane.

"I would not have thought Suzette so—so indiscreet," said Félice. There was a note of weariness in her voice.

Madame Arnault looked anxiously at her and then at Keith. The young man was staring abstractedly at the window, striving to recall the vision that had appeared there, and he felt, rather than saw, his hostess start and change color when her eyes fell upon the ring he was wearing. He lifted his hand covertly, and turned the trinket around in the light, but he tried in vain to decipher the irregular characters traced upon it.

"Let us go in," said the old madame. "Félice, my child, thou art fatigued."

Now when in all her life before was Félice ever fatigued? Félice, whose strong young arms could send a pirogue flying up the bayou for miles ; Félice, who was ever ready for a tramp along the rose-hedged lanes to the swamp lakes when the water-lilies were in bloom; to the sugar-house in grinding-time ; down the levee road to St. Joseph's, the little brown ivy-grown church, whose solitary spire arose slim and straight above the encircling trees.

Marcelite gave an arm to her mistress, though, in truth, she seemed to walk a little unsteadily herself. Félice followed with Keith, who was silent and self-absorbed.

The day passed slowly, a constraint had somehow fallen upon the little household. Madame Arnault's fine high-bred old face wore its customary look of calm repose, but her eyes now and then sought her guest with an expression which he could not have fathomed if he had observed it. But he saw nothing. A mocking red mouth; a throat made for the kisses of love; white arms strung with pearls—these were ever before him, shutting away even the pure sweet face of Félice Arnault.

"Why did I not look at her more closely when I had the opportunity, fool that I was?" he asked himself, savagely, again and again, revolving in his mind a dozen pretexts for going at once to the Beauvais plantation, a mile or so up the bayou. But he felt an inexplicable shyness at the thought of putting any of these plans into action, and so allowed the day to drift by. He arose gladly when the hour for retiring came—that hour which he had hitherto postponed by every means in his power. He kissed, as usual, the hand of his hostess, and held that of Félice in his for a moment; but he did not feel its trembling, or see the timid trouble in her soft eyes.

His room in the silent and deserted wing was full of fantastic shadows. He threw himself on a chair beside a window without lighting his lamp. The rose-garden outside was steeped in moonlight; the magnolia bells gleamed waxen-white against their glossy green leaves; the vines on the tall trellises threw a soft net-work of dancing shadows on the white-shelled walks below; the night air stealing about was loaded with the perfume of roses and sweet-olive; a mocking-bird sang in an orange-tree, his mate responding sleepily from her nest in the old summer-house.

"To-morrow," he murmured, half aloud, "I will go to Grandchamp and give her the ring she left in the old ball-room."

He looked at it glowing dully in the moon-light; suddenly he lifted his head, listening. Did a door grind somewhere near on its hinges? He got up cautiously and looked out. It was not fancy. She was standing full in view on the small balcony of the room next his own. Her white robes waved to and fro in the breeze; the pearls on her arms glistened. Her face, framed in the pale gold of her hair, was turned towards him; a smile curved her lips; her mysterious eyes seemed to be searching his through the shadow. He drew back, confused and trembling, and when, a second later, he looked again, she was gone.

He sat far into the night, his brain whirling, his blood on fire. Who was she, and what was the mystery hidden in this isolated old planta-tion house? His thoughts reverted to the scene in the rose-garden, and he went over and over all

its details. He remembered Madame Arnault's
agitation when the window opened and the girl
appeared ; her evident discomfiture—of which at
the time he had taken no heed, but which came
back to him vividly enough now—at his proposal
to visit the ball-room ; her startled recognition of
the ring on his finger ; her slurring suggestion
of visitors from Grandchamp ; the look of terror on Marcelite's face.   What did it all mean ?
Félice, he was sure, knew nothing.   But here, in
an unused portion of the house, which even the
members of the family had never visited, a young
and beautiful girl was shut up a prisoner, con-
demned perhaps to a life-long captivity.

"Good God !" He leaped to his feet at the
thought.   He would go and thunder at Madame
Arnault's door, and demand an explanation.
But no ; not yet. He calmed himself with an
effort. By too great haste he might injure her.
"Insane ?" He laughed aloud at the idea of mad-
ness in connection with that exquisite creature.

It dawned upon him, as he paced restlessly
back and forth, that although his father had been
here more than once in his youth and manhood,
he had never heard him speak of La Glorieuse
nor of Félix Arnault, whose letters he had read
after his father's death a few months ago—those
old letters whose affectionate warmth, indeed, had
determined him, in the first desolation of his loss,
to seek the family which seemed to have been
so bound to his own. Morose and taciturn as
his father had been, surely he would sometimes
have spoken of his old friend if— Worn out at

last with conjecture; beaten back, bruised and breathless, from an enigma which he could not solve; exhausted by listening with strained attention for some movement in the next room, he threw himself on his bed, dressed as he was, and fell into a heavy sleep, which lasted far into the forenoon of the next day.

When he came out (walking like one in a dream), he found a gay party assembled on the lawn in front of the house. Suzette Beauvais and her guests, a bevy of girls, had come from Grandchamp. They had been joined, as they rowed down the bayou, by the young people from the plantation houses on the way. Half a dozen boats, their long paddles laid across the seats, were added to the home fleet at the landing. Their stalwart black rowers were basking in the sun on the levee, or lounging about the quarter. At the moment of his appearance, Suzette herself was indignantly disclaiming any complicity in the jest of the day before.

"Myself, I was making o'ange-flower conserve," she declared; "an' anyhow I wouldn't go in that ball-room unless madame send me."

"But who was it, then?" insisted Félice.

Mademoiselle Beauvais spread out her fat little hands and lifted her shoulders. "*Mo pas connais*," she laughed, dropping into patois.

Madame Arnault here interposed. It was but the foolish conceit of some teasing neighbor, she said, and not worth further discussion. Keith's blood boiled in his veins at this calm dismissal of the subject, but he gave no sign.

He saw her glance warily at himself from time to time.

"I will sift the matter to the bottom," he thought, "and I will force her to confess the truth, whatever it may be, before the world."

The noisy chatter and meaningless laughter around him jarred upon his nerves; he longed to be alone with his thoughts; and presently, pleading a headache—indeed his temples throbbed almost to bursting, and his eyes were hot and dry—he quitted the lawn, seeing but not noting until long afterwards, when they smote his memory like a two-edged knife, the pain in Félice's uplifted eyes, and the little sorrowful quiver of her mouth. He strolled around the corner of the house to his apartment. The blinds of the arched window were drawn, and a hazy twilight was diffused about the hall, though it was mid-afternoon outside. As he entered, closing the door behind him, the woman at that moment uppermost in his thoughts came down the dusky silence from the farther end of the hall. She turned her inscrutable eyes upon him in passing, and flitted noiselessly and with languid grace up the stairway, the faint swish of her gown vanishing with her. He hesitated a moment, overpowered by conflicting emotions; then he sprang recklessly after her.

He pushed open the ball-room door, reaching his arms out blindly before him. Once more the great dust-covered room was empty. He strained his eyes helplessly into the obscurity. A chill reaction passed over him; he felt himself

on the verge of a swoon. He did not this time
even try to discover the secret door or exit by
which she had disappeared; he looked, with a
hopeless sense of discouragement, at the barred
windows, and turned to leave the room. As he
did so, he saw a handkerchief lying on the threshold of the door. He picked it up eagerly, and
pressed it to his lips. A peculiar delicate perfume which thrilled his senses lurked in its gossamer folds. As he was about thrusting it into
his breast - pocket, he noticed in one corner a
small blood-stain fresh and wet. He had then
bitten his lip in his excitement.

"I need no further proof," he said aloud, and
his own voice startled him, echoing down the
long hall. "She is beyond all question a prisoner in this detached building, which has mysterious exits and entrances. She has been forced
to promise that she will not go outside of its
walls, or she is afraid to do so. I will bring
home this monstrous crime. I will release this
lovely young woman who dares not speak, yet so
plainly appeals to me." Already he saw in fancy
her star-like eyes raised to his in mute gratitude,
her white hand laid confidingly on his arm.

The party of visitors remained at La Glorieuse
overnight. The negro fiddlers came in, and
there was dancing in the old-fashioned double
parlors and on the moonlit galleries. Félice was
unnaturally gay. Keith looked on gloomily, taking no part in the amusement.

"*Il est bien bête*, your yellow-haired Maryland-
er," whispered Suzette Beauvais to her friend.

"IT WAS ONLY FÉLICE"

He went early to his room, but he watched in vain for some sign from his beautiful neighbor. He grew sick with apprehension. Had Madame Arnault— But no; she would not dare. "I will wait one more day," he finally decided; "and then—"

The next morning, after a late breakfast, some one proposed impromptu charades and tableaux. Madame Arnault good-naturedly sent for the keys to the tall presses built into the walls, which contained the accumulated trash and treasure of several generations. Mounted on a step-ladder, Robert Beauvais explored the recesses and threw down to the laughing crowd embroidered shawls and scarfs yellow with age, soft muslins of antique pattern, stiff big-flowered brocades, scraps of gauze ribbon, gossamer laces. On one topmost shelf he came upon a small wooden box inlaid with mother-of-pearl. Félice reached up for it, and, moved by some undefined impulse, Richard came and stood by her side while she opened it. A perfume which he recognized arose from it as she lifted a fold of tissue-paper. Some strings of Oriental pearls of extraordinary size, and perfect in shape and color, were coiled underneath, with a coral necklace, whose pendant of amber had broken off and rolled into a corner. With them—he hardly restrained an exclamation, and his hand involuntarily sought his breast-pocket at sight of the handkerchief with a drop of fresh blood in one corner! Félice trembled without knowing why. Madame Arnault, who had just entered the room, took the box from her quietly, and closed the lid with a snap. The girl, accustomed to implicit obedience, asked no questions; the others, engaged in turning over the old-time finery, had paid no attention.

"Does she think to disarm me by such puerile tricks?" he thought, turning a look of angry warning on the old madame; and in the steady gaze which she fixed on him he read a haughty defiance.

He forced himself to enter into the sports of the day, and he walked down to the boat-landing a little before sunset to see the guests depart. As the line of boats swept away, the black rowers dipping their oars lightly in the placid waves, he turned, with a sense of release, leaving Madame Arnault and Félice still at the landing, and went down the levee road towards St. Joseph's. The field gang, whose red, blue, and brown blouses splotched the squares of cane with color, was preparing to quit work; loud laughter and noisy jests rang out on the air; high-wheeled plantation wagons creaked along the lanes; negro children, with dip-nets and fishing-poles over their shoulders, ran homeward along the levee, the dogs at their heels barking joyously; a schooner, with white sail outspread, was stealing like a fairy bark around a distant bend of the bayou; the silvery waters were turning to gold under a sunset sky.

It was twilight when he struck across the plantation, and came around by the edge of the swamp to the clump of trees in a corner of the home field which he had often remarked from his window. As he approached, he saw a woman come out of the dense shadow, as if intending to meet him, and then draw back again. His heart throbbed painfully, but he walked steadily forward. It was only Félice. *Only Félice!* She was sitting on a flat tombstone. The little spot was the Raymonde-Arnault family burying-ground. There were many marble head-stones and shafts, and two broad low tombs side by side and a little apart from the others. A tangle of rose-briers covered the sunken graves, a rank growth of grass choked the narrow paths, the little gate, interlaced and overhung with honeysuckle, sagged away from its posts; the fence itself had lost a picket here and there, and weeds flaunted boldly in the gaps. The girl looked wan and ghostly in the lonely dusk.

"This is my father's grave, and my mother is here," she said, abruptly, as he came up and stood beside her. Her head was drooped upon her breast, and he saw that she had been weeping. "See," she went on, drawing her finger along the mildewed lettering: "'Félix Marie-Joseph Arnault . . . âgé de trente-quatre ans.' . . . 'Hélène Pallacier, épouse de Félix Arnault . . . décédée à l'âge de dix-neuf ans.' Nineteen years old," she repeated, slowly. "My mother was one year younger than I am when she died—my beautiful mother!"

Her voice sounded like a far-away murmur in his ears. He looked at her, vaguely conscious that she was suffering. But he did not speak, and after a little she got up and went away. Her

dress, which brushed him in passing, was wet
with dew. He watched her slight figure, moving like a spirit along the lane, until a turn in
the hedge hid her from sight. Then he turned
again towards the swamp, and resumed his restless walk.

Some hours later he crossed the rose-garden.
The moon was under a cloud; the trunks of the
crêpe-myrtles were like pale spectres in the uncertain light. The night wind blew in chill and
moist from the swamp. The house was dark and
quiet, but he heard the blind of an upper window turned stealthily as he stepped into the latticed arcade.

"The old madame is watching me—and her,"
he said to himself.

His agitation had now become supreme. The
faint familiar perfume that stole about his room
filled him with a kind of frenzy. Was this the
chivalric devotion of which he had so boasted?
this the desire to protect a young and defence-
less woman? He no longer dared question himself. He seemed to feel her warm breath against
his cheeks. He threw up his arms with a gesture
of despair. A sigh stirred the death-like stillness.
At last! She was there, just within his doorway; the pale glimmer of the veiled moon fell
upon her. Her trailing laces wrapped her about
like a silver mist; her arms were folded across
her bosom; her eyes—he dared not interpret the
meaning which he read in those wonderful eyes.
She turned slowly and went down the hall. He
followed her, reeling like a drunkard. His feet

"HE THREW HIMSELF AGAINST THE DOOR"

seemed clogged, the blood ran thick in his veins,
a strange roaring was in his ears. His hot eyes
strained after her as she vanished, just beyond
his touch, into the room next his own. He
threw himself against the closed door in a transport of rage. It yielded suddenly, as if opened
from within. A full blaze of light struck his
eyes, blinding him for an instant; then he saw
her. A huge four-posted bed with silken hangings occupied a recess in the room. Across its
foot a low couch was drawn. She had thrown
herself there. Her head was pillowed on crimson gold-embroidered cushions; her diaphanous
draperies, billowing foam-like over her, half concealed, half revealed her lovely form; her hair
waved away from her brows, and spread like a
shower of gold over the cushions. One bare arm
hung to the floor; something jewel-like gleamed
in the half-closed hand; the other lay across her
forehead, and from beneath it her eyes were fixed
upon him. He sprang forward with a cry. . . .
At first he could remember nothing. The
windows were open; the heavy curtains which
shaded them moved lazily in the breeze; a shaft
of sunlight that came in between them fell upon
the polished surface of the marble mantel. He
examined with languid curiosity some trifles that
stood there—a pair of Dresden figures, a blue
Sèvres vase of graceful shape, a bronze clock
with gilded rose-wreathed Cupids; and then
raised his eyes to the two portraits which hung
above. One of these was familiar enough—the
dark, melancholy face of Félix Arnault, whose

portrait by different hands and at different periods of his life hung in nearly every room at La Glorieuse. The blood surged into his face and receded again at sight of the other. Oh, so strangely like! The yellow hair, the slumberous eyes, the full throat clasped about with a single strand of coral. Yes, it was she! He lifted himself on his elbow. He was in bed. Surely this was the room into which she had drawn him with her eyes. Did he sink on the threshold, all his senses swooning into delicious death? Or had he, indeed, in that last moment thrown himself on his knees by her couch? He could not remember, and he sank back with a sigh.

Instantly Madame Arnault was bending over him. Her cool hands were on his forehead. "*Dieu merci!*" she exclaimed, "thou art thyself once more, *mon fils*."

He seized her hand imperiously. "Tell me, madame," he demanded—"tell me, for the love of God! What is she? Who is she? Why have you shut her away in this deserted place? Why—"

She was looking down at him with an expression half of pity, half of pain.

"Forgive me," he faltered, involuntarily, all his darker suspicions somehow vanishing; "but—oh, tell me!"

"Calm thyself, Richard," she said, soothingly, seating herself on the side of the bed, and stroking his hand gently. Too agitated to speak, he continued to gaze at her with imploring eyes. "Yes, yes, I will relate the whole story," she added, hastily, for he was panting and struggling for speech. "I heard you fall last night," she continued, relapsing for greater ease into French; "for I was full of anxiety about you, and I lingered long at my window watching for you. I came at once with Marcelite, and found you lying insensible across the threshold of this room. We lifted you to the bed, and bled you after the old fashion, and then I gave you a tisane of my own making, which threw you into a quiet sleep. I have watched beside you until your waking. Now you are but a little weak from fasting and excitement, and when you have rested and eaten—"

"No," he pleaded; "now, at once!"

"Very well," she said, simply. She was silent a moment, as if arranging her thoughts. "Your grandfather, a Richard Keith like yourself," she began, "was a college-mate and friend of my brother, Henri Raymonde, and accompanied him to La Glorieuse during one of their vacations. I was already betrothed to Monsieur Arnault, but I— No matter! I never saw Richard Keith afterwards. But years later he sent your father, who also bore his name, to visit me here. My son, Félix, was but a year or so younger than his boy, and the two lads became at once warm friends. They went abroad, and pursued their studies side by side, like brothers. They came home together, and when Richard's father died, Félix spent nearly a year with him on his Maryland plantation. They exchanged, when apart, almost daily letters. Richard's marriage, which

8

occurred soon after they left college, strength-
ened rather than weakened this extraordinary
bond between them. Then came on the war.
They were in the same command, and hardly
lost sight of each other during their four years
of service.

"When the war was ended, your father went
back to his estates. Félix turned his face homeward, but drifted by some strange chance down
to Florida, where he met *her*"—she glanced at
the portrait over the mantel. "Hélène Pallacier
was Greek by descent, her family having been
among those brought over some time during the
last century as colonists to Florida from the
Greek islands. He married her, barely delaying
his marriage long enough to write me that he
was bringing home a bride. She was young,
hardly more than a child, indeed, and marvel-
lously beautiful"—Keith moved impatiently; he
found these family details tedious and uninter-
esting—"a radiant, soulless creature, whose only
law was her own selfish enjoyment, and whose
coming brought pain and bitterness to La Glorieuse. These were her rooms. She chose them
because of the rose-garden, for she had a sensu-
ous and passionate love of nature. She used to
lie for hours on the grass there, with her arms
flung over her head, gazing dreamily at the flut-
tering leaves above her. The pearls—which she
always wore—some coral ornaments, and a handful of amber beads were her only dower, but
her caprices were the insolent and extravagant
caprices of a queen. Félix, who adored her, grat-

"IT YIELDED SUDDENLY, AS IF OPENED FROM WITHIN".

ified them at whatever expense; and I think at
first she had a careless sort of regard for him.
But she hated the little Félice, whose coming
gave her the first pang of physical pain she had
ever known. She never offered the child a ca-
ress. She sometimes looked at her with a suppressed rage which filled me with terror and
anxiety.

"When Félice was a little more than a year old,
your father came to La Glorieuse to pay us a
long-promised visit. His wife had died some
months before, and you, a child of six or seven
years, were left in charge of relatives in Maryland. Richard was in the full vigor of manhood,
broad - shouldered, tall, blue - eyed, and blond-
haired, like his father and like you. From the
moment of their first meeting Hélène exerted all
the power of her fascination to draw him to her.
Never had she been so whimsical, so imperious,
so bewitching! Loyal to his friend, faithful to
his own high sense of honor, he struggled against
a growing weakness, and finally fled. I will never forget the night he went away. A ball had
been planned by Félix in honor of his friend.
The ball - room was decorated under his own
supervision. The house was filled with guests
from adjoining parishes; everybody, young and
old, came from the plantations around. Hélène
was dazzling that night. The light of triumph
lit her cheeks; her eyes shone with a softness
which I had never seen in them before. I watched
her walking up and down the room with Richard,
or floating with him in the dance. They were

like a pair of radiant god-like visitants from
another world. My heart ached for them in
spite of my indignation and apprehension; for
light whispers were beginning to circulate, and I
saw more than one meaning smile directed at
them. Félix, who was truth itself, was gayly
unconscious.

"Towards midnight I heard far up the bayou
the shrill whistle of the little packet which passed
up and down then, as now, twice a week, and
presently she swung up to our landing. Richard
was standing with Hélène by the fireplace. They
had been talking for some time in low, earnest
tones. A sudden look of determination came
into his eyes. I saw him draw from his finger a
ring which she had one day playfully bade him
wear, and offer it to her. His face was white
and strained; hers wore a look which I could
not fathom. He quitted her side abruptly and
walked rapidly across the room, threading his
way among the dancers, and disappeared in the
press about the door. A few moments later a
note was handed me. I heard the boat steam
away from the landing as I read it. It was a
hurried line from Richard. He said that he had
been called away on urgent business, and he
begged me to make his adieus to Madame Arnault and Félix. Félix was worried and perplexed by the sudden departure of his guest.
Hélène said not a word, but very soon I saw
her slipping down the stair, and I knew that she
had gone to her room. Her absence was not remarked, for the ball was at its height. It was

almost daylight when the last dance was concluded, and the guests who were staying in the house had retired to their rooms.

"Félix, having seen to the comfort of all, went at last to join his wife. He burst into my room a second later, almost crazed with horror and grief. I followed him to this room. She was lying on a couch at the foot of the bed. One arm was thrown across her forehead, the other hung to the floor, and in her hand she held a tiny silver bottle with a jewelled stopper. A handkerchief, with a single drop of blood upon it, was lying on her bosom. A faint, curious odor exhaled from her lips and hung about the room, but the poison had left no other trace.

"No one save ourselves and Marcelite ever knew the truth. She had danced too much at the ball that night, and she had died suddenly of heart-disease. We buried her out yonder in the old Raymonde-Arnault burying-ground. I do not know what the letter contained which Félix wrote to Richard. He never uttered his name afterwards. The ball-room — the whole wing, in truth—was at once closed. Everything was left exactly as it was on that fatal night. A few years ago, the house being unexpectedly full, I opened the room in which you have been staying, and it has been used from time to time as a guest-room since. My son lived some years, prematurely old, heart-broken, and desolate. He died with her name on his lips."

Madame Arnault stopped.

A suffocating sensation was creeping over her

listener. Only in the last few moments had the signification of the story begun to dawn upon him. "Do you mean," he gasped, "that the girl whom I—that she is—was—"

"Hélène, the dead wife of Félix Arnault," she replied, gravely. "Her restless spirit has walked here before. I have sometimes heard her tantalizing laugh echo through the house, but no one had ever seen her until you came—so like the Richard Keith she loved!"

"When I read your letter," she went on, after a short silence, "which told me that you wished to come to those friends to whom your father had been so dear, all the past arose before me, and I felt that I ought to forbid your coming. But I remembered how Félix and Richard had loved each other before she came between them. I thought of the other Richard Keith whom I— I loved once; and I dreamed of a union at last between the families. I hoped, Richard, that you and Félice—"

But Richard was no longer listening. He wished to believe the whole fantastic story an invention of the keen-eyed old madame herself. Yet something within him confessed to its truth. A tumultuous storm of baffled desire, of impotent anger, swept over him. The ring he wore burned into his flesh. But he had no thought of removing it — the ring which had once belonged to the beautiful golden-haired woman who had come back from the grave to woo him to her!

He turned his face away and groaned.

Her eyes hardened. She arose stiffly. "I will send a servant with your breakfast," she said, with her hand on the door. "The down boat will pass La Glorieuse this afternoon. You will perhaps wish to take advantage of it."

He started. He had not thought of going—of leaving her—*her!* He looked at the portrait on the wall and laughed bitterly.

Madame Arnault accompanied him with ceremonious politeness to the front steps that afternoon.

"Mademoiselle Félice?" he murmured, inquiringly, glancing back at the windows of the sitting-room.

"Mademoiselle Arnault is occupied," she coldly returned. "I will convey to her your farewell."

He looked back as the boat chugged away. Peaceful shadows enwrapped the house and overspread the lawn. A single window in the wing gleamed like a bale-fire in the rays of the setting sun.

The years that followed were years of restless wandering for Richard Keith. He visited his estate but rarely. He went abroad and returned, hardly having set foot to land; he buried himself in the fastnesses of the Rockies; he made a long, aimless sea-voyage. Her image accompanied him everywhere. Between him and all he saw hovered her faultless face; her red mouth smiled at him; her white arms enticed him. His own face became worn and his step listless. He grew silent and gloomy. "He is madder than the old colo-

nel, his father, was," his friends said, shrugging
their shoulders.

One day, more than three years after his visit
to La Glorieuse, he found himself on a deserted
part of the Florida sea-coast. It was late in November, but the sky was soft and the air warm
and balmy. He bared his head as he paced
moodily to and fro on the silent beach. The
waves rolled languidly to his feet and receded,
leaving scattered half-wreaths of opalescent foam
on the snowy sands. The wind that fanned his
face was filled with the spicy odors of the sea.
Seized by a capricious impulse, he threw off his
clothes and dashed into the surf. The undu-
lating billows closed around him; a singular las-
situde passed into his limbs as he swam ; he felt
himself slowly sinking, as if drawn downward by
an invisible hand. He opened his eyes. The
waves lapped musically above his head; a tawny
glory was all about him, a luminous expanse, in
which he saw strangely formed creatures moving,
darting, rising, falling, coiling, uncoiling.

"You was jess on de eedge er drowndin', Mars
Dick," said Wiley, his black body-servant, spreading his own clothes on the porch of the little fish-
ing-hut to dry. "In de name o' Gawd, whar
mek you wanter go in swimmin' dis time o' de
yea', anyhow ? Ef I hadn' er splunge in an' fotch
you out, dey'd er been mo'nin' yander at de plantation, sho !"

His master laughed lazily. "You are right,
Wiley," he said ; "and you are going to smoke
the best tobacco in Maryland as long as you

"'WHAR MEK YOU WANTER GO IN SWIMMIN'?'"

live." He felt buoyant. Youth and elasticity seemed to have come back to him at a bound. He stretched himself on the rough bench, and watched the blue rings of smoke curl lightly away from his cigar. Gradually he was aware of a pair of wistful eyes shining down on him. His heart leaped. They were the eyes of Félice Arnault! "My God, have I been mad!" he muttered. His eyes sought his hand. The ring, from which he had never been parted, was gone. It had been torn from his finger in his wrestle with the sea. "Get my traps together at once, Wiley," he said. "We are going to La Glorieuse."

"Now you *talkin'*, Mars Dick," assented Wiley, cheerfully.

It was night when he reached the city. First of all, he made inquiries concerning the little packet. He was right; the *Assumption* would leave the next afternoon at five o'clock for Bayou L'Éperon. He went to the same hotel at which he had stopped before when on his way to La Glorieuse. The next morning, too joyous to sleep, he rose early, and went out into the street. A gray, uncertain dawn was just struggling into the sky. A few people on their way to market or to early mass were passing along the narrow banquettes; sleepy-eyed women were unbarring the shutters of their tiny shops; high-wheeled milk-carts were rattling over the granite pavements; in the vine-hung courtyards, visible here and there through iron *grilles*, parrots were scolding on their perches; children pattered up and down the long, arched corridors; the prolonged cry of an early clothes-pole man echoed, like the note of a winding horn, through the close alleys. Keith sauntered carelessly along.

"In so many hours," he kept repeating to himself, "I shall be on my way to La Glorieuse. The boat will swing into the home landing; the negroes will swarm across the gang-plank, laughing and shouting; Madame Arnault and Félice will come out on the gallery and look, shading their eyes with their hands. Oh, I know quite well that the old madame will greet me coldly at first. Her eyes are like steel when she is angry. But when she knows that I am once more a sane man— And Félice, what if she— But no! Félice is not the kind of woman who loves more than once; and she did love me, God bless her! unworthy as I was."

A carriage, driven rapidly, passed him; his eyes followed it idly, until it turned far away into a side street. He strayed on to the market, where he seated himself on a high stool in *L'Appel du Matin* coffee-stall. But a vague, teasing remembrance was beginning to stir in his brain. The turbaned woman on the front seat of the carriage that had rolled past him yonder, where had he seen that dark, grave, wrinkled face, with the great hoops of gold against either cheek? *Marcelite!* He left the stall and retraced his steps, quickening his pace almost to a run as he went. Félice herself, then, might be in the city. He hurried to the street into which the carriage had turned, and glanced down between the rows of wide-eaved cottages with green doors and

batten shutters. It had stopped several squares
away; there seemed to be a number of people
gathered about it. "I will at least satisfy myself," he thought.

As he came up, a bell in a little cross-crowned
tower began to ring slowly. The carriage stood
in front of a low red-brick house, set directly on
the street; a silent crowd pressed about the entrance. There was a hush within. He pushed
his way along the banquette to the steps. A
young nun, in a brown serge robe, kept guard at
the door. She wore a wreath of white artificial
roses above her long coarse veil. Something in
his face appealed to her, and she found a place
for him in the little convent chapel.

Madame Arnault, supported by Marcelite, was
kneeling in front of the altar, which blazed with
candles. She had grown frightfully old and frail.
Her face was set, and her eyes were fixed with a
rigid stare on the priest who was saying mass.
Marcelite's dark cheeks were streaming with
tears. The chapel, which wore a gala air, with
its lights and flowers, was filled with people. On
the left of the altar, a bishop, in gorgeous robes,
was sitting, attended by priests and acolytes; on
the right, the wooden panel behind an iron grating had been removed, and beyond, in the nun's
choir, the black-robed sisters of the Carmelite
order were gathered. Heavy veils shrouded their
faces and fell to their feet. They held in their
hands tall wax-candles, whose yellow flames
burned steadily in the semi-darkness. Five or six
young girls knelt, motionless as statues, in their

midst. They also carried tapers, and their rapt
faces were turned towards the unseen altar within, of which the outer one is but the visible token.
Their eyelids were downcast. Their white veils
were thrown back from their calm foreheads, and
floated like wings from their shoulders.

He felt no surprise when he saw Félice among
them. He seemed to have foreknown always that
he should find her thus on the edge of another
and mysterious world into which he could not
follow her.

Her skin had lost a little of its warm, rich tint;
the soft rings of hair were drawn away under her
veil; her hands were thin, and as waxen as the
taper she held. An unearthly beauty glorified
her pale face.

"Is it forever too late ?" he asked himself in
agony, covering his face with his hands. When
he looked again the white veil on her head had
been replaced by the sombre one of the order.
"If I could but speak to her !" he thought; "if
she would but once lift her eyes to mine, she
would come to me even now !"

Félice! Did the name break from his lips in
a hoarse cry that echoed through the hushed
chapel, and silenced the voice of the priest? He
never knew. But a faint color swept into her
cheeks. Her eyelids trembled. In a flash the
rose-garden at La Glorieuse was before him; he
saw the turquoise sky, and heard the mellow chorus of the field gang; the smell of damask-roses
was in the air; her little hand was in his . . . he
saw her coming swiftly towards him across the

dusk of the old ball-room; her limpid, innocent eyes were smiling into his own .... she was standing on the grassy lawn; the shadows of the leaves flickered over her white gown. . . .

At last the quivering eyelids were lifted. She turned her head slowly, and looked steadily at him. He held his breath. A cart rumbled along the cobble-stones outside; the puny wail of a child sounded across the stillness; a handful of rose-leaves from a vase at the foot of the altar dropped on the hem of Madame Arnault's dress. It might have been the gaze of an angel in a world where there is no marrying nor giving in marriage, so pure was it, so passionless, so free of anything like earthly desire.

As she turned her face again towards the altar the bell in the tower above ceased tolling; a triumphant chorus leaped into the air, borne aloft by joyous organ tones. The first rays of the morning sun streamed in through the small windows. Then light penetrated into the nun's choir, and enveloped like a mantle of gold Sister Mary of the Cross, who in the world had been Félicité Arnault.

THE SOUL OF ROSE DÉDÉ

THE child pushed his way through the tall weeds, which were dripping with the midsummer-eve midnight dew-melt. He was so little that the rough leaves met above his head. He wore a trailing white gown whose loose folds tripped him, so that he stumbled and fell over a sunken mound. But he laughed as he scrambled to his feet—a cooing baby laugh, taken up by the inward-blowing Gulf wind, and carried away to the soughing pines that made a black line against the dim sky.

His progress was slow, for he stopped—his forehead gravely puckered, his finger in his mouth —to listen to the clear whistle of a mockingbird in the live-oak above his head; he watched the heavy flight of a white night-moth from one jimson-weed trumpet to another; he strayed aside to pick a bit of shining punk from the sloughing bark of a rotten log; he held this in his closed palm as he came at last into the open space where the others were.

"Holà, 'Tit-Pierre!" said André, who was half reclining on a mildewed marble slab, with his long black cloak floating loosely from his shoulders, and his hands clasped about his knees. "Holà! Must thou needs be ever a-searching! Have I not told thee, little Hard-Head, that she hath long forgotten thee?"

His voice was mocking, but his dark eyes were quizzically kind.

The child's under-lip quivered, and he turned slowly about. But Père Lebas, sitting just across the narrow footway, laid a caressing hand on his curly head. "Nay, go thy way, 'Tit Pierre," he said, gently; "André does but tease. A mother hath never yet forgot her child."

"Do you indeed think he will find her?" asked André, arching his black brows incredulously.

"He will not find her," returned the priest. "Margot Caillion was in a far country when I saw her last, and even then her grandchildren were playing about her knees. But it harms not the child to seek her."

They spoke a soft provincial French, and the familiar *thou* betokened an unwonted intimacy between the hollow-cheeked old priest and his companion, whose forehead wore the frankness of early youth.

"I would the child could talk!" cried the young man, gayly. "Then might he tell us somewhat of the women that ever come and go in yonder great house."

The priest shuddered, crossing himself, and drew his cowl over his face.

'Tit-Pierre, his gown gathered in his arm, had gone on his way. Nathan Pilger, hunched up

on a low, irregular hummock against the picket-
fence, made a speaking-trumpet of his two horny
hands, and pretended to hail him as he passed.
'Tit-Pierre nodded brightly at the old man, and
waved his own chubby fist.

The gate sagged a little on its hinges, so that
he had some difficulty in moving it. But he
squeezed through a narrow opening, and passed
between the prim flower-beds to the house.

It was a lofty mansion, with vast wings on
either side, and wide galleries, which were upheld by fluted columns. It faced the bay, and
a covered arcade ran from the entrance across
the lawn to a gay little wooden kiosk, which
hung on the bluff over the water's edge. A flight
of stone steps led up to the house. 'Tit-Pierre
climbed these laboriously. The great carved
doors were closed, but a blind of one of the long
French windows in the west wing stood slightly
ajar. 'Tit-Pierre pushed this open. The bedchamber into which he peered was large and
luxuriously furnished. A lamp with a crimson
shade burned on its claw-footed gilt pedestal in
a corner; the low light diffused a rosy radiance
about the room. The filmy curtains at the windows waved to and fro softly in the June night
wind. The huge old-fashioned, four-posted bed,
overhung by a baldachin of carved wood with
satin linings, occupied a deep alcove. A woman
was sleeping there beneath the lace netting. The
snow-white bed-linen followed the contours of
her rounded limbs, giving her the look of a re-
cumbent marble statue. Her black hair, loosed

from its heavy coil, spread over the pillow. One exquisite bare arm lay across her forehead, partly concealing her face. Her measured breathing rose and fell rhythmically on the air. A robe of pale silk that hung across a chair, dainty laceedged garments tossed carelessly on an antique lounge — these seemed instinct still with the nameless, subtle grace of her who had but now put them off.

On a table by the window, upon whose threshold the child stood atiptoe, was set a large crystal bowl filled with water-lilies. Their white petals were folded; the round, red-lined green leaves glistened in the lamp-light. One long bud, rolled tightly in its green and brown sheath, hung over the fluted edge of the bowl, swaying gently on its flexible stem. 'Tit-Pierre gazed at it intently, frowning a little, then put out a small forefinger and touched it. A quick thrill ran along the stem; the bud moved lightly from side to side and burst suddenly into bloom; the slim white petals quivered; a tremulous, sighing, whispering sound issued from the heart of gold. The child listened, holding the fragrant disk to his pink ear, and laughed softly.

He moved about the room, examining with infantile curiosity the costly objects scattered upon small tables and ranged upon the low, manyshelved mantel.

Presently he pushed a chair against the foot of the bed, climbed upon it, lifted the netting, and crept cautiously to the sleeper's side. He sat for a moment regarding her. Her lips were

9

parted in a half-smile; the long lashes which swept her cheeks were wet, as if a happy tear had just trembled there. 'Tit-Pierre laid his hand on her smooth wrist, and touched timidly the snowy globes that gleamed beneath the open-work of her night-dress. She threw up her arm, turning her face full upon him, unclosed her large, luminous eyes, smiled, and slept again.

With a sigh, which seemed rather of resignation than of disappointment, the child crept away and clambered again to the floor.

. . . Outside the fog was thickening. The dark waters of the bay lapped the foot of the low bluff; their soft, monotonous moan was rising by imperceptible degrees to a higher key. The scrubby cedars, leaning at all angles over the water, were shaken at intervals by heavy puffs of wind, which drove the mist in white, ragged masses across the shelled road, over the weedy neutral ground, and out into the tops of the sombre pines. The red lights in a row of sloops at anchor over against Cat Island had dwindled to faintly glimmering sparks. The watery flash of the revolving light in the light-house off the point of the island showed a black wedge-shaped cloud stretching up the seaward sky.

Nathan Pilger screwed up his eye and watched the cloud critically. André followed the direction of his gaze with idle interest, then turned to look again at the woman who sat on a grassy barrow a few paces beyond Père Lebas.

"She has never been here before," he said to

himself, his heart stirring curiously. "I would I could see her face!"

Her back was towards the little group; her elbow was on her knee, her chin in her hand. Her figure was slight and girlish; her white gown gleamed ghostlike in the wan light.

"Naw, I bain't complainin', nor nothin'," said the old sailor, dropping the cloud, as it were, and taking up a broken thread of talk; "hows'ever, it's tarnation wearyin' a-settin' here so studdy year in an' year out. Leas'ways," he added, shifting his seat to another part of the low mound, "fer an old sailor sech as I be."

"If one could but quit his place and move about, like 'Tit-Pierre yonder," said André, musingly, "it would not be so bad. For myself, I would not want—"

"The child is free to come and go because his soul is white. There is no stain upon 'Tit-Pierre. The child hath not sinned." It was the priest who spoke. His voice was harsh and forbidding. His deep-set eyes were fixed upon the tall spire of Our Lady of the Gulf, dimly outlined against the sky beyond an intervening reach of clustering roofs and shaded gardens.

André stared at him wonderingly, and glanced half furtively at the stranger, as if in her presence, perchance, might be found an explanation of the speaker's unwonted bitterness of tone. She had not moved. "I would I could see her face!" he muttered, under his breath. "For myself," he went on, lifting his voice, "I am sure I would not want to wander far. I fain

would walk once more on the road along the
curve of the bay ; or under the pines, where little white patches of moonlight fall between the
straight, tall tree-trunks. And I would go sometimes, if I might, and kneel before the altar of
Our Lady of the Gulf."

Nathan Pilger grunted contemptuously.
"What a lan'lubber ye be, Andry!" he said, his
strong nasal English contrasting oddly with the
smooth foreign speech of the others. "What a
lan'lubber ye be! Ye bain't no sailor, like your
father afore ye. Tony Dewdonny hed as good
a pair o' sea-legs as ever I see. Lord! if there
wa'n't no dif*fick*ulties in the way, Nathan Pilger
'd ship fer some port a leetle more furrin than
the shadder of Our Lady yunder! Many's the
deck I've walked," he continued, his husky voice
growing more and more animated, "an' many's
the vi'ge I've made to outlandish places. Why,
you'd oughter see Arkangel, Andry. Here's the
north coast o' Rooshy"—he leaned over and
traced with his forefinger the rude outlines of a
map on the ground ; the wind lifted his long,
gray locks and tossed them over his wrinkled
forehead ; "here's the White Sea ; and here, off
the mouth of the Dewiny River, is Arkangel.
The Rooshan men in that there town, Andry,
wears petticoats like women ; whilse down here,
in the South Pacific, at Taheety, the folks don't
wear no clo'es at all to speak of! You'd oughter
see Taheety, Andry. An' here, off Guinea—"

"All those places are fine, no doubt," interrupted his listener, "Arkangel and Tahee*tee*

and Guinee "—his tongue tripped a little over
the unfamiliar names — "but, for myself, I do
not care to see them. I find it well on the bay
shore here, where I can see the sloops come sail-
ing in through the pass, with the sun on their
white sails. And the little boats that rock on
the water! Do you remember, Silvain," he cried,
turning to the priest, "how we used to steal
away before sunrise in my father's little fishing-
boat, when we were boys, and come back at night
with our backs blistered by the sun and our arms
aching, hein? That was before you went away
to France to study for the priesthood. Ah, but
those were good times!" He threw back his
head and laughed joyously. His dark hair, wet
with the mist, lay in loose rings on his forehead;
his fine young face, beardless but manly, seemed
almost lustrous in the pale darkness. "Do you
remember, Silvain? Right where the big house
stands, there was Jacques Caillion's steep-roofed
cottage, with the garden in front full of pinks
and mignonette and sweet herbs; and the vine-
hung porch where 'Tit-Pierre used to play, and
where Margot Caillion used to stand shading her
eyes with her arm, and looking out for her man
to come home from sea."

"Jack Caillion," said Nathan Pilger, "was
washed overboard from the *Suzanne* in a storm
off Hatteras in '11—him and Dune Cook and
Ba'tist' Roux."

"The old church of Our Lady of the Gulf,"
the young man continued, "was just a stone's-
throw this side of where the new one was built;

back a little is our cottage, and your father's, Silvain; and in the hollow beyond Justin Roux has his blacksmith's forge."

He paused, his voice dying away almost to a whisper. The waves were beating more noisily against the bluff, filling the silence with a sort of hoarse plaint; the fog—gray, soft, impenetrable—rested on them like a cloud. The moisture fell in an audible drip-drop from the leaves and the long, pendent moss of the live-oaks. A mare, with her colt beside her, came trotting around the bend of the road. She approached within a few feet of the girl, reared violently, snorting, and dashed away, followed by the whinnying colt. The clatter of their feet echoed on the muffled air. The girl, in her white dress, sat rigidly motionless, with her face turned seaward.

André lifted his head and went on, dreamily: "I mind me, most of all, of one day when all the girls and boys of the village walked over to Bayou Galère to gather water-lilies. Margot Caillion, with 'Tit-Pierre in her hand, came along to mind the girls. You had but just come back from France in your priest's frock, Silvain. You were in the church door when we passed, with your book in your hand." A smothered groan escaped the priest, and he threw up his arm as if to ward off a blow. "And you were there when we came back at sunset. The smell of the pines that day was like balm. The lilies were white on the dark breast of the winding bayou. Rose Dédé's arms were heaped so full of lilies that you could only see her laughing black eyes

above them. But Lorance would only take a
few buds. She said it was a kind of sin to take
them away from the water where they grew.
Lorance was ever—"

The girl had dropped her hands in her lap,
and was listening. At the sound of her own
name she turned her face towards the speaker.

"*Lorance!*" gasped André. "Is it truly you,
Lorance?"

"Yes, it is I, André Dieudonné," she replied,
quietly. Her pale girlish face, with its delicate
outlines, was crowned with an aureole of bright
hair, which hung in two thick braids to her waist;
her soft brown eyes were a little sunken, as if she
had wept overmuch. But her voice was strangely cold and passionless.

"But . . . when did you . . . come, Lorance?"
André demanded, breathlessly.

"I came," she said, in the same calm, measured tone, "but a little after you, André Dieudonné. First 'Tit-Pierre, then you, and then
myself."

"Why, then—" he began. He rose abruptly,
gathering his mantle about him, and leaned
over the marble slab where he had been sitting.
"'*Sacred to the memory of André Antoine Marie
Dieudonné,*'" he read, slowly, slipping his finger
along the mouldy French lettering, "'*who died
at this place August 20th, 1809. In the 22d year
of his age.*' Eighty years and more ago I came!"
he cried. "And you have been here all these
years, Lorance, and I have not known! Why,
then, did you never come up?"

She did not answer at once. "I was tired," she said, presently, "and I rested well down there in the cool, dark silence. And I was not lonely . . . at first, for I heard Margot Caillion passing about, putting flowers above 'Tit-Pierre and you and me. My mother and yours often came and wept with her for us all—and my father, and your little brothers. The sound of their weeping comforted me. Then . . . after a while . . . no one seemed to remember us any more."

"Margot Caillion," said Nathan Pilger, "went back, when her man was drownded, to the place in France where she was born. The others be all layin' in the old church-yard yunder on the hill . . . all but Silvann Leebaw an' me."

She looked at the old man and smiled gravely. "A long time passed," she went on, slowly. "I could sometimes hear you speak to 'Tit-Pierre, André Dieudonné; . . . and at last some men came and dug quite near me; and as they pushed their spades through the moist turf they talked about the good Père Lebas; and then I knew that Silvain was coming." The priest's head fell upon his breast; he covered his face with his hands and rocked to and fro on his low seat. "Not long after, Nathan Pilger came. Down there in my narrow chamber I have heard above me, year after year, the murmur of your voices on St. John's eve, and ever the feet of 'Tit-Pierre, as he goes back and forth seeking his mother. But I cared not to leave my place. For why should I wish to look upon your face, André Dieudonné, and

mark there the memory of your love for Rose
Dédé?"

Her voice shook with a sudden passion as she
uttered the last words. The hands lying in her
lap were twisted together convulsively; a flush
leaped into her pale cheeks.

"Rose Dédé!" echoed André, amazedly. "Nay,
Lorance, but I never loved Rose Dédé! If she
perchance cared for me—"

"Silence, fool!" cried the priest, sternly. He
had thrown back his cowl; his eyes glowed like
coals in his white face; he lifted his hand men-
acingly. "Thou wert ever a vain puppet, André Dieudonné. It was not for such as thou
that Rose Dédé sinned away her soul! Was it
thou she came at midnight to meet in the lone
shadows of these very live-oaks? Hast *thou*
ever worn the garments of a priest? . . . They
shunned Rose Dédé in the village . . . but the
priest said mass at the altar of Our Lady of the
Gulf, . . . and the wail of the babe was sharp in
the hut under the pines, . . . and it ceased to
breathe, . . . and the mother turned her face to
the wall and died, . . . and my heart was cold in
my breast as I looked on the dead faces of the
mother and the child. . . . They lie under the
pine-trees by Bayou Galère. But the priest lived
to old age; . . . and when he died, he durst not
sleep in consecrated ground, but fain would lie
in the shadows of the live oaks, where the dark
eyes of Rose Dédé looked love into his."

His wild talk fell upon unheeding ears. 'Tit-
Pierre had come out of the house. He was nest-

ling against Nathan Pilger's knee. He held a lily-bud in one hand, and with the other he caressed the sailor's weather-beaten cheek.

"'Tit-Pierre," whispered the old man, "that is Lorance Baudrot. Do you remember her, 'Tit-Pierre?" The child smiled intelligently. "Lorance was but a slip of a girl when I come down here from Cape Cod — cabin - boy aboard the *Mary Ann*. She was the pretties' lass on all the bay shore. An' I — I loved her, 'Tit-Pierre. But I wa'n't no match agin Andry Dew-donny; an' I know'd it from the fust. Andry was the likelies' lad hereabout, an' the harnsomes'. I see that Lorance loved him. An' when the yaller-fever took him, I see her a-droopin' an' a-droopin' tell she died, an' she never even know'd I loved her. Her an' Andry was laid here young, 'Tit - Pierre, 'longside o' you. I lived ter be pretty tol'able old; but when I hed made my last v'ige, an' was about fetchin' my las' breath, I give orders ter be laid in this here old buryin'-groun' some'er's clost ter the grave o' Lorance Baudrot."

His voice was overborne by André's exultant tones. "Lorance!" he cried, "did you indeed love me?—me!"

Her dark eyes met his frankly, and she smiled.

"Ah. if I had only known!" he sighed—if I had only known, Lorance, I would surely have lived! We would have walked one morning to Our Lady of the Gulf, with all the village-folk about us, and Silvain—the good Père Lebas—would have joined our hands. . . . My father would have given us a little plot of ground; . . . you would have planted flowers about the door of our cottage; . . . our children would have played in the sand under the bluff. . . ."

A sudden gust of wind blew the fog aside, and a zigzag of flame tore the wedge-shaped cloud in two. A greenish light played for an instant over the weed-grown spot. The mocking-bird, long silent in the heart of the live-oak, began to sing.

"All these years you have been near me," he murmured, reproachfully, "and I did not know." Then, as if struck by a breathless thought, he stretched out his arms imploringly. "I love you, Lorance," he said. "I have always loved you. Will you not be my wife now? Silvain will say the words, and 'Tit-Pierre, who can go back and forth, will put this ring, which was my mother's, upon your finger, and he will bring me a curl of your soft hair to twist about mine. I cannot come to you, Lorance; I cannot even touch your hand. But when I go down into my dark place I can be content dreaming of you. And on the blessed St. John's eves I will know you are mine, as you sit there in your white gown."

As he ceased speaking, Père Lebas, with his head upon his breast, began murmuring, as if mechanically, the words which preface the holy sacrament of marriage. His voice faltered, he raised his head, and a cry of wonder burst from his lips. For André had moved away from the mouldy gravestone and stood just in front of him. Lorance, as if upborne on invisible wings, was floating lightly across the intervening space. Her shroud enveloped her like a cloud, her arms were extended, her lips were parted in a rapt smile. Nathan Pilger, with 'Tit-Pierre in his arms, had limped forward. He halted beside André, and as the young man folded the girl to his breast, the child reached over and laid an open lily on her down-drooped head.

The priest stared wildly at them, and struggled to rise, but could not. As he sank panting back upon the crumbling tomb, his anguish overcame him. "My God!" he groaned hoarsely, "I, only I, cannot move from my place. *The soul of Rose Dédé hangs like a millstone about my neck!*"

Even as he spoke, the cloud broke with a roar. The storm — black, heavy, thunderous — came rushing across the bay. It blotted out, in a lightning's flash, the mansion which stands on the site of Jacques Caillion's hut, and the weed-grown, ancient, forgotten graveyard in its shadow.

. . . And a bell in the steeple of Our Lady of the Gulf rang out the hour.

A MIRACLE

It was the Fourteenth of July. Dolly Lammitt came out on the gallery and looked at the bit of tricolor which floated from a tall staff on the lawn. The glories wreathed about the pillars, and, running along under the wide eaves, made a sort of frame for her slender young figure in its white gown.

Such glories! You would never dream of insulting them by placing before them such limiting adjectives as "morning" and "evening." For they bloom—the glories at San Antonio—all day and all night; great blue disks that sway in the wind and laugh in the sun's face, and call the honey-bees to their hearts with an almost audible murmur.

The green lawn sloped imperceptibly from the one-storied yellow adobe house to the river—the opalescent river San Antonio—which here made one of its unexpected curves, and then rippled away in the direction of the old Mission of San José, half a mile below.

The yuccas which hedged the lawn were in bloom, their tall white-belled spikes glistening

in the sunlight ; a double thread of scarlet pop-
pies marked the path to the river ; the jalousied
porch which jutted from one end of the house
was covered by a cataract of yellowish-pink roses,
whose elusive "tea" scent filled the morning air.

But Dolly's eyes came back from all this blos-
soming to dwell once more on the glories. She
loved them : she was even proud of them, as, indeed, she had a right to be. Did not her own
grandfather—or was it her grandmother— But
wait a bit ; the story is worth telling.

It was away back in the early fifties. The
Eclipse swung her way clear of the overhanging mustang grape-vines on Buffalo Bayou, and
shoved her nose against the muddy landing at
the foot of Main Street. The little town of
Houston lay as if asleep in the gray fog of early
morning. But at the shrill, prolonged sound of
the *Eclipse's* whistle everybody, it would seem,
came hurrying down the black, slippery bluff to
watch the landing of Count Considérant and his
colonists.

The chattering sallow-faced strangers thronged
the guards and the upper deck, gazing down with
curious eyes until the gang-plank — amid the
lusty whoops of the negro deck-hands — was
pushed out ; then they disappeared within.

The crowd on the bluff and along the single
straggling street had increased, and there was a
faint, questioning cheer when the French *émigrés*
came marching up the slope, keeping step, two
and two, men and women.

At the head of the column walked Monsieur le Comte himself—a commanding figure in his velvet coat and cocked hat, with his long hair floating over his shoulders. He carried a naked sword in his hand. The tricolor of France, borne by one of his lieutenants, waved above his head, mingling its folds with the stars and stripes. Madame la Comtesse stepped daintily along beside him. As he set foot on the soil of Texas he lifted his sword, and the self-exiled band burst with one voice into the "Marseillaise." The echoes of the unknown tongue arose, piercing, powerful, resonant, on the strange air, and sped away to die in the silences of the wide prairies.

"*Liberté! Égalité! Fraternité!*" said Monsieur le Comte, bowing right and left to the curious, silent, unresponsive American citizens and citizenesses.

Near the tail end of the procession walked, arm in arm, Achille Lemaître and Étienne Santerre. They fell a little silent when the song ceased. It was very deep, that sticky black mud, and their faces expressed a profound if momentary disgust for the free and untrammelled soil of the New Paradise. Both were young—mere lads, in fact. But both "came from somebody." Achille's grandmother, old Margot Lemaître, had spat in the Queen Marie Antoinette's face as she ascended the guillotine with her hands tied behind her; and Étienne was the grandson of the famous "tall, sonorous Brewer of the Faubourg St.-Antoine"—the formidable Santerre of the French Revolution.

"One has the head quite dizzy after all those days on shipboard," remarked Achille presently. "But behold us at last in the Promised Land !" He repeated between his teeth a snatch of the "Marseillaise." "How that was glorious," he exclaimed—"that time of our grandfathers, when the blood spouted from the mouth of Mother Guillotine !"

Étienne shivered a little, and Achille laughed. "You were ever a chicken-heart, Étienne," he said, with good-natured contempt, "and afraid of the very smell of blood. For myself—"

Étienne was not listening. They had come up the bluff, and halted on its brow while Monsieur le Comte made his little speech to the *Maire*. There was a brown, weather-beaten cottage on their right ; the magnolias shading it were full of blooms — white, mysterious cups, like those whose petals had dropped all night long on the deck of the *Eclipse*, where the lads lay a-sleeping. A girl leaned over the low gate, staring with blue, wide-open eyes at the *émigrés*. Étienne gazed at her like one in a dream ; when they moved on he blushed and sighed, pressing the arm of his companion.

And when, a week later, the Fourierists started on their long, crawling journey to found their *phalanstère* at Réunion, Jenny Lusk, the blue-eyed girl, who had in the meantime become Citoyenne Santerre, accompanied her husband.

Monsieur le Comte, ever restless, ever dreaming lofty Utopian dreams which never came true,

left the *phalanstère* at Réunion before it was fairly
established. Achille Lemaître, taking a dramatic
leave of Citizen Santerre and his wife, followed
the *Fondateur* to San Antonio.

He was very lonesome—Achille—the morning
after his arrival in the old Mexic-American town.
He wandered about the quaint, river - thridded
streets, with the sound of strange speech in his
ears, ready to cry, between wishing himself back
at Réunion with Étienne and thinking of his old
mother in France.

Suddenly, at a turn of the street—it was that
Flores Street where the *acequia* rushes limpid and
musical by the low adobe houses, and lithe, beautiful women swing in their hammocks on latticed
balconies—he met Dolores Concha and her wea-
zened, leather-colored old nurse.

"But you are much too young," said Monsieur
le Comte, frowning, when, cap in hand, and blushing all over his round young face, Achille presented himself, a few weeks later, to ask the
Fondateur's permission to marry. "You are
nothing but a boy."

"Pardon, M'sieu le Comte," stammered Achille,
"I am nearly twenty. I am the youngest of the six
sons of my father. The others all married before
they were nineteen; and my father himself, Jean
Lemaître—"

"Never mind Jean Lemaître." The Count cut
him short, and he promised the necessary papers.
"Since the Señorita is an orphan, and has a *dot*,"
he added. "But I am sorry you do not marry
an American. A brown-skinned Mexican—pah!"

10

"Ah! but when you see Dolores, M'sieu le Comte!" cried Achille.

And M'sieu le Comte, when he saw Dolores, admitted that it truly made a difference.

It was to the yellow adobe house—bought with her *dot*—whose yucca-hedged garden sloped down to the river's edge, that Achille took his wife the day after their marriage—at which Monsieur le Comte "assisted" in the old Cathedral on the Plaza.

A *propriétaire* in his own right! A land-owner! Monsieur Achille Lemaître's socialistic theories vanished into the soft air perfumed by his own roses. He continued to sing the "Marseillaise," and to talk fiercely about the charms of *La Mère Guillotine;* and he planted a flag-staff on his lawn, whence floated on each successive anniversary of the taking of the Bastille *ce brave étendard,* the tricolor of the republic. But he no longer dreamed of sharing his worldly possessions with a Fourierist *phalanstère.* No more, however, did Monsieur le Comte in his fine mansion just across the river.

One morning, some months after Achille became husband and *propriétaire* in one day, he came into the room where his young wife was sitting. His face wore a pleased expression; his lips parted in a smile beneath his budding mustache.

"Soul of my Soul!" cried Dolores, in the mixed Spanish and French which they employed in their intercourse with each other, "why, then, do you smile?"

"It is, Angel of my Life," replied Achille, "that I have planted a seed by my front door-step."

"In the soft little spot on the right, by the pillar?" demanded his wife, with lively interest.

Achille nodded.

"Ah," cried Dolores, triumphantly, "I have myself planted a seed in that very spot this morning."

Achille looked a little vexed. "But, my Soul's Love—" he began.

"It came from Monterey," she continued, "from a vine which grew over my mother's doorway. I remember it quite well. It has white flowers, like little silver trumpets, and the smell of them is heavenly."

"The seed I have planted," said her husband, "came from a vine on my grandmother's balcony at Auteuil. It has big red flowers—oh, red as the blood of Marat in his bath-tub."

"My mother's vine," murmured Madame Lemaître, dreamily, with her large dark eyes fixed on the ceiling, "has a long slim leaf that glistens in the sun."

"The vine of Margo Lemaître," remarked the *propriétaire*, looking out of the window, "has a leaf round as a saucer."

A coolness which lasted several minutes followed these reminiscences; but it melted in a couple of kisses.

Both planters, however, during the next week, inspected frequently—and surreptitiously—the flower bed under the edge of the veranda. They surprised each other there one morning before the sun was up. Both drew back, blushing guilt-ily; but both sprang forward again with a cry, for there, in very truth, was a little vinelet, with trembling, pale green twin leaves.

The leaves were heart-shaped.

"It is the vine of my mother," Dolores said, thoughtfully. "I now remember that the leaves were like hearts."

"It is Margot Lemaître's vine!" roared Achille. "I can see the leaves with my eyes shut. They were precisely of this fashion."

Upon this they quarrelled. Monsieur stamped his foot and swore, and madame fled to her own bedchamber, where she remained weeping, and refusing to come out even to dinner. Then they made up. But only for a little while.

The vine crept up and up, catching hold of the pillar and spreading out its heart-shaped leaves and shaking them in the wind. And Achille and Dolores watched it, and disputed over it, and be-rated each other in French and Spanish, and even in very imperfect "American."

"The flowers will be white, like little silver trumpets," cried the wife.

"The flowers will be red as the blood of Marat in his bath-tub," blustered the husband; "and if I have a son he shall receive under those red flowers his name of Maximilien Robespierre!"

"_Ay de mi! Santa Maria Purissima!_" wailed Dolores. "I will not bear a son to be called after a bloody monster! My son shall have the name of the good St. Joseph!"

It was a terrible time !

But one morning Achille came out of his house, where in the early dawn a night-light was still burning. His face was swollen with weeping, and he staggered as he walked, like a man in liquor.

He crossed the garden to the little gate which opened upon the river steps, and stopped, putting his hands out blindly to grasp the railing. "She will die !" he whispered hoarsely, looking around with blurred eyes which saw nothing. "Mother of God, she will die, never knowing how much I love her ! And I, who have made her weep, brute that I am ! Oh, if she will only live ! But she will die, she will die !" And he shook the railing with such fury that a loose piece at the end fell into the river and swirled around on the dimpling eddy.

"Señor !" It was the shrill voice of the old nurse calling him from the veranda.

But he durst not turn his head.

He heard her come pattering down the path, and his knees became as water.

"Señor," said Marta, "come and see your son."

His son! He shook from head to foot, staring at her with dazed eyes. "Dolores ?" he stammered.

"Santa Maria !" said Marta, impatiently. "Do you think your wife is such a fool that she cannot bring a man - child into the world without dying ?"

"I will tear down that monster of a vine before the red flowers bud upon it," he said within himself, following her, and wiping the glad, foolish tears from his eyes. He glanced up, from habit, at the subject of all their childish quarrels.

He stopped, open-mouthed.

The vine, in one unheeded night, had burst into bloom. The blossoms of it were not white, like little silver trumpets, nor red, like the blood of Marat in his bath-tub. A row of great heavenly blue disks starred the lintel like a crown.

He reached up and plucked one of these miracles, and tiptoed into the hushed and darkened room.

"Heart of my Body!" he sobbed, falling on his knees by the bedside, "our vine has blossomed!" and he laid the glory on her white bosom.

Dolores smiled — an adorable, weak, youngmother smile. "Life of my Soul!" she said, uncovering the little bundle which lay on her arm, "behold your son! He shall be called Maximilien Robespierre."

"But no!" said Achille, solemnly; "we will name our son *Jesus-Mary.*"

Such was the mysterious origin of the blue glories which to-day riot over every house in San Antonio. They may wish to tell you a different story down there, but it would be foolish to listen even, since this is the true one.

Achille Lemaître was killed in a charge at the

battle of Shiloh, and his wife, dying shortly after
of grief at his loss, left her young son in the care
of Monsieur le Comte, his godfather.

And by the time Jesus - Mary had reached the
age *convenable* for a Lemaître to enter the holy
estate of matrimony, and had fetched his American wife to the yellow adobe house by the river,
he had become, through persistent mispronun-
ciation and the American fashion in initial letters, Mr. J. M. Lammitt.

Dolly, baptized Dolores in memory of her beautiful grandmother, continued to look with un-
natural intentness at the glories, blushing, but
pretending not to see Mr. Steven Santer, who
had fastened his little skiff at the landing and
was coming up the poppy-bordered walk.

He took off his straw hat as he approached.

"Good-morning, Miss Lammitt," he said, boldly, though inwardly quaking at his own au-
dacity.

They sat down on the steps together.

Mr. Steven Santer was a good - looking blond
young man from somewhere near the East Fork
of the Trinity. He had come to San Antonio
some weeks earlier on account of business, and
stayed on account of Dolly Lammitt.

"What is that?" he asked, suddenly starting
up from his seat, for a puff of wind had caught
the pennant fastened to the staff on the lawn
and unfurled it.

"That," replied Dolly, "is a French flag. My
father always puts it out on the Fourteenth of
July. The Fourteenth of July," she explained,

with condescension, "is the anniversary of the taking of the Bastille."

"I know," said Santer. "My father," he added, as if apologizing for his own acquaintance with the subject—"my father always runs up a French flag on the Fourteenth of July."

"My grandfather," said Dolly, "came over from France with Count Considérant to the *phalanstère* at Réunion."

"So did my father! Why, they must have sailed together in the *Nuremberg!*"

"What an unheard-of coincidence!"

And so Dolly presently related the history of the glories, or as much of it as Jesus-Mary himself knew. She twirled one of the heavenly blue blossoms in her fingers while she talked; and when she had finished she stretched out her hand to pluck another, but got a splinter instead, which tore the delicate white flesh of her thumb.

She turned pale and bit her lip, drawing in her breath, while Steven Santer wiped away the blood with his handkerchief.

"The sight of blood always makes me ill," she murmured, closing her dark eyes.

Shade of great-great-grandmother Margot Lemaître!

And the great-grandson of Santerre the Sonorous, having thus strategically possessed himself of her hand, kept it in his own.

AT THE CORNER OF ABSINTHE AND ANISETTE

It was drizzling, and the banquette was overlaid with a black slush which seemed to ooze from the very paving-stones. The girl standing on the corner — her slim, white-gowned figure softly outlined against the pink stucco of the wall behind her—appeared curiously at variance with the November-afternoon gloom. The single passenger in a street-car crawling past glanced out at her with a momentary gleam of interest. "She looks like a bayou lily," he murmured, returning to his evening paper.

There is nothing earthly which can compare, for whiteness, with the bayou lily — hovering above the dark marsh like a tethered soul—pure, spotless, radiant ; exhaling an innocent perfume, its flexible stem rooted far below in the slime.

The drizzle became a downpour, and the few pedestrians scurried into shelter, leaving the narrow street quite deserted. The girl drew a little farther under the high, projecting balcony, with its wrought-iron balustrade. Her white gown, slightly open at the throat, as if designed for indoors, was drenched with the wind-blown rain: though, by some miracle, the hem remained unsmirched by the ooze beneath her feet. She was very young. The delicate, almost child-like face beneath her round hat was pale; her violet eyes had a strained, expectant look. She leaned against the wall of the old building, trembling, as if frightened or over-fatigued.

The heavy batten shutters were flung back; their enormous bolts turned aslant; the inner doors, whose upper halves were composed of fancifully shaped panes of ground glass, were closed.

On the same spot—christened by some dead-and-gone wag The Corner of Absinthe and Anisette—stood, in the year of our Lord eighteen hundred and thirteen, the self-same building. It was even then more than a quarter of a century old, and a conspicuous landmark in its isolated situation; a few low habitations only clustering between it and the outlying swamps, and but a thin scattering of houses stretching down to the river. The steep roof of the single squat story was tiled; a long arm thrust out from the eaves held a lantern over the muddy, unpaved street. It was a cabaret then as now; and then, as now, famous for its "green hours."

Its rough outer wall, one morning in the autumn of that year, was adorned with a large printed poster which set forth, in the three languages then current in the old town on the Mississippi, the misdeeds of one Jean Lafitte, smuggler, marauder, desperado, and pirate, and offered, in the name of his Excellency Governor Claiborne, a reward of five hundred dollars for the capture of the said Jean Lafitte and his delivery into the hands of justice.

The laughing eyes of a knot of apparent idlers on the wooden banquette were turned alternately from this placard to the tall, handsome man—no less a person than Jean Lafitte himself!—who leaned against the wall, the long, curling locks of his hair blown against the signature of his (late Provisional) Excellency. But there were covert flashes of malign intelligence in some of the laughing eyes, and an imperceptible movement of the crowd towards the batten door at the outlaw's right hand. His own glances, as he bandied jests with the leaders, toying the while with the fringed end of his green silk sash, went warily about. He knew himself to be in danger of arrest; he might, indeed, pay with his life for his seeming bravado. But he was not thinking of himself. His ear was strained to catch the slightest sound within the cabaret, where Henri Destréhan was blithely quaffing his glass of absinthe, unaware that his enemies, sworn to butcher him like a rat in a trap, were closing upon him.

It was the knowledge of his friend's impending peril which had drawn the pirate chief from his lagoon fastnesses.

"How about that last bale of smuggled silk brocade, Lafitte?" demanded a brawny, dark-browed man, lightly, edging nearer to the wall as he spoke.

"Sold at ten dollars the yard for the waistcoats of his Excellency, the Governor!" returned Lafitte, in the same tone.

"And the gold chain captured on the high seas from His Grace, the Mexican Bishop?" laughed another.

"Sold off in inches for the repose of his Grace's soul."

He had dropped the end of his sash. His hand, as he spoke, was on the door. "*A moi, Destré-han, à moi!*" he cried, bursting into the dimly lighted cabaret. And, catching the bewildered young officer into the sweep of his powerful arm, he lifted him from the floor, bore him through the very midst of his enemies, turned the corner with the leaping speed of a stag, and disappeared behind a clump of cabins in the direction of the swamp. A howl of rage and a volley of shot from the baffled plotters followed the fugitives, but they were already safe from pursuit.

A few days later Destréhan was about starting on his roundabout journey to France. A pirogue, dancing on the breast of the sinuous bayou which led away from the outlaw's stronghold at Barrataria, awaited him with its lithe, dark-skinned paddler. "If ever a Destréhan" —these were his parting words to Lafitte, with a warm hand-clasp—"if ever a Destréhan fails a Lafitte in the hour of need, may his soul die and his bones rot unburied."

Léonie Destran, apparently unconscious of the rain, which continued to fall, was waiting still.

The pallor of her delicate face had increased. She moved nearer to the closed door of the cabaret.

Within there was a drowsy silence. The fat, bald-headed proprietor was nodding over an out-worn copy of *La Mouche*.

It was midway between *les heurs vertes*—early and late—of the staid and respectable habitués who came with the regularity of unimpeachable clocks every day at noon, and every day before setting towards their late dinners.

The floor had been re-sanded since noon and swept into fresh geometrical figures, and the old-fashioned wooden bar with its simple fixtures was in readiness for the six o'clock *clientèle*.

There was, however, a single patron, who stood with his left hand resting lightly on the bar ; in his right hand he held a small tumbler ; the wan light filtering in through the ground glass of the door fell upon its cloudy green contents, giving them a strange, unearthly gleam.

The man, who was elegantly and fashionably attired, was young and extraordinarily handsome, though his face showed signs of dissipation, and his dark eyes beneath the thick brows had a bold, unpleasant expression.

He wore a white flower in his buttonhole.

He lifted the glass to his lips, but set it down hastily. *Octave Lafitte !* It was a whisper, a faintly dying breath, but he heard his own name distinctly pronounced. He looked at the deaf old man half asleep in his chair ; then he stepped noiselessly to the door. The rain, striking him full in the face as he opened it, blurred his vision for a second. "Mademoiselle Destran! Léonie!" he exclaimed, starting back surprised, his dark face flushing with pleasure.

She lifted her hand. "Stay, monsieur," she said, speaking rapidly and in French, "there is no time for words. I was following you, and I saw you enter here. I have been waiting for you to come out, but I dared wait no longer. You must leave this State—this country—at once. Stay"—for he was beginning to speak—"'Toinette Farge, on Bayou Desnoyers, near our plantation, has confessed to her father that it is you"—a wave of crimson dyed her face and throat, but she continued to look steadily at him—"that it is you who have disgraced her and ruined their home. Old Dominique Farge will kill you. He has sworn to hunt you down like a dog. My father is ill . . . we fear he is dying . . . he could not come himself to warn you . . . I did not even stop to change my dress . . . I have been travelling all day." She stopped, panting for breath, with her hand pressed to her side.

His eyes were glowing; he smiled exultantly. "And you have done this for me, Léonie, for me!" he whispered, tenderly, moving towards her with outstretched arms. "Then you do care for me! You do love—"

She drew away with a gesture of loathing. "You! God forbid!" she cried. "I do the duty of the Destréhan to the Lafitte," she added, calmly. "But you must go at once, monsieur.

Dominique Farge may reach the city at any moment. Go, before it is too late—"

It was already too late. There was a sound of footsteps above the rush of the rain, and Dominique Farge came around the corner—a large old man, with a swart, bearded face. His blue cotton shirt—he wore no coat—was open at the throat, showing his massive chest; and the unbuttoned sleeves fell away from his hairy wrists. His deep-sunken eyes were bloodshot; his long, grizzled hair, soaked and matted by the rain, clung to his cheeks. At sight of his prey his face lighted horribly. " *Li mové nomme!*" he hissed, with a forward spring.

Lafitte, with his eyes on the uplifted hand, stood rooted to his place. But there was a quick movement on the girl's part.

She had thrown herself in front of the intended victim; and the alligator knife in Dominique's hand, descending, sheathed itself in her bosom.

Without a cry, and like a bayou lily whose stem has been suddenly cut, the white figure sank into the ooze of the banquette, her spirting blood dyeing the stuccoed wall.

The old man passed his hand over his starting eyes. He did not even stoop to see if the child of his neighbor and old comrade-in-arms were dead; but stepping back a pace, he drew a revolver from his belt and placed the muzzle against his forehead.

His body fell heavily at her feet.

The report of the pistol brought a voluble, hurrying crowd into the drowned street, but there had been no witnesses of the double tragedy—which caused extraordinary comment. No one ever knew its meaning. 'Toinette Farge, cowering over her nameless infant in the cabin on Bayou Desnoyers; Henry Destran on his death-bed in the old Destréhan plantation-house—even these but dimly surmised the truth.

The deaf old cabaret-keeper came out to watch the removal of the dead bodies, leaving the little room quite empty.

The untasted glass of absinthe on the bar glowed like a huge, scintillating opal in the purple shadows.

A year later a man drifted at nightfall one day—alone—into a cheap pot-house on the out-skirts of Paris. There was an air of decayed gentility about him. His well-fitting clothes were shabby. The lining of the top-coat he carried over his arm was frayed and much soiled.

His face, covered with a stubble of black beard, was haggard. His dark, shifting eyes had a dull, outworn expression.

The hand which he stretched out towards the little glass pushed towards him by the gruff, ill-looking proprietor, shook almost as if with palsy.

He grasped the slender stem eagerly and raised the glass to his lips, but set it down again with a nauseate shudder and turned away. "I cannot drink it!" he muttered, dropping upon the rude bench outside the door, and drawing the brim of his hat over his eyes, as if to shut out something

from his sight.   " *God!* I am dying for it, yet I
cannot drink it !   There were exactly those green,
changing lights in her eyes that day !   And when
I remember "—he threw out his arms with a gesture of self-loathing—" when I remember that I
am, after all, a Lafitte only by adoption— !"

THE CLOVEN HEART

I

It was morning in the rose-hedged garden. The gardener, a dark-visaged old man, with strangely gleaming, deep-sunken eyes, and quick, adder-like movements, had just unearthed from among the roots of a stunted bitter-almond tree a small wooden box. It lay in the hollow of his hand. The carved lid was fastened with hasps of rusty metal. He was showing it to his companion.

She was a tall, slender woman, clad in a coarse, loose-sleeved robe, which aimed to hide but rather emphasized the fine outlines of her figure. Her blue eyes, beneath heavy, black-fringed lids, were sad—the eyes of one who had lived through an infinity of suffering or unsatisfied longing. Her forehead was banded with white linen; a veil, drawn over her head and under her throat, shaded her face, which was young, calm, and singularly joyless.

She looked silently on while the old man brushed the mould from the box with his fin-

gers and pried open the rotting lid. A handful of ancient gold coins lay within; underneath
them were some jewels in tarnished silver setting, and a ring of clumsy workmanship, on
whose dull-blue signet-stone was cut an odd de-
vice—a rosary drawn through a.cleft heart.

The woman eyed the gold incuriously. "It
may be used in payment for glass in the oriel,"
she said, lifting her eyes to a crumbling tower
of the building which flanked the garden.

The gardener stooped, laying hold of the
gnarled almond-tree to set it in its place—for
a heavy wind had overblown it in the night.
But he straightened himself abruptly, arrested
by a half-whisper which dropped from the woman's lips. It was spoken in a strange tongue,
with long, caressing syllables and curious inflec-
tions.

The shadow of a crumbling tower fell over the
spot where they stood. At the farther end of
the large garden three young girls were walking
to and fro along a sunlighted walk. Their low
voices sounded in the distance like the murmur
of bees.

With head averted the gardener listened while
the mistress spoke long and rapidly. Her speech
had in it the subtle monotony of the Eastern
juggler's incantation when he causes a seed to
swell and burst and spring into a tree before
the eyes of the spectator, waving his hand the
while, and fanning the budding leaves with a
branch of faded palm.

When she had concluded the old man replied

briefly in the same tongue. There was a tone
of awed entreaty in his voice. A fire shot into
her blue eyes, and her slight form stiffened
haughtily. He crouched to her feet and kissed
the hem of her coarse gown. She dropped the
antique coins into his outstretched palm and
turned away.

The young girls made a deep obeisance as she
passed them. She entered the high Gothic doorway, and moved slowly towards a dim point of
light which shone in the shadows beyond a fretwork of marble. Her hands, grasping the jewels,
were covered by her long, flowing sleeves.

II

A carriage stopped before a tall brick mansion fronting on a side street of the city. A
sign above the arched entrance showed the house
to be a hotel; a crowd of well-dressed idlers on
the veranda testified to its importance. These
looked down curiously as the carriage drew up
at the steps, and its single occupant—a woman—
leaned forward. The electric light—for it was
long past the close of the short winter day—fell
upon her muffled figure and veiled face. The
maskers in the street, excited by the mumming
and merriment of the Carnival, pressed against
the carriage wheels. The obsequious attendant
who had come out of the hotel laid his hand on
the carriage door. He was thrust aside by the
proprietor, who assisted his guest to alight. His

manner indicated that special orders had been given for her reception. He offered her his arm with a show of gallantry; she waved him aside without speaking, and signed him to precede her up the broad steps. She followed him with an air in which timidity and assurance were strangely blended.

The room into which she was conducted was large, and richly though quietly furnished. It was faintly illuminated by candles burning in silver sconces. The polished floor was overlaid with heavy rugs; the carved furniture was of a quaint, old-fashioned pattern.

On a low couch placed within a curtained alcove was spread a profusion of women's garments, exquisite in color and texture.

The woman, on entering, closed the door and walked to one of the gilt - framed mirrors set in the wall. She removed her veil and gazed long and fixedly at her own image, which looked back at her with steady, unsmiling eyes. Her bosom heaved. She snatched the veil across her face and stumbled towards the door; but her eyes caught the gleam of silk and lace on the couch, and she stopped, trembling, and began to unloose the clasps of her dark mantle.

III

A little before midnight the gayly decorated *salon* hard by began to fill, and presently a carnival rout was in full swing there. It differed

little in outward appearance from other pre-
Lenten revels. There were few maskers, and these
were gravely decorous beneath their masks and
dominoes. The inexperienced observer would
have failed to detect an almost imperceptible
undercurrent — the innuendo lurking beneath
the jest, the covert meaning behind a rapid in-
terchange of glances, the quick signal given and
returned in the passing crowd.

A group of young men in faultless evening-
dress stood, during an interval of the dance, near
the ball-room door. Most of them had a *blasé*
expression; nearly all showed signs of recent
dissipation. One only—a clean - shaven, handsome, ruddy-faced young fellow of twenty-five or
so—seemed fresh and unworn. He was apparently unknown to the others, who looked at
him with an amused contempt not unmixed with
envy.

He had been dancing — a little awkwardly,
it is true, but with an abandon and gallantry
which made the tired nerves of his dancer thrill
as they had not thrilled for many a long year.
He was looking about him now eagerly, as if
making mental choice of a partner for the waltz
whose lazy tones were beginning to pulse upon
the air.

At that moment a woman came down the narrow entrance-hall, unwinding from her head, as
she approached the door, a filmy lace scarf. It
was the same woman who had alighted at dusk
from her carriage at the door of the hotel in a
neighboring street.

She was extraordinarily and strangely beautiful in her ball-dress. This was composed of heavy, dull-yellow satin, foamy about the foot with lace so old as to be nearly the same color. A band of gold was fastened about the slim waist with an agraffe of diamonds sunk deep in unpolished silver. Clasps of the same jewels held together the narrow shoulder-bands of the low corsage, which left her perfect neck and arms bare. Her black hair was cut close, giving a singularly proud look to her erect, well-shaped head. Her blue eyes wore a startled, half-expectant expression, her red lips were parted, her bosom rose and fell pantingly.

An open murmur of admiration greeted this dazzling apparition. She pressed forward as if to taste it to the full, though at the same time a burning blush suffused her pale face and dyed her neck and bosom. It was as if the Angel of the Flesh shrank from that which the spirit within ardently desired. She stopped abruptly, passing her hands along her arms like one who draws down a long sleeve.

This movement was so constantly and apparently so unconsciously repeated during the evening that the spectators remarked it and commented wonderingly upon it.

Several of the young men near the ball-room door sprang forward to meet her. But it was the clean-shaven young stranger who first reached her side. He made scant ceremony of invitation, but placing his arm about her waist, he drew her into the circle of dancers. She quivered visibly

at his touch, and again the red passed like a
wave over her white skin. Then a soft yielding
smile dawned into her eyes, and her slight form
swayed to his embrace.

The onlookers followed their movements with
cynical, fascinated eyes. They danced with the
charming, untaught grace of children. The
waltz, at first rhythmic and languid, grew hurried. The dancers swept, by in circles, which
changed like the figures in a kaleidoscope. The
sound of so many light feet on the smooth floor
was like the shoreward rush of foamy waves.
The air throbbed. When the music ceased, with
a shrill clash, the frenzied waltzers reeled in
their places, looking about them with dazed
eyes, and laughing foolishly.

The woman in the dull-yellow gown and the
clean-shaven stranger were no longer among
them. They had passed, dancing, through one
of the long, open windows, to the veranda outside. There was a tangled close below, where
the shadows of the vines on the walks were heavy
in the starlight.

A mocking-bird was singing in the Spanish-
dagger tree in a corner of the close. It fell suddenly silent.

IV

In the old garden it was still dark, though a
hint of dawn thrilled the air.

There was a whir of wheels on the road outside ; a carriage stopped, and then crawled away,

its lights shining like baleful fires in the darkness.

Two persons came in at the small wicket cut in the high, enclosing wall. They were the gardener and the woman. Her forehead was banded with linen, and her coarse, dark robe trailed on the dew-wet walk.

The old man trembled so that he could hardly dig a place at the foot of the bitter-almond tree to receive the little carved box. The woman threw into the box, with a gesture of loathing, the jewels which she carried in her hands, and the money left from that which the gardener had obtained in exchange for the antique coins. He heaped the sod upon the box and pressed it down with his foot. Then he stood still with his arms hanging at his side, his face turned to hers in the darkness.

The moments passed ; the moist leaves rustled to the chill breeze ; a bird in an orange-tree twittered dreamily.

At length she spoke—always in the curious foreign tongue ; but the glow and the heart-beat were gone from it, and the sound of it was dull and lifeless. She seemed to be relating some story in which there was shame and anguish for them both ; for she twisted her hands wildly as she spoke, and the old man wept, with his arms hanging at his side.

When she had finished she writhed to his feet and lay prone with her face on the ground, her dark mantle covering her like a pall.

He lifted her, and sought with soothing whispers to draw her towards the wicket. But she put him aside, suddenly imperious. A single word of command came from her ashen lips.

The old gardener put his hand to his bosom and drew forth a small packet. He laid it in her palm, and, prostrating himself, he placed her sandalled foot upon his neck. Then he arose, and passed, without a backward glance, through the gate in the wall. The woman crossed the garden and entered the Gothic doorway. She felt her way towards the small point of light which burned steadily in the thick darkness beyond the fretwork of marble.

The next day—it was Ash-Wednesday—the dim aisles rang with cries of mourning. For the young Mistress had died during the night in the great hall. There they had found her kneeling, quite stiff and cold, with her forehead pressed against the marble fretwork.

The awe-struck young girls gathered about the bier and gazed, weeping, upon her beautiful, saint-like face.

The bell in the crumbling tower tolled the live-long day.

V

At sunset of the same day a clean-shaven young man, on the farther side of the old city, walked up and down a flower-set alleyway. His dark gown brushed the low hedge; the shadow of lichened walls fell athwart his path. He was reading from a small book, but ever and anon a vague smile came into his dark eyes, and he drew a ring from its hiding-place in his bosom and looked furtively at it.

On its dull-blue signet-stone was graven a string of prayer-beads drawn through a cloven heart.

III

FROM THE QUARTER

A HEART-LEAF FROM STONY CREEK BOTTOM

"JED HOPSON !" said the school-mistress, rapping sharply with a pencil on the edge of the slate which she held in her hand.

"Yethum," whimpered Jed, detected in his stealthy, stooping flight behind the last row of benches.

"What are you doing away from your seat ?"

"Pleathe, Mith Pothy, I wath juth goin' to give thith heart-leaf to Mary Ann Hineth."

"Bring it to me instantly, sir."

Mary Ann Hines pushed a red underlip out scornfully at her tow-headed adorer as he passed her on his way to the teacher's desk, with the long-stemmed, green, shining heart-leaf in his grimy hand ; and the other scholars giggled behind their calico-covered geographies.

Miss Posy Weaver's stern look restored order. She made Jed stand in a corner with his face to the wall, and she put the confiscated love-offering in her desk. But for the life of her she could not help bruising it between her fingers and sniffing it surreptitiously, with her head behind the desk-lid. Its aromatic, woodsy perfume floated out. permeating the warm, still air of the little school-room.

"Jeddy," said the young teacher, affectionately, "you may go back to your seat."

She looked furtively at the big silver watch hanging at her belt, and then glanced with longing eyes at the strip of blue sky which shone, all checkered with the swaying leaves of a young sassafras, between the unchinked logs. A ripple of excitement passed over the score of freckled faces turned expectantly towards hers. By some mysterious divination the scholars in the Stony Creek school-house were already aware that an extra half-hour was about to be prefixed to their two-hours noon play-time.

The school-mistress leaned forward and laid her hand on the small silver bell which used to stand on the work-table of Mrs. David Overall at Sweet Brier Plantation.

The children started up like a herd of young deer at the clear, tinkling sound; but they went out decorously, two and two. For Miss Posy had studied pedagogy in the Normal School at Greenhurst, and herself presided with great dignity once a month at the County Teachers' Association. But she smiled with girlish indulgence at the whoop which Pud Hines raised on the very threshold as he bounded out.

The isolated old log school-house was nestled in a wooded hollow between two long sloping pine-clad hills. A rutty, disused wagon-road rambled down one of these hills, and skirted the base of the other. It passed the school-house door, crossing, just below, a shallow, rippling branch which fell, a hundred yards or so down the hollow, into one of the deep pools of Stony Creek. Little paths, brown with pine-needles, led away in every direction, worn by the bare feet of Posy Weaver's scholars. A large water-oak shaded the low roof of the house; a grape-vine trailed down from one of the outstretched limbs and hoisted itself up again, forming a natural swing. The ground beneath was skirt-swept and bare, for that was the girls' side. Some pretty-by-night bushes and a straggling line of yellow nigger-heads marked the limit of their play-ground. On the other side the boys of several generations had trampled out a ball-field.

Tom Simmons, who was at one of the outer bases, came running in. "Boys! boys!" he cried, breathlessly. "Wish I may die if a wagin ain't comin' down the old road!"

It was an unheard-of thing, since the laying of the new turnpike, for anybody to drive along the old Stony Creek road.

Sure enough; an open wagon was bumping down the hill, between the tall, brown pine trunks, yawing first to one side and then to the other, in order to escape the red, rain-washed gullies of the road. The shambling, whity-brown horse which drew it stopped a moment at the foot of the descent to breathe; then jogged lazily on, of his own accord, to the branch, where he dipped his nose, with a snuffle of satisfaction, in the sun-

12

warmed water. The boys, and one or two of the
larger girls, hurried down to the reed-fringed
bank, and stood gazing, open-mouthed, at the
vehicle and its occupants.

The driver was a lean, sallow-faced lad about
fifteen years old. He sat on a plank laid across
the mud-splashed bed of the wagon. Behind
him, in a couple of rickety, hide-bottomed chairs,
were two old men—a white man and a negro.
Both were neatly dressed in threadbare black
broadcloth, with old-fashioned plaited shirt-
fronts of the finest white linen. The negro was
bent so nearly double that his brown, alert-looking face almost rested upon his knees. His
knotted hands trembled, as if shaken by palsy.
His companion sat stiffly erect, with his arms
crossed upon his breast. There was an air of unconscious dignity about him, though his sunken
eyes were humble and appealing. His face was
pale and emaciated, and his gaunt form was
shaken from time to time by a racking cough.

A large-patterned old carpet-bag and a bundle
tied up in a red cotton handkerchief were lying
in the back of the wagon, and a battered-looking
fiddle was tucked under the negro's chair.

"Mith Pothy," whispered Jed Hopson, laying
a timid hand on the teacher's arm.

She was sitting by the low, shutterless window; an open book was on her lap, and she
twirled the heart-leaf absently in her fingers.
A ray of sunlight falling across her head brightened her bronze-brown hair and drooping lashes. She was very young—hardly as old, in

fact, as Pud Hines or Tom Simmons, her oldest scholars.

She started at the light touch, and smiled at the small intruder. "Well, Jed, is it a thorn in the finger or a splinter in the foot, this time?"

"Mith Pothy"—his eyes widened as he spoke—"the po'-houthe wagin, with Tad Luker drivin' it, ith yonder at the branch, an' ole Cunnel Dave Overall an' Unc' Bine ith in it, goin' to the po'-houthe to live. Tad thayth he 'th takin' 'em to the po'-houthe 'cauthe they ain't able to work no more for theythelvth, an' if they don't go to the po'-houthe they'll thtarve. Oh, Mith Pothy, what 'th the matter?"

The girl had started to her feet; the color had left her cheeks, and she was staring at the child with frightened eyes.

There was a creaky sound of wheels outside. She ran out distractedly. Tad Luker grinned with bashful delight at sight of her, and drew his horse up so suddenly that the two old men were jerked forward in their chairs. Colonel David Overall recovered himself, and removed his rusty tall hat with a courtly bow. The schoolmistress leaned against the wheel, panting and speechless.

"Mornin', Miss Posy." The old negro lifted a hand with difficulty to his ancient beaver.

"Posy?" echoed the Colonel, turning inquiringly from one to the other, a faint flush rising to his hollow cheek.

"Yessah," returned Uncle Bine. "She de gran'chile o' we-all's las' 'fo'-de-wah overseer, sah,

Mist' Josh Mullen—you 'member Mist' Josh Mullen, Marse Dave—an' she name' Posy a'ter ole Mis', sah."

"Yes, sir," the teacher said, answering the sudden look of affectionate interest in the old man's eyes, "my name is Repose Cartwright Weaver. My mother was born at Sweet Brier Plantation, and she named me for your wife. She is buried near Mrs. Overall in the Sweet Brier burying-ground."

Colonel Overall opened his lips and then closed them, swallowing a lump in his throat.

"Won't—won't you put on your hat, Colonel?" she stammered, after a moment's silence, for the noon sun was beating hot upon his gray old head.

"Oh no, I could not think of it," he said, hastily, "in the presence of a lady." He reached down, as he spoke, and took her hand in his.

The scholars had all pressed up, and were standing in a ring about the poor-house wagon, staring in respectful silence at the dispossessed owner of the old Sweet Brier Plantation. Tad Luker, seeing Miss Posy's distress, and feeling himself in some sort implicated in the cause of it, had slid down, and was sheltering himself behind the placid old horse from the misery in her brown eyes.

"Ha!" It was the heart-leaf dropped from Posy Weaver's palm into his own which had brought an almost youthful light into the dimmed eyes. "A heart-leaf! I would wager, Byron"—he turned to the negro beside him—

"that it came from the Long Bend in Stony Creek bottom."

"Yeth, thir, it did!" cried Jed Hopson, thrusting his tousled head up under the teacher's arm.

"Are you a Hopson?" demanded the Colonel, looking down at him quizzically.

"Yeth, thir; Jed Hopthon, thir."

The Colonel laughed softly. "I thought so. Your grandfather had the same lisp and the same tow head when he was your age." His eyes went back to the leaf. "They grow," he said, "just beyond the Flat Rock in the Long Bend. You wade through a boggy thicket until you come to a fern-bed; a little further to the right there is a clump of beech-trees—four of them—set close together; the heart-leaves grow in a sort of square made by the beech roots."

"Yeth, thir!" shouted little Jed, quivering with excitement. "I've knowed the plathe nigh a year, but I ain't never told nobody."

"And your name is Repose, my dear? Well, well! And you teach the Stony Creek school? I used to go to school here myself, you know, when I was a boy, with little Posy Cartwright. Not in this house, to be sure. The old one was pulled down—some time in the forties, I think it was, eh, Byron? I found the heart-leaves in Stony Creek bottom one day at play-time. Byron here, my body-servant, was with me."

"I wuz bawn de same day Marse Dave wuz bawn, an' ole Marse gin me ter him fer a body-servant," interjected Uncle Bine.

"I must have been about eleven years old at the time. I slipped in the bog, and had to go home in wet clothes, but I sent the heart-leaf to Posy by Byron."

"Yas," said Uncle Bine, taking up the story as his old master relapsed into silence, "an' what you reckin Miss Posy done when I gin her de heart-leaf? She wuz settin' in de grape-vine swing long o' 'n'er lil gal. Dey wa'n't mo'n seven er eight year ole, na'r one o' 'em, an' Miss Posy's yaller hair wuz flyin' in de win'. I gin her de heart-leaf an' tole her dat Marse Dave saunt it, an'—'fo' de Lawd!—she up an' slap me spang on de jaw, an' th'o' de leaf on de groun'. She 'ten lak she gwine ter tromp on it in de bargain; but I done cut my eye on her roun' de cornder o' de school-house, 'caze I knowed she gwine ter pick it up."

"An' did she?" asked Mary Ann Hines, involuntarily; then hung her head, blushing red through tan and freckles.

"Yas, chile, co'se she did," chuckled Uncle Bine. He waited a moment; then proceeded, with a sidelong glance at his self-absorbed companion: "Fum dat day ontwel he went off ter collige Marse Dave wuz all de time sp'ilin' his britches wadin' roun' in dat bog a'ter heart-leaves fer Miss Posy; an' when he come back fum collige—de fines' young genterman dat ever kep' a pack o' houn's—he fairly hang roun' de Poplars, wher' Mist' Tom Cartwright live', fum mawnin' twel night. Ole Marse say he 'spec' Miss Posy leadin' Marse Dave a dance. An' at -

las', one night, he rid home fum de Poplars lookin' lak he plum desput. Nex' mawnin' he ax me ter saddle de hosses 'fo' day, 'caze he gwine huntin' down in Stony Creek bottom. I wuz 'bleedged ter go 'hine de stable ter laugh when he come out'n de house 'bout daylight, 'caze how Marse Dave gwine ter hunt 'dout a gun? We rid at a run down ter de Long Ben' o' de creek, an' fus' t'ing I knowed Marse Dave done flung me his bridle an' jump' onter de Flat Rock; an' dar he wuz wadin' thoo de bog, in his fine clo's, ter de beeches wher' de heart-leaf grow!

"Hit wa'n't mo'n breakfus'-time when we come ter de cross-road 'twix' Sweet Brier an' de Poplars. Den Marse Dave he check up de gray an' han' me de heart-leaf.

"'Tek it ter Miss Posy Cartwright,' he say. 'I'm gwine ter wait right here ontwel you come back. Hit's de turn o' my life, Bine.'

"I lef' him settin' straight ez a saplin' on de big gray, an' I rid on ter de Poplars. Dar wuz Miss Posy walkin' up an' down de gal'ry in her white dress, an' de win' blowin' her yaller hair. She look at me curus-lak wi' her blue eyes when she tuk de leaf. 'Fo' de Lawd, I wuz feared she wuz gwine ter th'o' it on de groun' an' tromp on it! But she turn her head, fus' dis way an' den dat, an' den she say, sof' an' sassy-lak, 'Mek my compliments to yo' marster, an' ax him do he want re-pose fer his heart.'

"I ain' sho', but seem lak I heerd Miss Posy call me back ez I onlatch de big gate, but

somep'n' inside me aiggd me not ter look roun'.
Marse Dave wuz pale ez death when I galloped
up ter de cross-road wher' he wuz waitin'. But
I ain' no sooner got Miss Posy's words out'n my
mouf dan he streck spurs in de gray an' mek fer
de Poplars lak a streak o' lightnin'. He done
fergot dat his clo's all splesh over mud fum dat
Long Ben' bog."

The Colonel was listening now, and he smiled
encouragement as Uncle Bine stopped to cough.

"I reckin dass huccum Miss Posy wore heart-
leaves stidder white flowers at de weddin'. Me
an' Marse Dave went down ter de bottom a'ter
'em on de weddin'-day mawnin'. An' dat
huccum every year, when de same day come
eroun', Marse Dave useter ride down ter Stony
Creek an' wade out ter dem beeches a'ter a heart-
leaf. But he never did fetch 'em ter Miss Posy
hisse'f. He useter stop in de summer-house an'
sen' me inter de house, wher' Miss Posy wuz settin' in de mawnin'-room, wi' de silver bell on de
wu'k-table 'longside her. She useter tek de
heart-leaf an' look at me out'n dem laughin' eyes
an' say, 'Mek my compliments to yo' marster,
an' ax him do he want re-pose for his *heart*.'
An' 'reckly Marse Dave 'd come bulgin' inter de
house an' tek her in his arms! Every year,
'cep'n' endurin' o' de wah, when Marse Dave an'
young Marse Cartwright, his onlies' son dat wuz
killed in de wah, wuz away fum Sweet Brier—
every year fer up'ards o' forty year, I fotch a
heart-leaf ter ole Mis', an' tuk dat same message
ter Marse Dave in de summer-house. But I

couldn't no wise mek out de meanin' o' Miss Posy's message, ontwel, all at once, one day, fetchin' dem words ter Marse Dave, I got de meanin'. It flesh over me in a minit. *Repose,* dat mean *res',* you know, an' de heart-leaf stan' fer Marse Dave's *heart. Does you want res' fer yo' heart?* I bus' out laughin' now ever' time I 'member how de true meanin' o' dem words flesh over me a'ter up'ards o' forty year!" He wagged his head up and down, laughing wheezily.

"Dass de las' time I ever fotch de heart-leaf," he added, in a subdued tone, "'caze Miss Posy died dat same year, an' Marse Dave hatter sell Sweet Brier."

Yes, Sweet Brier, tumble-down and dilapidated in the midst of its shrunken fields, had passed into alien hands. The household belongings—the quaint old furniture which had been handed down from one generation of Overalls to another—had been sold at auction. Posy Weaver longed to tell the last of the Overalls how she herself had bought, out of her first scanty earnings, the little silver bell which used to stand on his wife's work-table. But she could not, somehow. She stood silently looking back over the past few years—which seemed long in her brief life—during which Uncle Bine and his old master had lived together in one of the deserted negro cabins at Sweet Brier; keeping up, in the midst of the new and strange generation, their unequal struggle with poverty and sickness, until—

Colonel David Overall's thoughts, it would seem, had been travelling along with hers. "I am told," he said, abruptly, but with great gentleness, "that the—the place to which they are taking Byron and me is very comfortable. There is a wide gallery and shade-trees, and—" A violent fit of coughing interrupted his speech.

The young teacher leaned her head upon the tire of the wheel and wept silently. The older boys slunk away, ashamed and frightened at the sight of their teacher's tears. The girls turned their heads and pretended not to notice.

A sharp click disturbed the silence. It was the snapping of a string on Uncle Bine's old fiddle.

Tad Luker stooped under the horse's neck and came around to where the school-mistress was standing. "Miss Po-Posy," he whispered, desperately, "I orter go. I'll git a lickin' if I don't. An', Miss Posy, I—I fetched him over the old road so's to keep offer the 'pike, where folks might ha' seen him on his way to the poor-house."

Posy gave him a grateful look through her tears, and pressed eagerly between the wheels to murmur something which the children could not hear. But the old Colonel shook his head. "No, no, my dear, I cannot burden an orphaned child like you. It will not be long, for Byron and I are very old. Besides"—he straightened himself with dignity—"I am told that the county poor-house is quite comfortable—quite comfortable."

Tad clambered to his seat; he shook the reins, and the old horse pricked up his ears.

"Wait a moment, please," said Colonel David Overall, lifting his hand. "My dear," he continued, looking wistfully down into the girl's flushed and tear-stained face, "would — would you mind standing for a second upon the step?"

She sprang lightly upon the muddy wagon-step.

He laid his hand on her head. "Repose Cartwright! It was my wife's name," he muttered, kissing her on either cheek. And then he turned and laid his arm about Uncle Bine's bowed shoulders.

The wagon rattled away, jolting the old men in their chairs, and displacing the grotesque beavers on their heads. A turn of the red road presently hid them from view, and a moment later the silver bell was calling the scholars of the Stony Creek school to order.

I

FRANCIS UNDERWOOD glanced about him as the train whizzed away, leaving him the sole occupant of the narrow platform upon which he had alighted. His smaller luggage lay at his feet, but his travelling - trunk was nowhere in sight. The few idlers—a couple of sallow-faced, shock-headed crackers and a squad of noisy negro lads—who had collected about the little way-station while the train made its momentary halt, had disappeared. He walked to the end of the platform, where a dozen or more turpentine barrels stood on end, their contents oozing from the rifts in their sun-warped sides, and cast his eyes over the green flat, which was bounded in every direction by low, red, pine - clad hills. The dim haze of an early autumn afternoon hung in the pine-tops ; a thin spiral of smoke arose from the chimney of the single cabin within range of vision ; a rickety buggy, over whose sagging top fluttered the loose end of a woman's veil, was just turning the distant bend of a road. There were no other visible signs of life. The perplexed traveller strode back to the dingy waiting-room and looked in. The tripping click of the telegraph in the cubby beyond and a familiar opening in the thin board partition indicated the occasional presence, at least, of operator and agent; but the individual who combined these two functions was in momentary eclipse.

Underwood thrust his hands into his pockets and meditated, frowning impatiently.

"De telegraph is boun' fer ter clickety-click, sah," said a voice over his shoulder; "she jes keep on er-talkin' ter herse'f in yander same ez ef de boss was 'longside her ter write her down."

The young man turned quickly and found himself face to face with a negro, who held a carriage-whip in one hand, and in the other his own bag, top-coat, and umbrella.

"Scuse me, sah," the speaker continued, removing his hat. "I reckin you mus' be Mist' Onderwood?"

Underwood nodded assent.

"Dey's lookin' fer you at Pine Needles, Mist' Onderwood. Step dis way, sah. Yo' trunk is gone on in de cyart. But I ain' been able ter fetch up de cay'age ontwel de ingine stop her fool screechin', 'caze my hosses is kinder res'less."

He led the way as he spoke to a light trap, which had been driven up noiselessly, and was waiting near the steps of the low platform.

Underwood settled himself comfortably on the cushioned seat, and turned a gaze of wondering admiration on his conductor, who stood with a hand on the glossy flank of one of the horses, respectfully awaiting orders. He was himself of unusual height, slenderly proportioned, but with an athletic frame and well-knit muscles, which contradicted a rather boyish face, laughing blue eyes, and a sensitive mouth, whose weakness was not wholly concealed by a light, drooping mustache. But he seemed suddenly dwarfed. The negro towered like a giant above the tall mulatto who held the bridles of the horses. His large head, crowned with a bush of crisp, wiry curls, was set squarely upon shoulders of enormous breadth. Underwood examined almost with awe the broad chest and massive limbs; the latter were straight and well formed; the powerful wrist, indeed, and the hand, with its long fingers, perfect nails, and outward-curving palm, might have served for a sculptor's model. He was jet-black. His square-jawed face was beardless. His long, brown eyes had the melancholy softness characteristic of his race; the lips were thick, and the cheek-bones prominent, but the nose was straight and shapely, giving a curious and unexpected dignity to an otherwise typical negro physiognomy. He spoke the uncouth *patois* of the quarters, but his bearing was that of one who held a position of trust and confidence.

He was clad in a sort of homely livery of dark-blue flannel—a blouse, whose open collar exposed his full throat, and loose trousers held in at the waist by a broad leather belt.

Underwood waved his hand as he concluded

his brief, half-unconscious inspection, and the
black colossus took a seat beside him, the mulatto stepped aside, and the handsome bays
sprang forward at the loosening of the reins.
The road wound gradually up long, sloping hills,
dipping now and then into a moist hollow, where
the sturdy underbrush and the jungle-like growth
of trees were aflame under the first light touches
of the frost. A few belated spikes of goldenrod
nodded by the road-side, and an occasional cluster
of dim purple asters shone against the back-
ground of a fallen pine; but the Indian-pipe—
precursor of winter—was already thrusting its
waxen crook through the dark mould on the
sheltered slopes. The hill-sides were brown with
pine-needles. The sky, in the waning sunlight,
was a fine, soft purple; the plumy tops of the
lofty pines seemed to melt into it far overhead;
the warm air was charged with aromatic odors.
Underwood bared his head, and expanded his
lungs with an idle sense of well-being. His eyes
followed dreamily the flight of a hawk across the
sky. A faint smile curved his lips.

"Dar's a molly cottontail!" suddenly exclaimed the negro. A rabbit sped across the
road a few paces in front of the horses and scurried up a ridge, her gray ears laid back and her
white bit of a tail in the air. "Dat's bad luck,
Mist' Onderwood!"

Underwood recalled a half-forgotten super-
stition. "Not for me," he said, gayly. "I
carry a rabbit foot in my pocket! What is your
name—boy?" he continued, stumbling over the

last word, quizzically conscious of its inappropriateness.

" Marcas, sah," returned the "boy," promptly. " Dey calls me Blue-gum Marc," he added, with a side glance at the questioner and a suppressed chuckle.

" Blue-gum Marc ?" echoed Underwood, interrogatively.

The giant opened his mouth, drawing back his thick lips, and pointed significantly to a double row of glistening white teeth, set in gums of a dark leaden blue. "Dat's de reason, sah," he said, lightly. "I's a blue-gum nigger. An' dey 'lows ef I git mad at anybody, an' bite de pusson, dat bite gwine ter be wusser 'n rattlesnake pizen! Der ain' no whiskey in de jug dat kin heal up de bite of a blue-gum nigger !"

He threw back his head and laughed with a keen enjoyment of his own words.

" Have you ever tried it ?" asked Underwood, carelessly.

" Who? Me? Gawd-a-mighty !—no sah!" A sudden spasm of terror swept over the ebon face. "No, sah," he repeated, relapsing into decorous mirth. "I 'ain' never had no call ter bite anybody yit."

The horses shied violently as he concluded.

" What in de name o' Gawd is de matter wid you, Dandy ? Whoa, Jim !" he ejaculated, tightening his grasp on the reins, and peering to right and left with a frown on his forehead. Underwood saw the frown melt suddenly, and a light leap into the dark eyes. He followed the

direction of his gaze ; his own heart beat tumul-
tuously, and the blood surged into his cheeks.

The glade through which they were passing
was filled with the uncertain shadows of a fast-
gathering twilight, though the slanting beams of
the sun still illuminated the crest of the hills.
A little stream, whose rippling murmur filled the
silence, ran obliquely across the road and widened
into a broad pool in the thicket beyond. The
half-dried reeds on the margin, and the over-
hanging trees with their festooning vines, were
mirrored in the clear brown depths of this wave-
less tarn. A woman was standing on the farther side, her tall, lithe figure outlined by the
pale glimmer of her gown. One hand, which
held a cluster of vivid red leaves, hung at her
side ; the other was arched above her brows as
she leaned forward in a listening attitude. As
they whirled past, Underwood caught the gleam
of a bare, tawny wrist, and the glow of a pair of
large, lustrous eyes.

" Who was that ?" he demanded, abruptly.

" S'lome," responded his companion, with
affected indifference. "She Miss Cecil's own
maid," he added, after a pause.

" I thought at first that it was Miss Cecil herself," said Underwood, glancing back over his
shoulder.

" S'lome do look lak—" the negro checked
himself and averted his face, flecking Dandy's
arched neck with the whip-tassel.

Something in his tone struck the young man
at his side ; he drew the lap-robe closer about

13

his knees, for the air was growing chill, and remained silent until Marcas sprang to the ground to open the boundary gate of Pine Needles, Miss Cecil Berkeley's fine old country place.

"How old are you, Marc?" he asked, struck anew by the negro's noble physical proportions.

"Twenty-five, come Christmas, sah. Bawn jes inside o' freedom. Hit's mighty liftin' ter be bawn free, an' ter be raise' up free, Mist' Onderwood," he went on, resuming his seat and taking the reins from Underwood's hands. "But my old daddy 'ain' had no call ter complain whilse *he* was a slave."

"Where—" began Underwood.

"My daddy was a Affican prince—" the fine nostrils dilated and the broad chest heaved. "Colonel Berkeley bought him out'n a slave-pen in Charl's'n, wher he was dyin' lak a dog, an' fotch him home. An' fum dat day twel de day he died he had the treatments of a genterman at Pine Needles. Dere wa'n't a drap o' blood in his body dat he wouldn't ha' spill' fer de Berkeleys! An' dat huccome I 'ain' never lef' Miss Cecil, Mist' Onderwood. 'Caze dat ole Affican prince is layin' out yander in de fam'ly buryin'-groun' 'longside o' ole marster an' ole mis'; an' who gwine ter tek keer o' Miss Cecil ef I go?"

Underwood, moved by the simplicity and earnestness of the speaker, laid his hand on the brawny arm next to him, and opened his lips to speak. But Marcas shrank from the light touch. Underwood felt the firm flesh quiver beneath his fingers. "He knows that I have come to carry away his young mistress, and he is jealous," he thought, smiling with pardonable exultation.

His eyes roved curiously over the broad park. The kind of table‑land, from which the pine hills sloped away to the west and north, was covered with noble woodland trees, through whose trunks, in passing, he caught glimpses of orchards, vineyards, and fields. It was his first visit to Pine Needles, and he looked out eagerly for the house. A last turn of the smooth road brought it in view—a large, rambling country-house, embowered in greenery, with wide galleries, slanting roof, and square, red-brick chimneys.

"Yander's Miss Cecil, er-waitin'!" said Marcas, pointing with his whip. Underwood barely had time to catch the flutter of light garments through the foliage before the horses were drawn up beneath the veranda where she stood.

She came down the steps with outstretched hands. "Welcome to Pine Needles, Francis," she said, with a sort of shy pride. "This is my cousin, Mrs. Garland," she added, presenting the small, alert-looking personage who filled the agreeable office of companion to the young heiress.

Cecil Berkeley offered a pleasing contrast to the man upon whom she was about to bestow the ownership of herself and the Berkeley estates. She was tall and slender, with hair and brows of an almost startling blackness, and dark eyes in which a smouldering fire seemed to dwell; her high-bred oval face was singularly delicate in its outlines. There was a pliant softness in her movements and a hint of strength in her firm white chin and perfect mouth. She flushed as her lover's ardent eyes met hers in the fading light.

"Welcome to Pine Needles!" she cried again, springing lightly up the steps.

Underwood had not finished relating the common-place details of his southward journey when the soft fall of unshod feet sounded on the polished floor; a shadowy form glided across the dim-lit room in which they were seated, and bent over Miss Berkeley's chair. He felt, rather than saw, that it was the woman whom he had seen an hour before standing on the edge of the dark pool in the hollow.

"Thank you, S'lome," said her mistress, in a tone of affectionate familiarity, taking the leaves, whose color was lost in the semi-darkness. The quadroon bent her shapely head, and passed from the room as silently as she had entered it.

That night they sat late before a blazing pine-knot fire in the snug library. The hands of the slow-ticking old clock on the mantel pointed almost to midnight when the guest arose to bid his hostess good-night. As he opened the door a strain of music fell upon his ears, accompanied with a burst of noisy laughter.

Cecil smiled in reply to his questioning look. "Uncle Darius is fiddling on the kitchen gallery," she said, "and the negroes are doubtless dancing there, late as it is. Come, let us take a peep at them."

She led the way down the wide hall, and out upon a small vine-hung porch in the rear of the dining-room. The night was clear and still. The grassy yard and the garden beyond were bathed in the tranquil light of a full moon. But an enormous fig-tree, whose branches brushed the low eaves, swathed the long kitchen gallery in dense shadow, save where, from an open door, a broad glare of red light streamed across it. Uncle Darius, lean and brown, sat just within the doorway, fiddling with all his might, his chair tilted against the wall, his gray head thrown back, his big bare foot keeping time on the floor. Aunt Peggy, the old black cook, dozed on a stool beside him. A confused mass of dark forms were dimly visible in the shadow, lying about the floor, lounging on the low steps, squatting against the wall. Here and there a dusky face, a bare foot, an out-thrust arm, gleamed strangely in the muddy light. Lindy, big-limbed and black, and Mushmelon Joe, small, wizenèd, and wiry, sank on their heels against the door-posts, breathless and exhausted after a prolonged "break-down," as the invisible spectators drew aside the leafy curtain and looked out.

"I ain' gwine ter play nary 'nother tune ter-night," declared Uncle Darius, bringing his chair-legs down with a thump. "De chickens is fair crowin fer day now." But as a tall figure stepped noiselessly from the darkness into the shaft of light, he tucked his fiddle under his chin again with a whoop. "Now you gwine ter see *dancin'!*" he shouted, flourishing his bow. "Blue-gum Marc gwine ter teach the niggers how ter rack down de cotton row!"

Marc swayed his huge body from side to side rhythmically, then paused. "Ain' you gwine ter rack down de cotton row 'long o' me, S'lome?" he demanded, turning his face towards a group of women at the farther end of the gallery.

" No," drawled a low, musical voice there.

" Den you can ontie de fiddle - strings, Unc' Darius," said Marc, joining good - naturedly in the loud laugh at his own expense.

Underwood bent forward, straining his eyes in the darkness. But Aunt Peggy had already shut the kitchen door, and a moment later they all trooped away, singing, to the negro settlement in the pines, which had replaced the old - time quarters.

II

One morning about ten days later Miss Berkeley came out of the house alone and walked slowly across the lawn. Her step was listless; her eyes were downcast; her cheek had lost its brilliant color. She seated herself on a rustic bench under a low - branched oak, and opened the book which she held in her hand. But her gaze wandered absently from the printed page. It fell at length upon Marcas, who was moving to and fro among the flower-beds, whistling joyously. He carried a small garden hoe, and the splint basket on his arm was heaped with tufts of violets. His face brightened as his eyes caught those of his young mistress. He took off his hat and came over to where she was sitting.

"Hit's edzackly de weather ter transplan',
Miss Cecil," he said; "de groun' is dat meller
an' sof'—"

"Marcas," she interrupted, imperiously, leaning her head against the dark tree-trunk and
looking fixedly at him, "is it true that you carry
poison in your teeth like a rattlesnake?"

"Lawd-a-mussy, Miss Cecil!" he cried, falling back a step or two in his amazement. "I
dunno. Yes, 'm. I 'ain' never projecked none
wi' dat foolishness. But my ole daddy useter *say*
so, an' I reckin a Affican prince oughter *know!*"

Her eyes dropped on her book, and he returned
with a bewildered air to his work. She watched
him abstractedly as he placed the moist roots
one by one deftly in the ground, and patted the
loose earth about them with a large, open palm.

"The dwarf-marigolds are nearly all gone,"
she remarked, after a long silence.

"Yes, 'm," assented Marc, glancing at a triangular plot in the centre of the lawn, where a few
small yellow flowers shone on their low stalks.

"S'lome has been gathering them—" she went
on, musingly, and as if speaking to herself.

"S'lome do hone a'ter yaller, dat's a fac'!" he
commented, with a pleased laugh.

"—for Mr. Underwood," she concluded, in a
monotonous tone.

The negro rose slowly to his feet. A sombre
fire shot into his eyes. He stood for a moment
silently looking down at her. Then he dropped
again to his knees and drew the basket to him.

She went away presently, leaving the book.

which had slipped from her lap, lying face downward in the yellowing grass.

He watched her furtively until she entered the house. Then, without a glance at the overturned basket and neglected tools, he passed across the grounds, leaped the low fence, and plunged into the silent reaches of the pines.

That night when the mistress of Pine Needles came down from her own room, whither, under pretext of a headache, she had withdrawn after the mid-afternoon country dinner, she found the house wearing an unwonted air of festivity.

"Ah, there you are at last, Cecil dear!" cried Mrs. Garland, bustling into the hall to meet her. "Everything is waiting for you. I've arranged what Uncle Darius calls a *speckle-tickle* for your Mr. Underwood," she added, dropping her voice.

She drew the girl into the long parlor, whose polished floor reflected the clustered lights in the old-fashioned crystal chandeliers. Wax tapers burned softly in the tall silver candelabra on the mantel; roses were stuffed in the wide-mouthed vases; the furniture was pushed against the wall; a couple of quaint high-backed chairs were placed side by side in the broad curve of the bow-window.

"You and Francis are to sit here, like the king and queen in a play," said Mrs. Garland, gayly. "Don't lift an eyebrow, Cecil, pray, if you recognize the contents of your own armoires and jewel-cases."

Cecil sank into the chair with a wan smile.

She looked frail and almost ghost-like in her trailing white gown. Underwood, who seemed possessed by a sort of reckless gayety, seated himself beside her. He wore pinned upon the lapel of his coat a small yellow flower.

There was a moment of almost painful silence. Then Mrs. Garland, leaning on the back of her cousin's chair, touched a small silver bell. The heavy portière which draped the entrance to the library was pushed aside, and Uncle Darius, arrayed in an antiquated blue coat with brass buttons, light trousers, and ruffled shirt-front, entered pompously, fiddle in hand, and seated himself on the edge of a chair. Mushmelon Joe, Scip, 'Riah, Sara-Wetumpka—a motley gang of field hands and house servants—swarmed in after him. They ranged themselves, grinning and nudging each other, about him, and began to pat a subdued accompaniment to his music. At a scarcely perceptible signal from the fiddler, Lindy bounced into the room. A scarlet sash was wound turbanwise about her kinky head, and an Oriental shawl draped her blue cotton skirt. The black arms and neck were encircled with strings of many-colored beads. She looked preternaturally solemn as she dropped her arms and began the heavy "hoe-down" for which she was famous in the settlement; but a broad grin presently stole over her face; her glistening eyeballs rolled from side to side; the perspiration streamed from her forehead.

"Wire down de crack, nigger, wire down de crack!" exhorted Uncle Darius. "Pick up dem battlin' sticks you calls yo' feet, gal, an' tromp in de flo'!"

"She sho is made de flat o' her foot *talk* ter de fiddle," remarked Mushmelon Joe, as she executed a last breathless whirl, and retired giggling into the admiring circle of clappers.

The clear tinkle of the little bell echoed on the air. Blue-gum Marc appeared suddenly in a doorway that gave upon a side gallery, and, folding his arms on his breast, leaned his great bulk against the frame. At the same moment S'lome stepped from behind the portière.

An involuntary exclamation burst from Underwood. Cecil closed her eyes, dazzled by the wild and barbaric beauty of the tawny creature before her.

She wore a short, close-clinging skirt and sleeveless bodice of pale, shimmering yellow satin; a scarf of silver gauze girdled her slender waist, and was knotted below her swelling hips. Her slim brown ankles and shapely feet were bare. Bands and coils of gold wreathed her naked arms; a jewelled chain clasped her throat; a glittering butterfly, with quivering outspread wings, was set in the crinkly mass of black hair above her forehead. Her eyelids were downcast, their long fringes sweeping her bronze-like cheeks. A curious light, defiant and disdainful, played over her face as she stood motionless, with her arms hanging loosely at her sides, while Uncle Darius played the first bars of the *bamboula* which had been brought by Marcas's father from the heart of Africa.

The music was low and monotonous—a few
constantly recurring notes, which at first vexed
the ear, and then set the blood on fire.

The girl hardly appeared to move ; there was
a languid swaying of the hips from side to side,
and an almost imperceptible yet rhythmic stir of
the feet. But as the music gradually quickened
its time, a thrill seemed to pass along her sinuous
limbs, and a subtle passion pervaded her movements ; her arms were tossed voluptuously above
her head ; her breast heaved ; a seductive fire
burned in her half-closed amber eyes ; the sound
of her light feet on the floor resembled the whir
of wings.

The negroes, huddled mute and breathless
against the wall, gazed at her with wide, fascinated eyes. Suddenly, as if moved by some mysterious and irresistible impulse, they rushed forward and closed in a circle around the flashing
figure, whirling about her with strange evolu-
tions and savage cries.

. . . A powerful, penetrating odor thickened
the air. . . .

Underwood had started from his seat ; he stood
as if transfixed, breathing heavily, his arms unconsciously extended, his eyes aflame, and the
veins in his forehead swollen almost to bursting.
Marcas, curiously impassive in the doorway, kept
his gaze fixed steadily, not upon the dancer, but
upon his young mistress, who leaned back in her
chair, faint and dizzy, the rose-tint on her cheek
fading to a death-like pallor.

The movement of the *bamboula* became by

degrees less rapid; the panting circle opened
and fell back. S'lome paused, and stretched her
arms slowly upward with the supple grace of a
young panther. She looked full at Underwood,
and her lips parted in an exultant smile.

The blood surged into Miss Berkeley's white
cheeks; she lifted her head haughtily; her nostrils quivered; her eyes met those of Marcas for
an instant, then rested, flashing, upon S'lome,
decked for triumph, as it were, in her own hered-
itary jewels.

With a roar like that of a wild beast, Marcas
leaped across the room. His hand fell with a
vise-like grasp upon the gleaming shoulder of the
quadroon; he stooped with a second ferocious cry,
and buried his teeth deep in the smooth flesh of the
rounded arm. A single agonizing shriek pierced
the sudden stillness; before it had ended he had
caught the slight form in one hand, and bearing
her high above his head he bounded through the
open door and disappeared in the darkness.

Underwood, heedless of the terrified confu-
sion and wild clamor which reigned around, was
springing after him, when he felt a hand upon
his arm. "For Heaven's sake come and help
me, Francis," said Mrs. Garland; "Cecil has
fainted!"

III

The next afternoon Miss Berkeley passed
through a small gate into the pine woods which
stretched away to the south, forming a part of

her own domain. She walked slowly along the well-worn path, halting now and again with an air of indecision. Once she stooped mechanically and plucked a yellow daisy which grew in a drift of warm brown pine-needles, but cast it from her with a gesture of loathing. Her black garments gave her an appearance of uncommon height. Her face was livid, her lips compressed, her dark eyes dull and suffering. She turned at length into the narrow lane which led to the negro settlement. As she drew near the outermost cabin she saw Underwood standing in the shadow of a scrubby pine that overhung the picket-fence. Aunt Peggy, the mistress of the cabin, was leaning over the low gate; her arms were uplifted, as if in entreaty or adjuration.

He started at sight of the approaching figure, and walked rapidly forward. He had a white flower in his hand. His face was turned away, and for a moment it seemed as if he were about to pass his betrothed without a greeting. But as she stepped aside he paused, and said, abruptly:

"I am going away, Cecil. I—I think it is best." His eyes were fixed upon the althea blossom which he was twirling awkwardly in his fingers.

"You are quite right," she returned, coldly; "it is best."

She left him without another word. He lingered a moment, gazing irresolutely after her, then struck into the beaten road that led to the railway station.

Aunt Peggy had come out of the gate. "Miss Cecil, honey," she said, hoarsely, "dis ain' no place fer de likes o' you! Go back ter de house, chile—go back!" she entreated. "Mist' Onderwood yander he's been here, off an' on, 'mos' all day. But I ain' dassen ter lef him go inter de cabin. I ax him fer Gawd's sake ef he ain' mek enough trebble a'ready 'd'out showin' hisself wher' Blue-gum Mare kin see him. He say he wan' ter see S'lome! My Gawd! I gin him a althy flower fum offin de corpse, an' saunt him erway. Doan go in de cabin, Miss Cecil!" she panted, following her mistress into the little dooryard, and laying hold of the folds of her gown. "Blue-gum Mare is in de cabin. He ain' never lef' de gal sence he pizen her. Nobody dassen ter go er-nigh him 'cep'n' me, an' he ain' lef me tech her, not even ter put on de grave-close. He say he gwine ter kill the pusson dat steps inside dat cabin do'. De mo'ners is 'bleedge' ter mo'n in Lindy's cabin yander. Fer Gawd's sake. Miss Cecil—fer Gawd's—"

Cecil put the old woman gently aside and pushed open the cabin door. The little room had been hastily put in order. The large four-posted bed was spread with white ; the bare floor was swept clean ; the pine table, piled with blue-rimmed dishes, was placed in the chimney-corner. Uncle Darius's fiddle hung in its accustomed place on the wall, with his Sunday coat on a nail beneath it. The level rays of a setting sun came in at the single window ; a light breeze moved the white curtains to and fro.

The dead girl was lying in the centre of the room on a rude bier, her head resting on a pillow. She was still clad in the fantastic costume in which she had danced the night before ; the gold bands and jewelled ornaments sparkled in the red light which streamed over her. Her eyes were closed ; their silken lashes made a black line against the dusky pallor of her checks. Her lips were slightly parted, and an inscrutable smile seemed to hover about their corners. One arm was laid across her breast, a fold of silver gauze was drawn over the purpling wound just below the shoulder ; the other arm hung to the floor, the closed hand grasping the filigree chain which she had torn, in the death agony, from her neck. A few white altheas were scattered on her bosom, and some sprigs of lavender and rue were lying on the rough boards about her bare feet and ankles. A short, large-handled, keen-bladed knife was laid across the pillow above her head. She looked like a savage queen asleep on her primitive couch.

Marcas sat by the head of the bier. His body was erect and rigid ; his powerful hands rested on his knees ; his feet were drawn close together ; his head was turned towards the dead girl, showing his curiously fine profile. It was the attitude and pose of the Pharaoh of the Egyptian monuments.

He did not move as Cecil entered the room. She stood for a second as motionless as the dead and the watcher of the dead, with her hands clasped before her, the fingers interlocked. Then

she stumbled across the floor, and halted at the
foot of the bier.

The buzzing of some bees about the pots of
flowering moss on the window - sill filled the
silence with a low, droning sound. The wail of
the mourners in Lindy's cabin came in fitfully,
softened by the distance.

"Miss Cecil," he said, presently, without turning his head or lifting his heavy eyelids, "I jes'
waited fer de tu'n o' yo' eye, 'caze I didn' know
which you was gwine ter p'int out fust—S'lome
or *him*. De knife is fer *him*, soon ez de gal is
onder groun'."

Cecil shuddered and put out her hands.

"Doan fret, Miss Cecil," he went on, in the
same sombre tone. "No stranger ain' gwine ter
turn de rosy cheek o' Colonel Berkeley's chile
white ez cotton—*an' live!* Not whilse de blood
o' de ole Affican prince is hot in de vein o' his
son!" His voice shook with sudden rage as he
concluded; his breast rose and fell spasmodically.
When he spoke again, it was almost in a whisper,
strangely soft and musical : "S'lome ! *S'lome!*
I doan 'member de time, Miss Cecil, when I 'ain'
been lovin' S'lome ! Fum de day when she wa'n't
ez high ez de pretty-by-nights in Aun' Peggy's
do'-yard I is had my heart sot on her. . . . She
was swif' ez a fiel'-lark, Miss Cecil, an' her eyes
is ez sof' ez de eyes of a dove when she look at
me an' say she ain' gwine ter love nobody 'cep'n'
me ez long ez she is 'bove de groun'. . . . She is
de onlies' one in de settlemint dat ain' 'feard
o' de pizen in de gum o' Blue-gum Marc . . .

dat's de fam'ly blood in her . . . de Berkeley blood—"

Cecil Berkeley threw up her arms convulsively
and sank to her knees; her forehead pressed the
feet of the dead girl, and she shivered as if the
chill of death had passed from them into her
own benumbed veins.

"I'll do it! *I'll do it!*" exclaimed Mr. Gish, aloud. But the mere thought of what he was about to do made him so light-headed and faint that he had to cling for support to the spear-like points of the low iron fence; the music took on a confused, far-away sound; the forms of the dancers gliding past the long, open windows became hazy and indistinct, as if suddenly enveloped in mist. He came to himself in a spasm of fright lest the policeman leaning idly against the gate, or the liveried coachmen lolling on the box-seats of the waiting carriages, might have heard his outburst. Apparently his indiscretion had passed unnoticed, and he took heart to repeat more emphatically still, but in an inaudible whisper, "As sure as my name is Benjamin Franklin Gish, I'll do it!"

It was a soft Southern winter night. The large, many-galleried residence in front of which he stood was brilliantly illuminated. Within, the dancers were weaving intricate and symmetrical figures to the airy music of a band stationed behind a screen of palms; women in trailing robes and men in faultless evening dress loitered in groups about the wide, old-fashioned halls, and sauntered up and down the lantern-hung verandas; a few couples had ventured down into the large garden, where Duchesse roses bloomed in great dewy clusters, and straggling sprays of sweet-olive scented the air. A tall girl in a fluffy pink gown even strayed along the flower-bordered walk by the fence; she leaned lightly upon the arm of her companion; her round, bare shoulder brushed Mr. Gish's worn coat-sleeve in passing.

The little man on the banquette heaved a profound sigh. It was a sigh of unutterable longing.

Mr. Gish — christened Benjamin Franklin, though his employers called him Gish, his fellow-clerks "B. F.," and his family Benjy (they even wrote it Bengie)—was an assistant book-keeper in the office of T. F. Haley & Co., cotton-buyers. He was short, fat, and quite bald, being in fact a bachelor nearing his fifties. He had been brought up (by his mother, relict of the late Samuel Gish, Esq.) to regard dancing as a frivolous, not to say sinful, amusement. Naturally timid and retiring, he had from his boyhood avoided all gatherings which included the element that, with bashful, antiquated courtesy, he called "the fair sex." Two or three times, indeed, in earlier years, in company with his sisters, the six Misses Gish, he had attended a church sociable or a conversation party. But his sufferings on these occasions had been so great that he had mildly but firmly declined to expose himself to a repetition of them. Year in and year out, always at the same hour of the morning, he walked down to the office of Haley & Co., where he worked methodically over his ledgers until business hours were over, when he went home—in a street-car—to his late dinner. Once a week, on Monday evenings, he escorted his mother and "the girls" to prayer-meeting. On Sundays he sat with the oldest Miss Gish in the choir. He did not sing; the habit dated from the time when—a boy in roundabouts—he blew the bellows of the long-discarded wind-organ. The neighbors were unanimous in the opinion that Mr. Benjy was an exemplary son, a good brother, and a consistent church-member.

Latterly, however, Mr. Gish's feelings had undergone a mysterious change. He could not himself have explained the phenomenon, but he could lay his finger, as he often declared to himself, upon the exact moment when the idea first took hold of him. They were coming home from Monday-night prayer-meeting; his mother was on his arm; the girls trailed along behind, two and two. A light streamed out from the wide-open windows of a house set well back from the street and embowered in roses; a rhythmic strain of waltz music pulsated on the air; couples embracing each other moved down the long room, floating, floating, as if borne on unseen wings. It was but a flash, a momentary glance; "but that done it," groaned Mr. Gish, inwardly, "and I've never been the same man since." He con-

"THEY WERE COMING HOME FROM MONDAY-NIGHT PRAYER-MEETING"

tinued to blush and tremble if by chance he en-
countered one of the fair sex. But a new and
strange fever burned in his veins. An extraordinary passion haunted him day and night. The
truth is, Mr. Gish was beset with an overwhelming desire to dance. His mother, had she been
aware of this shameless ambition of her only son,
would no doubt have declared that Benjy was
being tempted of the devil. But she did not
know. He kept it to himself, gloating over it in
secret; taking it out, so to speak, when he was
alone, and turning it over and over in his mind,
stealthily, as a girl counts her trinkets and shoves
them hurriedly back into the box when she hears
some one coming. Standing at his high desk
in the office of Haley & Co., his mild blue eyes
fixed on the columns of figures, his finger slipping mechanically from line to line, his heart
would give a sudden thump, and a vision would
swim before his eyes—a marvel of radiant beings
swaying, wheeling, advancing, retreating, winding in and out in squares and rings and loops, to
the music of unheard melodies !

For nearly two years past he had been accustomed to loiter at night about the great mansions
in the Garden District ; the echo of dance music
from any point whatsoever drew him as a magnet
draws the needle, from the tall, narrow tenement-
house on a side street where the Gishes lived, to
stately avenues, where he leaned for hours, as he
was now doing, jostled by a rabble of small boys,
elbowed by unkempt idlers, and gazed into open
windows, or stood out in the middle of the street

watching the moving shadows on drawn shades. Now, at last, a resolution which had been slowly gathering in his brain for many weeks had taken definite shape. "Yes! I'll do it," he repeated a third time, as he turned away and hurried homeward; for he was supposed at such times to be overworked by the sordid and avaricious firm of Haley & Co.—for shame, Benjy!—and his mother always sat up until he came in.

A day or two later a good-humored, bustling crowd thronged the streets, for the holiday-loving old town was making ready for one of its great annual holidays. Mr. Gish came out of the office about noon and walked down towards Canal Street. His round, clean-shaven face wore an unwonted look of excitement. He seemed to be searching, in a covert sort of way, for some one or some thing. He paused at the street corners, casting hurried glances in either direction; once he made a few steps towards a knot of boys gathered in front of a peanut-stand, but he changed his mind, a pink flush mounting to his cheeks as he moved hastily on.

His conference, far down in the French quarter, with a slim, dark, foreign-looking gentleman who wore immense hoops of gold in his ears, and whose shoulders went up and down in incessant shrugs, was an animated one. Mr. Gish talked a good deal, and seemed to be giving minute directions. The foreign-looking gentleman listened attentively, and nodded understandingly from time to time. Presently they walked together, threading the crowd, across

Canal Street, and a few squares up Carondelet.
From the opposite sidewalk Mr. Gish pointed
out the office of his employers. There was a
quick movement from hand to hand, and they
separated. "All-a rright-a!" said the gentleman, showing his beautiful white teeth. Around
the corner he stopped to examine the crisp bill;
he grinned, and puckered his lips into a whistle,.
slapping his knee. The transaction was evidently a business one, and the shabby little ac-
countant had not been niggardly.

The next day was the eve of the festival.
"Mr. Haley," said Mr. Gish, looking up from
his books as the senior partner was about quitting
the office, "I—I think, sir, I will come back to-
night and finish this piece of work."

"Very well, Gish," said Mr. Haley, carelessly,
from the doorway. "It is of no great importance; you can let it stand over if you like."

"You'd better come along and have a blow-
out with the boys, B. F.," remarked Bob Haight,
shaking himself into his overcoat and watching
for the look of horror which these unseemly
suggestions always brought into that modest
gentleman's face.

"No, I thank you, Mr. Haight," Mr. Gish
replied, nervously, the blood rushing into his
cheeks; "I—I have made other arrangements."

Haight stared at him a moment in amazement.
"Blest if I don't believe old B. F. is sowing some
oats on his own account!" he muttered to himself. But he forbore any comment.

The assistant bookkeeper left the office a little

late. He walked rapidly up the street some four
or five blocks and turned to the right, plunging,
a few doors from the corner, into a small, dingy
shop, whence a minute later he reappeared, carrying under his arm a good-sized bundle done up
in thick brown paper.

In the crowded car he held the bundle carefully on his knees; but when he alighted he
hugged it to his breast, folding his overcoat
closely about it, and stole along the street, de-
voutly hoping to gain his own room without
being seen. It was twilight when he reached the
gate and slipped across Miss Charlotte's trim
little flower-garden to the front door. He let
himself in as softly as he could with his latch-
key. Fortunately the narrow hall was dark and
deserted. He bolted up the stair, his heart beating like a trip-hammer, his knees trembling beneath him. Inside the small hall room where he
slept he drew a long breath of relief. But the
troubled look returned to his face as he cast
about for a safe hiding-place for the brown-paper
package. He had at first thought of slipping it
between the mattresses of his bed, but he drew
back in sudden terror. Sister Mary-Lou would
certainly sniff it out when she came up to take
off the ruffled day pillows and turn down the
covers. He dropped it into the flat clothes-bas-
ket and threw some soiled linen carelessly over
it; it bulged frightfully, and Mary-Lou's eyes
were so keen ! The rickety old armoire, which
contained, besides his own well-worn best coat,
sundry articles belonging to the girls, was not to

be thought of.   After much hesitation, and with
many qualms, he laid the bundle in the top
drawer of the high bureau, and—for the first
time in his life—turned the key in the lock and
put it in his pocket.   Then he went guiltily
down to dinner.

Mrs. Gish and the six Misses Gish were already
at table.   The Misses Gish, with the exception
of Miss Martha, the youngest, just turned of
thirty-nine, all "took after" their mother, who
was tall and spare, and very brisk and alert in
spite of her seventy-five years.   Miss Martha was
short and plump, like her brother, with a round,
fresh face and a dimpled chin.   Time was when
Benjamin Franklin came, or believed he came,
fourth in due order of age in the family circle.
Certain it is that the names of Caroline, Amelia,
and Mary-Lou preceded his own in the list re-
corded on the yellowed register of the big family Bible, while those of Jane, Charlotte, and
Martha came after.   But, by some occult calcu-
lation on their part, he had found himself suddenly, half a score of years ago, older than Mary-
Lou and Amelia.   A year or two later he had
stepped above Charlotte herself, and now bore
himself as became the first-born and the head of
the house.   This, however, by the way.

"Benjy," said his mother, passing him a plate
of thin soup, "you are late.   It is almost time
for the first bell."

Sure enough ! it was Monday night !

Benjy turned scarlet.   "I'm s-sorry," he
mumbled, with his face in the napkin, "but

I have to go back to the office—a little business—"

Mrs. Gish shook her head mournfully. She
had her opinion of the hardened and inhuman
taskmasters who were " working the life " out of
Benjy.

"I am sure," said Miss Martha, rebelliously,
pushing away her plate, "*I* don't pity Benjy!
I'd a great deal rather add up figures than go to
prayer-meeting! I *hate* prayer-meeting."

A shiver of horror went around the table. Mrs.
Gish dropped her knife and fork and stared
aghast at Miss Martha, who threw up her head
defiantly, then dropped it and burst into tears.

Benjamin Franklin did not hear the storm of
reproach which followed. A wild scheme revolved in his brain as he gazed absently at the
culprit.

"I did not know Martha was so—so nice!" he
murmured. "I'll ask her to go with me. But
no," he added, after a moment's reflection, "I
could never manage it. Poor Martha!"

He watched them trooping off to prayer-meeting, a forlorn and straggling procession, with the
penitent Miss Martha bringing up the rear. A
slight pang of remorse stirred within him, but
he stiffened himself against it. Indeed, no
sooner were they out of sight than he went
boldly out into Miss Charlotte's flower-garden
and began cutting her cherished roses with his
pocket-knife. He looked uneasily over his
shoulder during the operation, it is true; he
even had a prophetic vision of Delphy, the fat

black cook, undergoing suspicion, arraignment, perhaps dismissal, on account of the crime he was committing. But he did not desist until he had a generous handful of dewy, long-stemmed buds. To these he added cluster after cluster of scarlet and pink geranium blossoms, snipped recklessly from Miss Charlotte's well-trimmed borders.

He hurried up to his room, closing and locking the door behind him. When he had lighted the smoky lamp, he took the bundle from the drawer and spread its contents on the bed. It was an evening suit of black cloth—coat, vest, and trousers. A smaller parcel within contained a pair of dancing-pumps, a white silk handkerchief, a white tie, and a small round cap.

Mr. Gish contemplated these things for a moment in abstracted silence. Then, with a sort of feverish haste, he began to put them on.

The low-cut vest gave him a queerish sensation; the coat made him blush. He pulled uneasily at the claw-hammer tails, with much the same feeling that a ballet-girl may be supposed to have when she dons her short skirts for the first time. But, twisting and squirming in front of the tilted looking-glass, with the lamp on the floor, he passed abruptly from gloom and anxiety to rapture. The coat wrinkled between the shoulders, and the gentleman who had hired the suit last had bagged the trousers at the knee. These, however, were but trifles. Mr. Gish had undergone a transformation! He swelled with pride as he surveyed himself from head to foot, and from foot to head again.

He hesitated a moment before he could make up his mind to put on the little silk cap, but he ended by setting it rather jauntily on his bald head. He got gingerly into his light overcoat, and drew on his overshoes—a precaution he never neglected in any kind of weather—and tiptoed out. carrying the flowers wrapped in a bit of newspaper.

He left the car a few blocks above the office of Haley & Co., and walked down, keeping well in the shadow of the tall buildings.

There were noise and bustle enough a stone's-throw away; here the street was quite deserted. But a woman was sitting on the lowest step of the long, dark stairway that led up to the office. She had a child in her arms, and a little bundle of rags with its head on her knees was sobbing in its sleep.

"I can walk home," muttered Mr. Gish. He dropped his only remaining coin in her lap, and groped his way up the stair.

He unlocked the door, and refastened it on the inside. When he had removed his overcoat and overshoes, he lighted the gas, every jet of it, turning up each tongue of yellow flame as high as possible. He pushed the chairs and office stools against the wall, and thrust the roses into a dusty glass that stood on the head bookkeeper's desk. Finally he threw open the three large windows that looked down upon the street. Then he seated himself gravely in Mr. Haley's revolving arm-chair and waited.

The hands of the small clock over his own desk pointed to a quarter of nine.

"HE FACED ABOUT WITH A LOW BOW"

The minute-hand moved slowly. The big bell in a church steeple not far away boomed nine.

Mr. Gish began to fidget. A cold perspiration gathered on his forehead. "Can it be possible," he whispered, with his eyes glued to the clock, "that there has been a mistake?"

The disappointment was too great. He covered his face with his pudgy hands and groaned. Half-past nine. Ten. He got up slowly and began to turn out the lights, one by one.

Suddenly his face cleared; a hand-organ sounded in the street below. The preliminary notes of "The Maiden's Prayer" floated up on the night wind, which came in a little chill through the wide windows. Mr. Gish hastily relighted the gas, and, crossing to the farther side of the room, he faced about with a low bow, smiling and extending his hand.

And then, he danced!

The repertory of the somewhat rickety organ consisted of five "tunes," including "The Maiden's Prayer." The others were "The Evergreen Waltz," "The Tower Song," from *Trovatore,* "Monastery Bells," and "Carry Me Back to Ole Virginny." To all of these, and to each one of them over and over, did Benjamin Franklin Gish dance. He glided, he leaped, he bounded, he swung corners, he chasséd, he fanned an imaginary partner, he ogled her as he pranced back and forth with her, he gazed down at her with a blissful smile as he revolved slowly and laboriously with her in a supposed waltz.

At the conclusion of each set of tunes he walked

about, red and panting, but delicately mindful of the (imaginary) tall girl in a fluffy pink gown whose hand rested on his arm.

Once there was an abrupt break in the music. Mr. Gish looked at the clock, and then ran to the window, dizzy with apprehension. A spirited dialogue was going on between the organ-grinder in the street below and an occupant of one of the rooms of the lofty building across the way. A head was thrust out of an upper window and a string of impotent missiles whizzed downward. But the sash presently dropped, and the cheery notes of "Carry Me Back" rang once more on the air.

Mr. Gish was no longer young; he was fat and short-winded. As the evening wore on he took fewer steps; he sat down between dances, mopping his face with his handkerchief; and it must be confessed that he became at times a little forgetful of his partner. But when the big bell struck twelve and the music broke off with a jerk in the midst of a strain, a pang shot through his heart. He stared blankly about him, and choked down a mournful sigh.

The ball was at an end.

"I must contrive somehow to pay for the gas," he muttered, as he turned off the last jet.

The long tramp homeward was dreary enough. His feet were bruised and blistered, his knees trembled, his arms hung limp from his shoulders, his back ached, his temples throbbed, and his eyes burned. But all this was a trifle as compared with the state of his mind. A moral reaction had set

"AND THEN HE DANCED"

in. The thought of his mother sitting up for him
hung on him like a weight, and he groaned outright as he approached the gate. He opened the
door cautiously and slipped in. His foot was already on the stair.

"Benjy!" called his mother from the little sitting-room.

"Yes, 'm," he gasped. The perspiration broke
out anew on his forehead as he limped slowly
down the hall.

Mrs. Gish sat in a low rocking-chair in front
of the grate, where the handful of coals had long
ago fallen to ashes. Her head and shoulders were
wrapped in an old-fashioned black-and-white plaid
shawl. Her slim old hands were crossed over the
Bible which rested on her knees. When Benjamin Franklin entered she looked up, and began,
severely, "Do you know, Benjy, that it is after
one o'—" But at sight of his woe-begone face
her voice changed. "Why, my son," she cried,
"what is the matter?"

Benjy had no heart for further concealments.
He dropped on his knees and hid his face in
his mother's lap, like a boy, and there fairly
sobbed out the whole story. He went over
it all with simple directness—the first fleeting
vision of the dance, the long evenings spent in
gazing through open windows at the airy inhabitants of another world, the growing desire to
taste this unknown and forbidden joy, the final
resolution, the bargain with the organ-grinder,
the hiring of the dress-suit, even the surrepti-
tious clipping of Miss Charlotte's roses, and then

the ball, the delight of those untaught steps! He told it all, or nearly all. His dream of the tall girl in a fluffy pink gown, with red lips and laughing eyes, *that* he kept to himself.

"Benjamin Franklin," said Mrs. Gish, when he had finished, "stand up."

He got upon his feet. Something unwonted in his mother's voice penetrated his troubled senses and gave him a curious thrill.

"Take off your overcoat," she added, peremptorily, "and let me look at you."

He obeyed, giving the tails of the claw-hammer a vigorous pull towards the front.

The old lady put out a thin, blue-veined hand, and turned him slowly around and around.

"La, Benjy," she exclaimed at last, "how han'some you are! You look exactly like your pa did the night me and him stood up to be married!"

Benjy stared at her in blank amazement. She had risen to her feet and dropped the shawl from her shoulders. Her white old head went up proudly; her sunken eyes flashed. "As for *dancin'*," she cried, "there wa'n't a lighter foot in Pike County than Sam Gish! He could dance all night without losin' his breath, Sam could! And *when* me and him led off *together*"—she paused to chuckle softly—"the balance of the girls and boys had to stand back, I tell you! La, Sam—Benjy, I mean—it's been a long time since I've heard a fiddle talk. But I believe in my soul if I was to hear 'Rabbit in the Cotton Patch,' or 'Granny, does yo' Dog Bite?' I couldn't no

"BENJY HAD NO HEART FOR FURTHER CONCEALMENTS"

more keep my foot off the floor than I could when I was Polly Weathers and Sam Gish was holdin' out his hand!''

She laughed so gayly that Benjy, whose heart was wellnigh bursting with relief, caught the infection and laughed too. The sound of their mirth penetrated the thin partition and echoed through the next room, where Miss Charlotte and Miss Martha were sleeping. Miss Martha turned upon her pillow, half awake, and a wistful smile flitted ghost-like over her round face.

"I'd like to have seen you at the ball, Benjy," the old lady went on, with a youthful ring to her cracked voice. "I'll be bound you stepped out like your pa."

All Benjamin Franklin's weariness had vanished. His face was beaming. He tossed away his tear-wet handkerchief, glided backward, laid his hand on his heart, and bent his short body in a graceful bow. A roguish gleam shot into his mother's dark eyes. She shook out her scant black skirts, and sank nearly to the floor in a sweeping courtesy, extending her finger-tips as she rose to lay them on Benjamin Franklin's arm. Thus, slowly and with measured steps she made the circuit of the dim little room, halting near the fireplace with another wonderful reverence. Then, softly humming a by-gone tune, she tripped lightly through the mazy turnings of an old-fashioned reel. Mr. Gish, radiant, bobbed after her, clumsily imitating her mincing steps. Her tall, erect figure had an almost girlish grace; a smile hovered about her thin lips; her small feet

15

in their loose felt slippers fairly twinkled. More than once she held up a warning finger and glanced over her shoulder, fearful lest the girls should awake. At last, with a quaint little twirl, she stopped, her hands set saucily upon her hips, and looked at her son with laughter-wet eyes.

"Go 'long to bed, Benjy," she said, presently, giving him an affectionate little shove; "it's high time the chickens was crowin' for day!"

He kissed her, and ran, breathlessly, up to the ·little hall bedroom, the happiest assistant book-keeper that ever gave a ball.

"DEY tells me you gwine ter be de centre figger at de 'Mancipation Day ter-morrer, Aun'
Calline," said Uncle Jake Prince, halting in the
dusty road outside the gate, and shifting his
white-oak split basket from one arm to the other.

"I sholy is, Unk Jake," responded Aunt Calline, with dignity.

The other cabins in the long, double row of low
two-roomed houses which had once made up the
quarters of the old Winston plantation had fallen
into disuse and decay; grass grew in their afore-
time trim door-yards; "jimson" weed and mullein choked their garden-patches; their window-
shutters swung loose on broken hinges; their
floors were mildewed and rotting; their very
chimneys were crumbling; the broad walk which
led past them and on to the "great-house," just
showing its white-pillared galleries and peaked
dormer-windowed roof through the trees, was a
tangled thicket of undergrowth. The "great-
house" itself, seen more closely, wore an air of
dilapidation, mournful enough to those who remembered it in the time of the old colonel, when

its hospitable doors stood wide open winter and summer, and even the pickaninnies swinging on the big gate grinned a welcome to the incoming guest.

But Aunt Calline's cabin preserved its old-time look of thrift and comfort. In the little garden there were beds of cabbages and beans and okra, bordered with sage and rosemary ; hollyhocks and larkspur and pretty-by-nights blossomed in the door-yard ; a multiflora rose, entangled with honeysuckle, clambered up the squat chimney, and sent its long, glossy green branches over the comb of the sloping roof and down to the over-hanging eaves ; a box of sweet-basil stood on the window-sill, and a patch of clove-pinks by the gravel-walk filled all the June morning with spicy fragrance. Within, the floor was yellow and shining from immemorial scrubbings ; the rough walls were adorned with newspaper pictures ; and the counterpane and old-fashioned valance of the bed were snowy white and sweet with the smell of lavender. A perpetual fire blazed or smouldered in the wide fireplace, while on the cracked hearth were ranged spiders and skillets and ponderous three-footed ovens with huge lids, suggestive of the rich, brown, salt-rising loaf, the crusty pone, hand-imprinted, the steaming pot-pie, the dainty "snowball," of days when self-respecting cooks looked with scorn and contempt on a cooking-stove.

Aunt Calline herself, as she sat on the door-step beating cake batter in a deep pan resting on her knees, was a reminder of the old *régime*. A fantastically knotted turban encircled her head; a spotless "handk'cher" was folded across her ample bosom; her scant skirts were hitched up under a long blue-check apron, and her rusty feet and ankles were bare. Her kindly old face was creased with wrinkles, but in her great soft brown eyes dwelt that curious look of eternal youth which belongs to her people.

"Big Hannah, whar useter b'long ter we-alls fambly, wus de centre figger las' year," continued Uncle Jake, sociably, drawing nearer to the gate.

"Humph!" grunted Aunt Calline; "mighty fine centre figger dat corn-fiel' gal mus' er made, dough she *is* er sister in Zion! But I ain' seen Big Hannah ez de centre figger. I ain' nuver *been* to no 'Mancipation Day."

"De Lawd, Aun' Calline!" ejaculated the old man, with a well-feigned air of astonishment, "ain' you nuver been ter de 'Mancipation Day? Huccum you ain' nuver been dar?"

"We-el," replied Aunt Calline, reflectively, dipping up a spoonful of batter and letting it drip slowly back into the pan, "hits edzackly dish yer way. De *fus* year dey celerbate 'Mancipation Day hit wuz jes' er leetle a'ter li'l Marse Rod lef' home. Co'se *you* 'members, Unk Jake, when ole Marse Rod an' young Marse Ed wuz kilt in de wah an' fotch home."

Uncle Jake nodded. He had set down his basket and placed his elbows on the low gatepost that he might listen more at his ease to the familiar story.

"De fambly trebbles wuz mo' beknownst ter

me an' my ole man, 'caze we wuz 'mongs' de
house-servants lak, dan dey wuz ter you-all fiel'
han's.   An' 'pear lak ole mis' an' missy wuz
gwine clean crazy when dey fotch home, fus ole
marse, an' den Marse Ed.   Den hit wa'n't no
time 'fo' de bre'k-up an' freedom.   An' all de
fool niggers dey up an' swarm erway fum de
place same ez ef dey wuz er swarm er bees.   All
two er dem boys o' mine wuz 'mongs' de fus ter
go ; an' you wuz 'mongs' de fus yo'se'f, Jake
Prince.   An' whar is you fool niggers now ?"
she demanded, abruptly, her voice rising, and a
look of scorn flashing into her eyes.   " Whar is
you fool niggers now, I axes you ?   *You* is
traipsin' roun' de lan', callin' yo'se'f a'ter de low-
life nigger-trader whar sol' you ter ole marse,
'stidder takin' de name o' de mos' 'spectable
fambly in de county.   An' mighty nigh all o'
you-all is lazy an' good-fer-nothin', whilse heah I
is in de cabin dat de cunnel gimme de same
night Ab'm an' me stood up in the gre't house
dinin'-room an' got married."

   "Dass so," admitted her listener, with a dep-
recatory grin.

   "'Reckly dey wa'n't nobody lef' on de plantation 'cep'n' jes me an' Ab'm an' Dick, dat
younges' chile o' mine dat grow up 'longside o'
li'l Marse Rod.   Lawd ! li'l Marse Rod, he wuz
de beatenes' white chile fum de *cradle*, mun !   I
nussed him at de same breas' wi' Dick, an' dem
two chillen wuz jes lak br'er and br'er.   Dey run
terg'er fum de cradle."

   " *To* be sho !" assented Uncle Jake.   " I 'members dem two chillen myse'f, mighty well. Dey useter pester me 'bout fishin'-lines an' wums, twel I—"

"Li'l Marse Rod's ha'r wuz dat yaller an' curly," she went on, heedless of the interruption, "twel I useter tell ole mis' hit wus jes lak er twist er sugar-candy; an' when dat chile laugh an' ax fer sumpn, Lawd! you is jes boun' fer ter gin hit ter him. An' dem chillen all de time terge'r. Ef Dick wa'n't at de gre't-house, li'l Marse Rod wuz in dis cabin. 'Pear lak I kin heah him yit, comin' runnin' down de walk yander, bar'headed, an' hollerin' ter me, settin' edzackly whar I is now, 'Mammy, tell Dick ter wait fer me; I'm comin'!'"

"*To* be sho!" interjected Uncle Jake. "I 'members dat mighty well, myse'f."

"He wuz er high-spirited chile; an' when he look erbout him an' see de ole plantation lef' ter rack an' ruin, an' nobody ter tek keer o' his ma' an' missy, 'cep'n' Ab'm an' me, he seem lak he couldn't 'bide dat. He wuz jes tu'n o' fo'teen den; jes de age o' my Dick. An' one mawnin' li'l Marse Rod wuz *gone*, mun! An' ole mis' foun' er letter onder de do' whar say dat he gwine some'ers fer ter wuk twel he git er pile o' money, an' den he comin' back an' tek keer o' ole mis', an' missy, an' Ab'm, an' me, an' Dick. An' he lef' er good word fer Dick in de letter. An' dass de las' we uver heerd tell o' li'l Marse Rod. But I tells you, Jake Prince, I jes ez sho dat chile gwine ter come back ez I is dat I settin' on dish yer do'-step. He gwine ter come back in er cayidge an' er pa'r er high-steppin' hosses, like dem Ab'm useter drive fer ole mis' 'fo' de wah."

She rested the spoon on the edge of the pan for a moment, while her eyes sought the dingy "great-house" among its embowering trees.

"We ain' nuver heerd fum him sence," she resumed, with a deep sigh. "Ole mis' and missy dey bofe werry twel dey sick 'bout Marse Rod, an' dat huccum I didn' go ter de *fus* 'Mancipation Day."

"Ole Aun' Dilsey Cushin' wuz de centre figger dat time," remarked Uncle Jake.

"Den de *nex* year missy wuz on de p'int er gettin' married ter Cap'n Tom Ramsay, fum Richmon', an' me an' ole mis' we wuz makin' de weddin'-cake, an' I ain' had no *time* fer ter fool 'long o' 'Mancipation Day. An' de *nex* year wuz de time dat my Dick wuz fotch home drownded from de bayou. Den Ab'm wuz tuk down. Mussy, Unk Jake, you 'ain' fergot dem seven year whar Ab'm wuz *down*?"

"Cert'n'y, Aun' Calline, I 'ain' fergot Unk Ab'm's rheumatiz. Dough dat ain' hender Unk Ab'm fum settin' in er cheer yander by de fiah an' pickin' de banjer. Mun! how Unk Ab'm could pick de banjer!"

"Dat he could! Dey wa'n't nobody in de quarter could tech Ab'm when it come ter pickin' de banjer. De quality useter come down fum de gre't-house 'fo' de wah ter heah him pick 'Billy in de low groun's,' an' 'Sugar in de gode,' an' de lak o' dat. Well, I 'ain' had no *call* ter go whilse de ole man wuz down , an' me er tukin' keer at de same time o' ole mis' an' missy, an' missy's chillen."

"An' missy er widder at dat."

"An' missy er widder at dat. Den de sweet chariot done swung low fer Ab'm, an' he tuk'n ter glory. An' *den* sometimes one an' sometimes an'er o' missy's chillen had de measles, o' de whoopin'-cough, o' de chicken-pox, o' de scyarlet-fever, an' 'pear lak I couldn't spar' er *minit* fer er frolic. Co'se, a'ter missy tuk'n de consomption an' die, an' de chillen gone ter Cap'n Tom Ramsay's folks, I couldn' leave ole mis'. Who gwine ter stay 'long o' ole mis' whilse Calline fla'ntin' herse'f ter 'Mancipation Day? Year befo' las' ole mis' *she* tuk down, an' I 'ain' lef' her night ner day twel she pass on ter glory las' Sat'day week. An' now, sence de fambly is all brek up, an' de gre't-house shet, an' I has de *time*, I gwine ter de 'Mancipation Day."

"Ez de centre figger," respectfully suggested Uncle Jake.

"Ez de centre figger. I has been invited by all de conjugations o' all de chu'ches ter set in de head cheer. But, kingdom come, Unk Jake!" she broke off, rising energetically to her feet, "I 'ain' got time ter be foolin' 'long o' you, an' all my cake ter bake. Dish yer batter ready for de oven now."

"Dass so, Aunt Calline! I is in er mons'us hurry myse'f. I done promise Miss Botts ter fotch her er settin' er domineker aigs 'fo' sun-up dis mawnin'. I gotter be gwine." And he picked up his basket and shuffled away.

It was late that night when Aunt Calline went to bed. Her hamper carefully packed and covered with a clean cloth was placed on the little table ; beside it on a chair was laid out the black bombazine gown reserved for state occasions, the sheer kerchief, and the freshly ironed turban. She surveyed these last preparations with great satisfaction before turning down the wick of the smoky kerosene lamp. "Bless de Lawd," she muttered, "I is gwine ter feel my freedom at las' ! I is gwine ter de 'Mancipation Day dis time, *sho!* An' I boun' Big Hannah, wi' de res' o' de corn-fiel' niggers, gwine ter laugh de wrong side o' dey mouf when dey sees me settin' in de head cheer ez de centre figger, an' all de conjugations o' all de chu'ches comin' up an' makin' dey bow ter Sister Calline Wins'n."

She was up betimes the next morning. The first long slanting rays of sunlight came in through the half-open shutter as she gave a last twist to the wonderful knot in her turban. "Now," she said aloud, "I gwine ter feed de chickens, an' tie up ole Rove, an' kiver up de fiah, an' den I *kin* say I ready."

She opened the front door as she spoke, but she started back with an exclamation of anger and surprise. A man, evidently a tramp, was huddled upon the step, his head resting upon his arms, which were crossed upon the door-sill. "Look a-heah, white man," she began, in a shrill, high voice, "what you doin'? Whar you come fum? I gwine ter set de dog on you dis minit ef you doan git up fum dar an' go 'long 'bout yo' business."

The bundle of rags at her feet stirred. He lifted his head and threw back the long, matted hair from his forehead. A pair of dim blue eyes looked up at her appealingly; a wan smile played over the emaciated and sunken features; the pale lips parted as if for speech. But there was no need. She had gathered him up in her arms, rags and all, and was carrying the light burden across the threshold, laughing hysterically.

"Lawd, li'l Marse Rod!" she cried, as she placed him in the big split-bottomed chair in a corner of the fireplace, "I know'd you wuz gwine ter come back! I is know'd it all de time. An' yo' po' ole mammy so blin' dat she didn' jes edzackly *place* you at de fus' look. 'Sides, you didn't had no *mustache* when you lef' home." The tears were streaming down her old cheeks as she hovered over him in an ecstasy of joy. He essayed to speak, but a hollow cough wrenched his frail body, and his head dropped helplessly against the faithful breast which had pillowed it in infancy.

"Doan you try ter talk, honey," she said, stroking his cheek with her hand. Then, leaning over him and interpreting a look in his haggard eyes, she cried, "My Lawd a' mighty, de chile is *hongry!*"

She dragged the table to his side with feverish

haste, and spread upon it the contents of the basket. She affected not to notice while he ate —almost ravenously. "You sees, Marse Rod," she said, now down on her knees before him, removing the tattered shoes from his blistered and travel-worn feet—"you sees dat de quality doan nuver put on dey fine cloze fer ter travel in, an' I might o' *know'd* dat you wa'n't gwine ter come home all dress up in broadcloth, same ez ef you wa'n't no mo'n po' white trash."

Rodney Winston smiled pitifully. He had pushed away his plate, and was leaning back in his chair, exhausted and panting.

"Mammy," he interrupted, speaking for the first time, and laying a thin hand caressingly on her shoulder, "where is my mother?"

"I 'clar' ter goodness," she went on, with tender volubility, pretending not to hear, "you look edzackly lak you did, edzackly! I gwine ter cut yo' ha'r 'reckly—dat same yaller ha'r whar me an' ole mis' useter say look lak er twis' er sugar-candy—an' den you kin put on some o' Ab'm's cloze yander in de chis; dey waz all yo' pa's, honey, an' you ain' gwine ter be 'shame' ter w'ar 'em twel yo' trunk gits heah; an' den—"

"Mammy," he began again. But at this moment a confused and tumultuous sound began to float in on the fresh morning air.

"Jes you wait er minit, li'l marse," she said, starting up; and throwing a light covering across his knees, she went out into the yard, closing the door behind her.

The procession was coming—the great, good-

humored crowd which had been gathering since
long before daylight about the doors of Antioch
Church. Every negro in the county, big and
little, young and old, was there—the congrega-
tions of the churches marching on foot and carrying banners; the Sunday - schools under the
leadership of the elders; societies with badges;
Sisters of Rebecca and Daughters of Deborah in
blue cambric shoulder-capes and wide belts; Sons
of Zion in the wrinkled and creased broadcloth
coats and the well-preserved silk hats of a dead
and gone generation; wagon loads of old people
and babies; back-sliders with banjos and fiddles;
hardened sinners who had never even been seek-
ers at the mourners' bench—they were all there,
and the long line had just turned the corner
of the field beyond the "great-house." It was
headed by an open wagon which carried the choir
of Antioch Church. Jerry Martin, big, black,
and sleek, one of the chief holders in Zion, stood
on the front seat, swaying from side to side, and
shouting:

" *Ole Satan he thought dat he had me fus'.*"

The shrill voices of the women took up the re-
frain:

" *March erlong, childern, march erlong!*"

" *But I is broke his chains at las'.*"

And the whole line joined in the chorus:

" *March erlong, childern, for de Promis' Lan' is nigh.*"

The sound rolled away triumphant, mighty unctuous, and came echoing back from the distant woodland.

The carriage destined for that sister in Zion whose virtues entitled her to the foremost place of honor followed Jerry and his choir. Aunt Calline's heart thrilled with pride as it rattled up to the gate and stopped. It was the old Winston family carriage, dilapidated, and somewhat the worse for wear, but strong and serviceable still. Two sleek mules trotted under the ragged harness, and Uncle Jake Prince sat on the driver's seat. Brother 'Lijah Vance, the pastor of Antioch, got out. The vast procession halted, and a sudden hush fell upon the people.

Brother Vance lifted the latch of the gate. "Good-mawnin', Sister Wins'n," he said, pompously, removing his tall hat and extending a gloved hand. "De centre figger will please ha' de goodness ter tek er seat in de cayidge, an' be druv ter de 'Mancipation Groun's."

"Much erbleege ter you, Br'er Vance," replied Sister Winston, with her grandest courtesy, "an' I meks my compli*ments* ter de chu'ches an' de chu'ch-members. But I has comp'ny dis mawnin', an' I axes you ter scuse me fum bein' de centre figger."

"Lawd, Aun' Calline!" exclaimed Brother Vance, dropping in his dismay into every-day manners, "who gwine ter be de centre figger ef you ain' ?"

"Mr. Rodney Wins'n done come home, 'Lijah," she replied. A murmur of surprise swept down the line; many of the old Winston negroes were near, and these left their places and came crowding about the gate. "Li'l Marse Rod done come back," she continued, her head raised majestically, and her hands folded across her bosom; "he ain' ter say *rested* yet, but ter-morrer he gwine ter open up de gre't-house yander. He axes you all howdy, an' he say you mus' come up an' shek han's at de gre't-house."

" *To* be sho !" ejaculated Uncle Jake from his perch.

"Dass de li'l Marse Rod whar Mis' Calline Wins'n been jawin' 'bout ever sence I bawn," giggled one of the girls in the choir-wagon, a pretty mulattress with a saucy face. "Whar's de cayidge, an' de pa'r er high-steppin' hosses, an' de baag er gol' he gwine ter fotch home fum yander, Aun' Calline ?"

Aunt Calline turned upon her wrathfully. "Yer lazy, good-fer-nothin', low-down nigger," she blazed, "ef you doan shet yo' mouf, I gwine ter hise myse'f in dat wagin an' w'ar you ter a plum frazzle."

The girl cowered down behind her companions, subdued and frightened. Brother Vance re-entered the carriage, much perplexed by the unexpected turn of events. Jerry Martin lifted up his powerful voice again, and the procession passed on.

She went back into the cabin. Her guest unclosed his eyes as she entered, and looked about him vaguely for a moment, as if he hardly knew where he was. Then a quick flush mounted to his cheek. "Mammy," he insisted, "where is my mother?"

"Well, honey," she admitted, reluctantly, "yer ma ain' ter say *livin'* edzackly; she done—"

"And my sister?"

"Marse Rod, you *knows* dat missy wuz po'ly fum de *cradle;* an' de consomption bein' 'mongs' de fambly—'mongs' de *women*-folks, min' you; 'tain't 'mongs' de *men*-folks—an' hit seem lak missy jes *hatter* go."

"Dick?"

"Lawd, chile, I ain't nuver *spected* ter raise *Dick!* Dick wuz dat venturesome dat when dey fotch him home fum de bayou drownded I ain' ter say *'stonish'.* Dick he layin' out yander in de fambly buryin'-groun', jes 'cross de foot o' yo' pa an' yo' ma; an' Ab'm he in de cornder, whar dey is lef' a place fer me."

He covered his face with his hands and groaned.

"Doan be trebbled, honey," she said, soothing him as one would soothe a hurt child—"*doan* be trebbled."

When she had clipped his hair and dressed him in the spotless linen and the old, blue, brass-buttoned suit, which had once been his father's, he lay on the bed, following with grateful eyes her bustling movements about the room.

"Mammy," he said, suddenly, "I've come back poorer than I went away. I've been everywhere; I've tried everything. In all these years I have somehow not been able to make my bread, much less—I was ashamed even to write to my mother until I could tell her that I was coming home to take care of her ; and now—"

"Dat doan matter, honey," she interrupted, eagerly. "Doan you fret yo'se'f. We gwine ter git erlong. Yo' ole mammy kin wuk. Lawd, dey ain't no young gal in dish yer county whar kin do day's wuk lak I kin ! An' when you gits fa'r rested, you is gwine ter tek up de ole plantation, an' men' de fences, an' patch up de cabins, and hiah de mules an' de niggers. Mun ! de niggers gwine ter be mighty proud when dey gits er chance ter come back ter de old plantation ; an' den—"

Even as she spoke his eyes closed, his head dropped, a mortal pallor crept over his already pale face.

" O Lawd, doan let de chile die !" she sobbed, chafing his pulseless wrists and rubbing his cold feet. He presently rallied, and sank into a peaceful slumber, which lasted well on into the afternoon. She sat watching him while he slept, her old brain teeming with visions of the renewed glories of Winston Place. The doors of the "great-house" once more stood wide open ;—the sound of music and laughter rang out from the windows ; —horses were hitched in the lane ;—carriages rolled around the drive, and ladies in long, rustling silk dresses got out and passed up the steps ; —children were at play on the smooth lawn— children with skin like the snow of apple blossoms, and coal-black pickaninnies with laughing eyes and shining teeth ;—a pack of hounds leaped and yelped about the stable-yard, where the

16

young master and his friends were mounting for a fox-hunt;—the long table in the dining-room blazed with crystal and silver under the light of the lamps;—the house-girls ran in and out, carrying trays of glasses, wherein the ice tinkled and wherefrom the sprigs of bruised mint perfumed the air;—outside, in the lane, the field-hands were going by with cotton-baskets on their heads and singing;—in the big kitchen fireplace the flames roared—

Suddenly a clear young voice filled the room. Could it be the curly-haired lad coming running bareheaded down the walk from the "great-house"? "Mammy, tell Dick to wait for me; I'm coming!" he cried, a boyish smile playing about his lips, and a boyish light sparkling in his dying eyes.

"De las' o' we-alls fambly," moaned the faithful soul, straightening his limbs and smoothing back the still, silken curls from his forehead.

An hour or two later she came out into the yard. The sun had set; the first stars were coming into the soft gray sky, and under the horizon hung the pale crescent of a new moon. "I gwine ter put some pinks an' some honeysuckle in his han's," she murmured, "'caze ole mis' gimme dem pinks an' dat honeysuckle fum onder her winder yander ter de gre't-house. An' I gwine ter bury him 'longside o' Dick, 'caze Dick he been er waitin' er long time fer li'l Marse Rod."

The evening wind was rising, and on it came borne the sound of singing. She lifted her head, listening. It was the 'Mancipation Day proces-

sion. Brother Vance was leading his flock homeward through the gathering dusk.

"*I is wuked all day in de br'ilin' sun,*"

sang Jerry Martin, the mellow tones of his voice
ringing clearly out across the open fields.

"*Lawd Jesus, call me home!*"

responded the people.

"*Now de sun is down an' de wuk is done.*"

"*Lawd Jesus, call me home!*"

"Dass so!" said Aunt Calline, softly. "Dass
so! De wuk is sho done. Lawd Jesus, call me
home!"

"You, 'Lijah !" called Aunt Cindy from within the cabin, "ef you doan keep out'n dat water, I is sholy gwine ter w'ar you ter er plum frazzle."

"Yass'm," replied 'Lijah, continuing to wriggle his small dusky body about in the water, and feeling with his toes for the ground, as he swung by the tips of his fingers from the gallery. But when his mother suddenly appeared in the doorway, with a well-seasoned bunch of switches in her hand, he crawled, chuckling, up on the wet planks, and stretched himself there like a baby alligator in the warm noonday sun.

Three days before the levee over on the big swollen river had broken, and the waters from the crevasse were swirling about Aunt Cindy Washington's cabin, and rushing away, yellow and foaming, in an angry current that was cutting a huge channel for itself across the very heart of the country. From the high gallery it looked like a vast sea, spreading as far as the eye could reach to the south and west, and gaining hour by hour upon the line of forest trees far away under the eastern horizon. Back of the cabin the ground rose a little; in one corner of the straggling turnip-patch a bit of green even showed itself when a breeze rippled the waves.

The first swift onslaught of the flood had carried away nearly all the cabins and out-houses scattered about the isolated negro settlement of Bethel Church; those that remained threatened every moment to topple over into the widening stream, on whose surface floated the forlorn mass of wreckage—beams, shingles, doors, window-shutters, odds and ends of household goods, bales of hay, chicken-coops, tree-stumps, animals living and dead—that told its own pitiful story of destruction. The inhabitants had been removed to a place of safety by the relief-boats that passed and repassed, distributing provisions and caring for the needy and homeless.

But Aunt Cindy had stoutly refused to abandon her cabin. "De onderpinnin' o' dish yer cabin," she declared, "ain' lak de onderpinnin' o' dem yander triflin' no-'count cabins. 'Caze Sol Wash'n'ton, my ole man, is put up dish yer cabin wi' his own han's befo' he was tuk'n ter glory, an' I *knows* hit's gwine ter stan'!"

The queer ramshackle little structure which Uncle Sol Washington had put up "with his own hands" had one room and a front gallery, and in ordinary times its peaked and lop-sided roof amply sheltered Aunt Cindy, her four well-grown girls—Polly, Dicy, Sal, and Viny—and her one eleven-year-old boy 'Lijah. Just now, however, it must be confessed, the cabin was somewhat crowded. At the first note of warning, Pomp, the old white mule which assisted in the making of Aunt Cindy's modest "crap," had been guided up the rickety steps, and quartered on one end of the gallery, where he munched contentedly all day long from the pile of corn and fodder supplied by the government relief boat. A new-born calf, which had drifted against the back door, and had been lifted in and warmed to life on the wide hearth-stone, stood beside him, or trotted like a kitten in and out of the open doorway. A big flop-eared hound-dog had buffeted his way, swimming, to the edge of the gallery, and looked up with red, appealing eyes; he now lay in a corner of the fireplace, sleek, brown, and dry, and sniffed hungrily at the frying-pan. A turkey-cock strutted about the floor. A litter of pigs grunted in a corner.

"I 'clar' ter goodness," said Aunt Cindy the second morning, as she fished out a coop of half-drowned chickens, which came bumping against the wall, "hit's edzacktly lak de Zark dat ole Noah done builded at de comman' o' de Lawd!"

A few hours later a 'possum crept in, and made his way stealthily to one of the blackened rafters under the roof, whence he looked gravely down; and a lame blackbird hopped upon the snowy counterpane of Aunt Cindy's big four-post bed, and nestled among the pillows.

"Hit's er Zark!" repeated Aunt Cindy, cheerfully, "an' I *knows* dat de onderpinnin' is gwine ter stan'. An' wi' gov'ment bacon an' de catfish dat me an' de chillen kin ketch frum de gall'ry, we ain' gwine ter starve."

'Lijah sunned himself in his wet clothes, now staring dreamily at the soft blue March sky overhead, now watching Polly, who was fishing from the other end of the gallery close to old Pomp's inoffensive heels. Suddenly he scrambled to his feet and gazed intently out over the yellow sea. The next moment he plunged headlong into the water, where for a second he disappeared, then rose, spluttering and blowing.

Polly threw down her pole at the splash and ran forward. "You, 'Lije," she gasped, "come out'n dat water dis minute! Does you wanter *drown* yo'se'f? Mammy gwine ter w'ar you ter er—"

She stopped abruptly; her mouth remained wide open and her eyes dilated. 'Lijah was pushing his way slowly against the incoming waves. The water, at first a little below his shoulders, presently lapped against his chin. Once or twice he slipped, and then only the top of his woolly head was visible in the foam. Finally he struck out, and swam with unsteady, childish strokes towards the object upon which his eyes were fixed. It was a whitish mass, which floated slowly, as if driven by a light wind, towards the rapid current of the deeper channel a few yards away. As 'Lijah approached it caught in the scraggy tops of some altheas that marked the boundary of the cabin door-yard; there it stopped a moment, swaying from side to side, as if about to sink; then, caught in an eddy, it turned suddenly and shot forward. 'Lijah made a desperate spurt and laid hold of it, drawing it cau-

tionsly to him; his lean, brown arm glistened in
the sun as he stretched it out. He turned with
difficulty, and labored back, pushing the drift
before him. As he came up, Polly, who had
been too terrified to utter a word, seized him,
and drew him upon the gallery, where he dropped,
exhausted and panting. Then she looked down
at the jetsam he had towed in, and gave a screech
which brought Aunt Cindy, the girls, and the
dog flying out.

It was indeed a strange little craft which lay
alongside the Zark—a tiny cradle mattress, water-
soaked and stained. Lying upon it—its single
passenger—was a four or five months' old girl
baby, white and delicate as a snow-drop. She
was clad in a long night-gown, which clung in
dripping folds about her plump little body; it
was open at the throat, showing her round, dimpled neck, encircled by a string of coral with a
broad clasp of gold. The soft rings of brown
hair that curled about her forehead were wet and
glistening. Her eyes were closed, her lips were
blue, and her cheeks cold and pale. In one tiny
benumbed fist she grasped a green leaf, which
she had probably caught from some overhanging
vine.

"Get de kittle er hot water, Dicy," ordered
Aunt Cindy, as she lifted the mattress in her
arms and carried it into the cabin. "Stir
yo'se'f, gal! Polly, fetch 'Lijah er swaller o' pep-
per-sass. Punch up de fiah, Sal. Po' li'l' gal
chile! Deir ain' much bref lef' in yo' body,
honey. *Is* de worl' comin' ter er een?"

Half an hour later the baby, lying on Aunt Cindy's lap, opened her blue eyes languidly, and looked at the wondering group gathered around her.

"Dar now!" said Aunt Cindy, comfortably, "I gwine ter git her somefin ter eat, an' den I be boun' she gwine ter be lively."

The little creature pursed up her pretty mouth and began to whimper as her eyes went from face to face. But catching sight of 'Lijah, who had recovered his breath in rebellion against the pepper-sauce, some mysterious sense within her seemed to stir; she smiled, reached out her little hand, and clasped a finger of one of his brown paws with a gurgle of content.

'Lijah picked up from the hearth the bit of green vine which had dropped unnoticed from the baby's unconscious hand. "Hit's de dove," he said, "dat de Lawd is done saunt inter de Zark wi' 'er green leaf in her han'."

From that moment the baby grew and thrived in the water-girt cabin. Its inmates, from Aunt Cindy herself down to Viny, the youngest child, adored her. Viny declared that even the pigs tried not to grunt when she was asleep. But it was to 'Lijah most of all that she clung with all the strength of her baby heart, and 'Lijah never wearied of "toting" her around the crowded room, or up and down the littered gallery. Aunt Cindy, mindful of the past grandeurs of her own white folks, cast about for some high-sounding name for the precious waif. But they called her Dovie; and there she abode, a white flower ringed around by dark, loving faces, while the water rose and fell and rose again as the crevasse was partly closed or the levee broke afresh.

One morning, nearly two months later, Aunt Cindy, carrying a basket of fresh eggs, and followed by 'Lijah, approached the little railway station a mile or so from Bethel Church just as the train whizzed away.

A light carriage, drawn by two sleek horses, was waiting at the station. Its owner, busy about the harness, looked around as Aunt Cindy came up.

"Dullaw !" she exclaimed, breaking into a broad grin. "Ef dat ain' li'l' Marse Jack Mannin'! Howdy, Marse Jack ?"

The young man shook hands with her heartily. "Why, Aunt Cindy," he said, "who ever would have thought of seeing you away up here ?"

Aunt Cindy laughed. "Sol Wash'n'ton wuz er pow'ful han' ter travel," she replied. "Huccum you here yo'self, Marse Jack ? An' whar is you lef' Miss Nannie ?"

His bright face clouded anxiously. "I have bought the Four Oaks Plantation, over on the river," he said. "Nannie is inside. Go and see her, Aunt Cindy."

The young and delicate - looking woman who was seated in the little waiting-room threw herself with a wild sob into the arms of the faithful soul who had nursed her when she was a baby.

"Oh, mammy ! mammy !" she moaned.

"What's de matter, honey?" Aunt Cindy asked, tenderly stroking her dark curls.

The story which Mrs. Manning told, through her tears, was a sad one. Four Oaks Plantation, where they had been living but a few months, was quite near the river. When the levee gave way, and the water began rapidly to rise, they had taken refuge, with their baby and some of the house-servants, in the manager's cottage, a short distance in the rear. There they passed a day and part of a night in the greatest anxiety. Towards midnight the rush of water became so threatening that they determined to take again to the skiffs that had brought them over. She herself was on the gallery, helping her husband and the negroes to get the boats ready, when the house suddenly parted in the middle, as if cleft by a knife, and in the dense darkness one end of it crashed down into the roaring flood. The baby, sleeping in her crib within, was drowned.

"And oh, mammy," the young mother sobbed, when she had finished the story, and told how they were finally taken, half drowned themselves, from the wreck, by a relief-boat, "if I could only have seen my baby once more! But her little body was swept away with the broken timbers. The deepest channel of the crevasse now is just where the house stood. My baby — my little baby!"

Aunt Cindy started involuntarily. "Miss Nannie," she said, after a moment's silence, "hit wuz er pow'ful 'fliction de losin' er dat baby boy."

"My baby was a girl, mammy," interrupted Mrs. Manning, sobbing afresh, "with blue eyes, and brown hair that curled all over her head."

"Jes lak yo'n useter, honey." Aunt Cindy's voice had a ring of excitement in it. She got up, and went out to where 'Lijah sat on the edge of the platform swinging his heels. A moment later he set off, whooping, by a short-cut towards home, with the hound running alongside. Mr. Manning was walking dejectedly up and down the platform. "Marse Jack," said Aunt Cindy, in a wheedling tone, "you knows dat I is knowed you an' Miss Nannie sence you wa'n't knee-high ter er duck."

"Indeed you have," said Mr. Manning, feeling in his pocket for some loose change.

"An' dat I nussed Miss Nannie when she wuz er baby; an' dat I close her ma's eyes when she died."

"Yes," he said again, kindly.

"An' I wants you ter 'suade Miss Nannie ter drive down ter my cabin. You has plenty o' time. Hit ain' fur, an' Miss Nannie might be hope up by seein' o' de chillen."

It needed no coaxing to induce Mrs. Manning to go. She clung to Aunt Cindy, whose familiar presence seemed to soothe her, and they got in the carriage.

The road was a roundabout one, owing to the gullies and pitfalls left by the flood, and by the time they came in sight of the cabin the young woman was quiet and almost cheerful.

The Zark looked forlorn enough; a dingy line around the walls showed the point at which the water had stood for many weeks; the gallery was rotting and falling in; the steps, which had been swept away, had been replaced by a shaky contrivance of boards. The fences were all down, and the door-yard was heaped with tangled drift. But the garden-patch was thriving; and neat furrows in the field showed that old Pomp and Aunt Cindy had been at work there. The cabin door was closed, and no one was in sight.

"Sol Wash'n'ton is put up dish yere cabin wi' his own han's," said its mistress, proudly, leading the way up the steps. "De onderpinnin' is made fer ter *stan'!* Ever' cabin in Bethel Chu'ch is squish down 'cep'n' jes mine. We done call hit de Zark, 'caze—" Mrs. Manning's eyes were filling with tears again at the mention of the fatal crevasse. Her husband gave Aunt Cindy a look of warning, but she went on, cheerfully: "We done name hit de Zark, 'caze we tuk 'n' tuk in ever'thing dat come er pass dis way, same ez ef hit wuz de comman' er de Lawd! Yes, honey, we tuk 'n' tuk in chickens an' dawgs an' mules— ever'*thing!* 'Possums an' 'coons — *ever*'thing! Birds an' calves an'—*babies;* yes, honey, *ev-er'- thing!*" She had her arm around her foster-child, and was drawing her gently towards the cabin door. A deadly pallor had crept into Mrs. Manning's cheeks, and her eyes were wide with entreaty. "Yes, chile, *ef* er li'l' white *gal* baby come floatin'—er long—*on* er crib mattress—" she pushed open the door.

The stained mattress was in the middle of the floor. Dovie, clad in the little gown—which she had sadly outgrown — that she wore when she came to the Zark, had been placed carefully upon it. But she was in the very act of crawling off; one bare, rosy foot was thrust out, her dimpled hands grasped the torn sheet, her lips were parted in a roguish smile, her blue eyes sparkled. Polly, Viny, Sal, and Dicy hung around the mattress, giggling; 'Lijah stood guard over her; the hound by his side looked gravely on. Dovie looked up as the door opened, and frowned inquiringly; then, as usual in any emergency, she reached up and laid firm hold of 'Lijah, stuck her thumb in her mouth, and stared at the intruders.

Mrs. Manning stumbled forward, and sank with a cry to the floor.

"Doan you be skeered, Marse Jack," said Aunt Cindy, "she ain't gwine ter die. Dat kin' er joy doan kill." She laid the frightened child in the mother's outstretched arms. "Why, honey, I might er knowed dat dis baby b'long ter we-alls fambly. Polly, 'ain' you got no manners? Fetch er cheer fer Marse Jack! An' Dicy done read de plain word 'Nannie' all de time on dat gol' clasp! I 'ain' shout sence Bethel Chu'ch is tumble inter de flood, but I sholy is gwine ter shout now. *Glory! Glory!*" And the high, triumphant cry of the old negress went echoing away like a trumpet tone on the clear morning air.

Second only to Dovie herself in importance at the Four Oaks Plantation great-house is 'Lijah Washington. He waits on Marse Jack and runs errands for Miss Nannie. But for the most part his business is to walk around, in company with the flop-eared hound, after Dovie, who is just be-

"MRS. MANNING STUMBLED FORWARD"

ginning to walk. Sometimes he proudly "totes" her in his arms.

"What a beautiful baby!" a visitor exclaims, patting Dovie's dimpled cheeks.

"Yass'm," 'Lijah responds, showing his white teeth in a delighted grin; "dish yere is de dove dat come ter de Zark endurin' er de flood wi' er green leaf in her li'l' han', an' I done tuk 'n' tuk her in. Yass'm!"

I

"Can you 'cunjur,' Maum Hagar?"

The words were carelessly spoken, but Hagar, keenly sensitive to every shade of feeling in her foster-son's voice, detected an unwonted thrill beneath their airy lightness.

The speaker was a tall, slightly built man about thirty years of age. His thin, sallow face was very handsome, though there were lines of dissipation about the dark, smiling eyes and the low forehead shaded by crisp, reddish-brown curls. His mouth, partly hidden by a drooping mustache, was rather feminine, but the smooth chin was firm almost to hardness.

His clothes were of irreproachable cut and fit; an air of high-bred ease pervaded his whole person as he swayed lightly to and fro in the low rocking-chair, fanning himself with a wide hat whose crown was encircled by a band of crape.

The old negress who stood before him in an attitude at once familiar and respectful was likewise tall and slender. Her brown, furrowed face beneath her gayly colored turban was curiously

impassive ; only the sunken eyes seemed alive.
They glowed like smouldering fires within their
half-closed lids. Her arms were folded across
her breast ; her bare feet and ankles were visible
beneath her short, scant skirts.

There were signs of a past grandeur about the
large room. A stucco frieze, representing a procession of mythological personages, ran around
the dingy walls under the lofty ceiling. The
arched windows were surmounted by elaborate
moldings; the high wooden mantel, upheld by
slim pillars of twisted brass, was delicately
carved ; the double doors, opening upon an inner
gallery, were set with panels of stained glass.

The massive sideboard and the claw-footed tables, which in an earlier day furnished forth this
ancient dining-hall, had long since disappeared.
But the floor was clean ; the humble bed, piled
with wholesome-smelling unlaundered garments,
was covered with a snow-white counterpane and
ornamented with stiff, fringed valances; the
hearth was reddened ; the tall brass fire - dogs
glistened like gold.

An ironing-board, with a partly ironed shirt
upon it, was supported on the backs of two chairs
near the fireplace ; a charcoal furnace, with some
flat-irons plunged into its bed of red coals, occupied a corner of the hearth.

Floyd Garth idly noted these commonplace details as he repeated his question, "Maum Hagar,
can you 'cunjur'?"

Old Hagar looked down at him a moment before speaking. "I ain't shore," she said, slowly,

17

"dat I kin conjur to suit *you,* Mars Floyd. It 'pends on what you *wants.*"

A flush darkened the young man's face; he shifted his position and cleared his throat.

"What is you honin' after, little Mars? You sholy ain't 'shamed to tell yo' black mammy. honey," she said, caressingly, her face suddenly losing its impassiveness.

He laughed gayly. "You make me half be-lieve that I am a boy again, and back on the old plantation, mammy! Do you remember how I used to steal down to your cabin at the quarter when I wanted anything? And you never failed to get me what I wanted, either! The old cabin looks just as it did when you left it. How long has it been since you came away from Garth Place?"

"It's seventeen year come Christmas," she re-plied, huskily, as if a lump had arisen in her throat.

"Ah, yes! it was the year my father took me abroad. You came this far with us, I remember. How I yelled and kicked, half - grown boy as I was, when they tore me away from your arms! Yes, the old place remains the same in spite of all our drifting about. But now that my father is dead—it is just three weeks to-day since I saw him laid beside my mother in the old burying-ground at the plantation—now that he is gone, it is too dreary there. I shall place everything in the hands of the manager and live in the city myself. I may open the old town-house. You will come and keep house for me, eh, maum? Do

you know, Maum Hagar," he continued, musingly, "I can just recollect living in that old house !
My father closed it, I know, when my mother
died. I was not more than three or four years
old, was I ? But I can dimly remember my pretty dark-eyed mother bending over me, with her
long curls falling about her shoulders, as they do
in her portrait."

His reckless face had softened, his eyes were
fixed upon the floor, and he did not see the sombre lightning which flashed into those gazing
down upon him.

"And then my father gave me to your care,
Maum Hagar."

"I nussed you fum de day you was bawn," she
interrupted, fiercely.

"So you did, mammy," he said, heartily—"so
you did. And spoiled me well into the bargain.
I must be going," he added, rising. "I have had
a precious hunt for you this time, and I never
would have found you if—" He checked himself suddenly; then asked, "How long have you
been living in this tumble-down old rookery ?"

"De cunjur, honey ?" she said, ignoring his
outstretched hand. "You axed me kin I cunjur."

The softened look vanished from the young
man's face. "Yes," he said, setting his teeth together, "I want you to cunjur—a woman." His
protruding chin had an ugly look and an uneasy
fire burned in his eyes. "A woman, by God ! who
eludes me, and tantalizes me, and holds me at
arm's-length, child though she is in years !" He

was speaking more to himself than to his old nurse. She watched him with narrowing eyelids.

"Is it de love-spell you wants, or de hate-spell, honey ?" she asked, moving a step nearer and laying her hand on his arm.

He laughed shortly. "Oh, the love-spell—first ! What nonsense !" he continued, shrugging his shoulders. "It just came into my mind how they used to say up at Garth Place that you could *throw Wanga*. I was only joking. Good-bye, Maum Hagar. Come to me when you need anything." He dropped some silver coin into her apron-pocket, and turned to go.

"I'm goin' to fetch you de love-spell, little marse," she said, softly.

He seemed not to have heard her. "Where is Lisette ?" he asked, as if prompted by a sudden thought. "She must be almost grown."

"Lisette is hired out," Hagar returned, in a preoccupied tone. "She's nigh on to seventeen year old, Lisette is."

She followed him out upon the gallery which overlooked the court, crossed and recrossed with flapping lines of wet garments, and watched him descend the shaky stair. He stopped to tap with his cane one of the great marble bath-tubs placed side by side on the slippery flag-stones. For this decayed and mildewed edifice had been, in the first quarter of the century, the luxuriantly appointed bath and club house of the *jeunesse dorée* of the old French quarter. He tossed a handful of nickels into the group of wide-eyed babies squatted within the tub, and nodded good-hu-

moredly, in passing, to a cobbler standing in the
doorway of one of the disused bath-cells.

"He's got all de ways of de Cunnel, his father,"
sighed the old woman, "fair a-drawin' de heart
out'n yo' body, an' den not keerin' fer it when
he gits it. I've ached a'ter him fer nigh thirty
year, an' he 'ain't studied 'bout me, not sense
he was weaned fum de breas', less'n he wants
sompn!" She went back into her own room and
closed the door. "So Cunnul Floyd Garth is
dead," she muttered, pacing back and forth with
rhythmic step. "What diffunce does dat make
to old Hagar, now? But de boy is got to have
what he *wants* ef I have to spill de las' drap o'
blood in my body to git it fer him. Ez to de
woman, white er black, dat is holdin' back fum
him, ef I kin git my hands on her I'll twis' her
neck same ez I twis' de neck of a chicken!"
Her voice rose with sudden ferocity, and sank
again to a hoarse whisper. "I kin *th'ow Wanga*,
me! I knows de hate-spell!" She thrust her
hand into her bosom and took out a small black
sea-bean, highly polished, and fitted, like a miniature flask, with a silver stopper. She shook it
lightly and held it to her ear as if to assure herself
of its contents, and returned it to her bosom.
"Yes, I knows de hate-spell. But I don't know
de love-spell. I 'ain't had no *call* to use de love-
spell, me!" The suggestion of a grim smile
played over her withered lips. "But de boy is
boun' to have what he *wants*. I mus' git dat love-
spell fum Voodoo Jean!"

A few moments later she came out into the

streets. The noonday sun was hot, though it was
but the middle of February. The breeze that
travelled along the narrow street was heavy with
the perfume of the orange-trees abloom in the
square a stone's-throw away. Swarms of bare-
footed children basked on the banquettes; they
shouted after the old *blanchisseuse* in pure baby
wantonness. She seemed as oblivious of them as
of the older idlers lounging in doorways or dozing
on the iron benches in the old *Place d'Armes*. She
walked up the street, rigidly erect, and with a
firm, brisk step, looking neither to right nor left,
and presently turned into a dim corridor, which
opened at the farther end into a small, ill-smell-
ing, triangular court. The enclosing walls, formed
by the rear of tall brick buildings, were pierced
by doors and windows, whose heavy batten shutters were closed. A large archway on one side
was boarded up; the huge spikes which clamped
the cross-pieces were rusty, as if a century might
have passed since they were driven in.

Hagar paused a moment and looked about her,
as if taking her bearings; then she crossed the
slimy brick pavement, and tapped upon a low
door half hidden by the leaky cistern in a corner
of the triangle. There was an interval of silence;
then a light shuffling sound within, and the door
was opened by an old negro. He was of almost
gigantic proportions; the shrewd, repellent face
was jet-black; the large, sensual mouth showed
when open a double range of tusks rather than
teeth of surprising whiteness; the small eyes shone
beneath their bushy white brows. A red turban

was twisted about his head; his coarse blue cotton shirt was open, exposing his massive, scarred chest. A necklet of oddly shaped bits of wood encircled his short throat; his feet were bare, and silver anklets tinkled on his brown ankles as he moved.

Hagar pushed past this forbidding figure and entered the small room.

Voodoo Jean regarded his visitor with mute, frowning inquiry. She turned back her sleeve without speaking, and pointed to a small tattoo-mark on her arm, just below the elbow. A quick gleam of intelligence leaped into his face. He uttered a guttural ejaculation and touched a similar hieroglyph on his own wrist. When they spoke it was in the gibberish-like tongue of their African forefathers.

The den in which they stood was bare, except for an arm-chair placed by the single window, and a rude table, which was strewn with pebbles, bunches of feathers, bits of bone and straw, and knotted fragments of rope. Lighted candles in flat candlesticks burned at either end of the table. On a narrow shelf above the open fireplace there were two or three tattered books, a wooden rod bound with brass, and a small box with iron clasps. A peculiar musty odor permeated the damp, close apartment.

"Is it for a woman you desire the spell?" Voodoo Jean demanded, when Hagar had finished speaking.

"No, for a man," she replied, briefly.

He walked over to the mantel and opened the

little box which stood there. "Those things"
—he waved his hand contemptuously towards the
table—"are for common and ignorant fools who
must be fed with lies, and furnished with dead
men's fingers, and lizard's blood, and graveyard
worms. This"—he took from the rude casket a
small white sea-shell, whose rosy lining glistened
in the candlelight, and laid it in the yellow
palm of his long, shapely hand — "this is for
those who wear *the mark.*" He touched with his
forefinger the cipher upon his wrist.

Hagar approached eagerly.

"Stay!" He lifted a warning hand. "Is the
man *of our blood?*" he demanded, with a searching look.

She hesitated; great drops of perspiration
gathered upon her forehead; her lips opened
in a vain attempt to speak. "Yes, yes!" she
panted, as he made a movement to return the
talisman to the box.

"I will help no dog of a white man to a woman," he said, with calm ferocity. "Take it,
Woman of the Mark! Let him give it himself
into the hand of the woman he desires. It is
powerful. It cannot fail."

He dropped the shell, as he spoke, into her
hand. She slipped it into the bosom of her
dress, where the sea-bean was already lying.

He waved away the silver she offered him—
the silver which her foster-son had given her
at parting. She laid her lips humbly upon the
tattoo-mark on his arm and went away. He
stood on the threshold, and watched her pass

across the court and turn into the alley. A look
of contempt, not unmixed with pity, rose for an
instant into his cunning eyes. Then he re-entered his lair and closed the door.

II

Some one was singing in Hagar's room; the
fresh voice went echoing about the ancient galleries and cobwebbed corridors. She heard it as
she mounted the stair, and her face lightened.
She opened the door and stood unnoticed on the
threshold. "Lisette was bawn in freedom," she
murmured, exultantly, "an' she cert'n'y *looks* it!"
The girl was bending over the ironing-board
with a heavy iron in her hand; her calico frock
was pinned back and her sleeves pushed up above
her rounded elbows. She was tall, like her
mother, but her slim figure had the tender and
graceful outlines of youth. Her skin was almost
abnormally white, the mixed blood showing
only in the colorless cheeks, the large eyes with
the purple, crescent-shaped shadows underneath
them, the full, voluptuous lips, and the crinkly
hair, which was drawn back from the low brow
and woven into innumerable little plaits, each
closely wound with cotton thread.
"Howd'ye, mammy," she cried, looking up
brightly as the old woman entered. "You see,
I've been doin' yo' ironin' whils I was waitin' for
you to come home."
Hager smiled at her affectionately. "Yo'

arms is younger dan mine," she said.   "Lawd ! how de i'on do skim over dat shirt !"

"I can't stay," Lisette said, slipping the garment from the board and folding it deftly. "My madame sent me on a erran', an' I just run by to fetch you some cold vittles."   She picked up her white sunbonnet.

"Dat's right," her mother remarked, following her to the door.   "Don't fool erway yo' mistiss's time.   An' min' you be a good gal. honey !"

"I will," laughed the girl, laying her soft arms about her mother's brown neck.

The next morning Hagar hung around the street corner near the hotel where Garth was stopping until she saw him come out.   He repulsed her almost roughly when she produced the talisman.   "Take it, little marse," she whispered, looking furtively around.   "It's de love-spell.   You ha' to give it into de woman's hand yo'se'f.   It's boun' to work."

"I don't want it," he said, averting his face. "Good God ! Hagar, couldn't you see I was jesting ?   Besides, you don't know—"   He stopped abruptly and walked up the street, leaving her staring vacantly after him, with the shell in her hand ; but half a block away he turned and came swiftly back.   "Where is the cursed thing, Hagar ?   Give it to me."   He seized it fiercely. "I shall not use it," he continued, with a short laugh.   "I am going away—up to Garth Place —abroad.   I may be gone six months—a year, perhaps.   I will come and see you as soon as I return." He shook her hand nervously and strode away.

"*He called me Hagar!*" said his nurse, looking after him with dazed eyes. "Fer de fus' time in his life, he called me *Hagar!*"

III

"Her mistiss mus' sholy bear a hard han' on Lisette," sighed the old washer-woman one morning nearly a month later. "I ain't seen de chile sence de day I come back fum Voodoo Jean, an' foun' her over my i'nin'-board."

She spoke in a half-audible tone to herself, as she moved to and fro among her tubs in the court-yard.

"What for you no make-a yo' dotter work-a with-a you?" interrupted a swarthy, smiling Italian near by, her fine brown arms rising and falling in the white froth of the suds. "Me, when Cesca git-a grown"—she stooped to pat the round cheek of the half-naked cherub clinging to her skirts—"I wouldn' lef' her leaf-a me for a hund'ed dolla, no!"

Hagar deigned no response. "Ef dey wa'n't so many low-down Dagos an' triflin' niggers in dis cote-yard"—she glanced disdainfully at her loquacious neighbor, then at a buxom mulatress leaning over the gallery railing above, exchanging doubtful jests with the ear-ringed Sicilian who was washing vegetables at the hydrant—"ef dis cote-yard wa'n't so onchristian I'd fetch

de chile home to-morrer. Praise de Lawd ! here
she come, now !"

There was a light foot-fall in the corridor,
and Lisette appeared, threading her way daintily
through the rubbish that strewed the court, and
through the net-work of lines overhead. "Run
along, honey," Hagar called, cheerily. "Soon
ez I wring out dis tubful an' pin up, I'll come."

Lisette, in the clean, cool, shadowy room above,
took off her sunbonnet and drifted aimlessly
about, touching a homely article here and there,
and looking at it with absent eyes. A subtle
change had taken place in her appearance. Her
dress was the same—the dark-blue calico gown
and freshly ironed apron ; the leather belt about
her slender waist ; the coarse shoes and cheap
stockings. But a new and indefinable charm
enveloped her ; a languid grace pervaded her
slow movements ; an exultant light came and
went in her dark eyes.

Her mother gazed at her in silence from the
doorway.

"Whyn't you wrop yo' hair, Lisette ?" she demanded, sharply.

A dull color rose in Lisette's cheeks ; her eyelids drooped ; she raised her hands as if instinctively to her head. The twisted plaits had been
combed out, and the wavy mass was drawn back
into a loose knot at the nape of her neck ; a fringe
of crinkly curls fell over her forehead.

"I ain't had time to wrop it this mawnin',"
she said, half sullenly. "I've got sompn to do
besides wrop my hair. The madame is down

sick," she went on, volubly, "an' the children has all got the measles. I was 'fraid you might get oneasy, an' I come to let you know, mammy."

"I don't know when I can come again," she called up from the court-yard when she went away; and after she had reached the corridor she ran back to say, breathlessly, "I forgot to tell you, mammy! My madame don't allow me to have comp'ny now. So's I can't ask you to come till the children gets well. But don't you be oneasy."

"De chile seem like she low-sperrited," Hagar mused, unpinning the snowy, sweet - smelling clothes from the lines. "Her mistiss mus' sholy bear a hard han' on her. I'm gwine to hurry up my starchin' an' rough i'nin', so I kin go an' he'p take keer o' dem measly chillen. Comp'ny, *hump! I* ain't no comp'ny!"

It was late in the afternoon of the next day when she closed and locked her door behind her and went out into the street. She was a noticeable figure in her old - fashioned, full - skirted, black bombazine gown, her spotless lace - edged 'kerchief and curiously knotted tignon. She moved along the uneven banquettes with a firm, quick step, but her form seemed to have lost some of its erectness, and her face had grown visibly older during the past month.

"Ef I could only see de boy!" she muttered. "I'm fair eatin' my heart out fer a sight of de boy! He called me *Hagar* fer de fus time in his life! He called me *Hagar*, an' den lef' me d'out so much ez lookin' back over his shoulder!"

She had halted unconsciously. The corner
was a quiet one ; wide-eaved cottages and dingy
shops shouldered each other along a maze of in-
tersecting streets beyond. The tall church-spire
above her cast its shadow across their pointed
roofs. She leaned against the church-wall, her
eyes fixed on the ground, her head upon her
breast. She drew a long breath and looked
around like one awakened from a dream.

"*Gawd—a—mighty!*" she cried, recoiling as
if she had received a blow.

Facing the church, set back from the street
and flanked on one side by a high wall that in-
closed one of those quaint gardens still to be
found in the very heart of the French quarter,
stood an old-fashioned brick mansion, with wide
verandas, long, high windows, and steep, dormer-
windowed roof. It had been newly painted ; the
iron grille which barred the corridor on one side
of the house was tipped with fresh gilding. The
window-shutters were flung back ; filmy curtains
within were swaying in the light breeze ; a bird-
cage hung in a shaded corner of the upper gallery.

A silver plate on the front door bore the name
Floyd Garth.

Hagar drew her sleeve across her eyes and stared
again. Her face twitched ; a sob rose in her
throat. "I didn't know wher' I wuz. De ole
house ! De ole house ! Where de slave was trod
onderfoot !"

The words came in broken jerks that seemed
to tear her breast.

"De mistiss in de front room. De slave in de
kitchen. Sarah in de tent. Hagar in de wilder-
ness. Twenty-five year an' mo' sence I've seen
de sin-stained house! Twenty-five year and mo'
sence de slave watched de mistiss twis' herse'f on
her big fo'-pos' bed an' die! . . . Die in yo' tent,
Sarah! Twis' yo'se'f on yo' bed an' die! . . .
But de boy is mine—de curly hair, roun'-cheek
boy, wi' his arms roun' Hagar's neck!"

Her voice softened as she uttered the last
words; a smile of unutterable tenderness played
about her mouth. She walked on mechanically,
but turned as if struck by a new thought. "De
boy must ha' come back," she murmured. "He
sholy is come back! He's done open up de ole
house! He's been studyin' 'bout what he said
when he ax me to come an' keep house fer him!
He ain't fergot his black mammy! He didn't
mean nothin' when he called me Hagar! *He
loves me!* . . . It's been a long time sence ole
Hagar has cried fer joy," she whispered, wonderingly, staring at the drops which splashed on the
back of her hand. "Mebby he's in de ole house
now—in de ole house where he was bawn! Lessn
he's gone down to de ole cote-yard to fetch me
home!"

She crossed the street, half-running. The
grille was unlocked; she pushed it open and
went in. The long-flagged corridor was filled
with purple shadows; a little stream of yellow
river-water ran along by the wall, and fell with
a gurgling sound into the open gutter outside.
Within the wide court a low-branched magnolia

was in bloom, the great white cups pouring their
pungent incense upon the air ; a row of annun-
ciation lilies bloomed at the foot of the garden-
wall. A thin spray of water arose from a foun-
tain set in the midst of prim, white-shelled walks,
and fell noiselessly into a mossy marble basin. A
hammock was slung on an overhanging balcony ;
a wicker chair knotted with ribbons was placed
beside it.

The kitchen door beyond the court stood open
and a fire burned in the range, but there was no
one in sight. Hagar hesitated, looking around.
A hall door stood open and a negro lad came out
of the house ; he carried a silver tray with a long-
stemmed goblet upon it.

"Miss July Jackson, de cook, has jes' stepped
roun' de cornder, m'am," he said, politely ;
"she'll be back in a minit."

"I 'ain't come to see no cook," said Hagar,
haughtily. "I come to see Mr. Floyd Garth. Is
he at home ?"

"No'm," replied the boy, overawed by her
manner, "he 'ain' come yit. *Dough* he ginerally
comes in 'bout dis time, m'am. But de madame,
she's at home. *Dough* I don' 'spec' she wanter
be *dis*-turb. But I'll ax her kin you see her,
m'am. *Dough*—"

Hagar put him aside unceremoniously. "I
nussed Mr. Floyd Garth fum de day he was
bawn," she said, "an' de madame 'll be glad to
see Mr. Floyd's black mammy."

"De shell 'ain't failed in its work," she breathed. triumphantly, threading her way through one

well-remembered room after another, heedless of the familiar objects they contained. "De curly hair boy has got what he *want*. An' it was old Hagar gin him de love-spell! He's gwine to turn his sof' laughin' eyes on me like he useter, an' say: 'Mammy, *you* gits me what I *want*. *I love you, mammy!*' Ez to de madame—" She laughed significantly, with her hand on a fold of the heavy portière.

She lifted the curtain.

On the wall just opposite were the portraits of the late Colonel Floyd Garth and his wife— the one blue-eyed and blonde, with a somewhat haughty turn to his patrician head; the other, dark, fragile, and beautiful in her wedding-gown of shimmering silk. Between them hung a medallion portrait of their only son, Floyd—an exquisite, angelic head, set in an aureole of luminous cloud.

Nothing surely had changed here in all these years: the same big canopied bed in the alcove, the rosewood work-table by the window, the high-backed sofa and deep-bosomed chairs, the dainty *peignoir* thrown across the foot of a lounge with a man's coat tossed carelessly beside it!

A woman was standing in front of the muslin-draped Psyche mirror. Her back was turned towards the door. A cloud of mist-like white drapery enveloped the slight figure; there was a gleam of gold in the dusky hair; her arms were stretched above her head, the filmy sleeves falling away from them, leaving them bare to the shoulders; the wrists were encircled with brace-

18

lets ; the shoulders rose dimpled and shining
above the loose, low gown.

She turned at the slight noise.

"*Lisette!*" The name broke in a hoarse whisper from the mother's lips.

"*Lisette!*" She dropped the curtain and
stepped into the room, glaring about her like
a wild animal, her lips frothing, the veins of her
neck swelling, her whole body quivering.

The girl gazed at her with horror - stricken
eyes, a bluish pallor creeping into her face.

A door closed somewhere, jarring the stillness.
A step sounded on the bare, polished floor of the
hall outside, a hand thrust the portière aside,
and Floyd Garth appeared. His face, flushed
with his walk, wore a look of boyish pleasure.
He stopped, confused and uncertain, on the
threshold. The flower which he held dropped
from his fingers.

At sight of him a low, appealing moan escaped
Lisette's lips. She started forward with outstretched arms ; but an imperious gesture from
Hagar restrained her, and she sank, trembling,
into a chair, and leaned her head against the high
back.

The shell attached to a slender gold chain about
her neck rose and fell with the frightened heav-
ing of her bosom.

Hagar lifted her shrivelled arms. "De Voodoo
spell has done its work," she said, looking sternly at the master of the house. "It has holp you
to de woman you *want*. But de spell ain't finish'
yet. Dis half is for you, little Mars Floyd ! De

yether half is fer de gal, Lisette ! Dis half is de
spell of Voodoo Jean. De yether half is de spell
of old Hagar." She paused, glancing around the
room as if in search of something. Her eyes fell
upon a silver filigree basket on the window-ledge
filled with fruit. She crossed the room hurriedly and took an orange from it. The two young
people watched her with fascinated eyes while
she swiftly stripped off the golden rind and parted the pulpy layers within.

"Has you ever heerd tell of de *love-stranche,*
little Mars Floyd ?" she asked, with a sort of
ferocious lightness. "*Dey say* it's de mos' certain of all de love-spells."

She held out between her thumb and forefinger
one of those small crescent-shaped sections known
locally as the *tranche d'amour,* the "love-slice."

Garth, rooted to the spot where he stood, was
vaguely aware of a quick movement of her hand
to her bosom. He saw, as if in a hideous night-
mare, wherein he was numb and helpless, some
dark shining object gleam for a second in the
long fingers. His eyes followed her panther-like
spring to where Lisette lay panting in the high-
backed chair.

"De spell of Voodoo Jean for one. De love-
stranche of Hagar for de yether. De love-stranche
is de stronges'. A'ter you try de love-stranche
you don't ax for no mo' love-spells—nor hate-
spells !"

She stooped over the girl, whose large eyes were
rolling wildly.

Garth saw Lisette's blanched lips open, the tiny

morsel drop upon her dry tongue, her throat contract in the effort to swallow.

Hagar looked down at her, mute and rigid. A second of silence followed, broken only by the soft pad of the negro lad's bare feet on the floor without, and the airy tinkle of ice in a goblet. Then a short, sharp shriek rang through the room ; a gasp shook the slight form in the chair, running like an electric thrill along her limbs ; a wave of purple mounted to her face and neck, and receded ; the eyes closed, the head fell back. The gold band, loosened from the dark locks, rolled to the carpeted floor.

"God Almighty! Fiend! Devil! What have you done?" Garth's hand was upon the old woman's throat, and he was shaking her to and fro in a frenzy of wrath and anguish. "She is my *wife!* Do you hear me? She would not listen to me until my mother's wedding-ring was on her finger! She is my wedded wife!"

She shook him off with a strength far beyond his own. His words evidently fell on unheeding ears. She stooped quietly and lifted the arm of her dead child, passing her hand gently over the smooth wrist. Then she let it fall, and, drawing herself up to her full height, she turned with a savage cry upon the man whose wild eyes were fixed upon her. "You axed me kin I cunjur," she said, in a terrible voice. "Yes, *son of Cunnel Floyd Garth and his slave Hagar—yes, I kin cunjur!*"

THE END

By RUTH McENERY STUART

SOLOMON CROW'S CHRISTMAS POCKETS, and Other
Tales. Illustrated. Post 8vo, Cloth, Ornamental. (*In Press.*)

CARLOTTA'S INTENDED, and Other Tales. Illustrated. Post 8vo, Cloth, Ornamental, $1 50.

They all are simple, pathetic, and full of humanity.
They are told wonderfully well, and the author reveals herself as exceptionally skilful alike in studying and describing
racial and personal characteristics. The volume is one of the
best and most entertaining of its class which we have read
in a long time.—*Congregationalist*, Boston.

Mrs. Stuart has a way of her own to charm her readers
withal. In these stories she is at her best; they are all
good, very good.—*Independent*, N. Y.

A GOLDEN WEDDING, and Other Tales. Illustrated. Post 8vo, Cloth, Ornamental, $1 50.

The ten or twelve sketches in "A Golden Wedding" re-
veal a mingled web of humor and pathos but rarely found in
the dialect writing of the day. Only one thrown into inti-
mate contact with the simple-hearted black people—brought
up with them — could have drawn their features and their
natures in outlines so true, steadfast, and dramatic.—*Critic*,
N. Y.

THE STORY OF BABETTE : A Little Creole Girl. Illustrated. Post 8vo, Cloth, Ornamental, $1 50.

The story is charming, and will be read as frequently by
grown people as by children.—*N. Y. Times.*

Not only does "Babette" thrill with interest, but it is
sweet and wholesome in its attractiveness.—*Cincinnati Com-
mercial-Gazette.*

PUBLISHED BY HARPER & BROTHERS, NEW YORK.

☞ *The above works are for sale by all booksellers, or will be sent by the
publishers by mail, postage prepaid, on receipt of the price.*

By CHARLES DUDLEY WARNER

THE GOLDEN HOUSE. Illustrated by W. T. SMED-
LEY. Post 8vo, Ornamental Half Leather, Uncut Edges and Gilt Top, $2 00.

It is a strong, individual, and very serious consideration
of life; much more serious, much deeper in thought, than the
New York novel is wont to be. It is worthy of companion-
ship with its predecessor, "A Little Journey in the World,"
and keeps Mr. Warner well in the front rank of philosophic
students of the tendencies of our civilization.—*Springfield Re-
publican.*

A LITTLE JOURNEY IN THE WORLD. A Novel.
Post 8vo, Half Leather, Uncut Edges and Gilt
Top, $1 50; Paper, 75 cents.

THEIR PILGRIMAGE. Illustrated by C. S. REIN-
HART. Post 8vo, Half Leather, Uncut Edges
and Gilt Top, $2 00.

STUDIES IN THE SOUTH AND WEST, with Comments
on Canada. Post 8vo, Half Leather, Uncut
Edges and Gilt Top, $1 75.

OUR ITALY. Illustrated. 8vo, Cloth, Ornamental,
Uncut Edges and Gilt Top, $2 50.

AS WE GO. With Portrait and Illustrations.
16mo, Cloth, Ornamental, $1 00. (" Harper's
American Essayists.")

AS WE WERE SAYING. With Portrait and Illustrations. 16mo, Cloth, Ornamental, $1 00.
(" Harper's American Essayists.")

THE WORK OF WASHINGTON IRVING. With Portraits. 32mo, Cloth, Ornamental, 50 cents.

PUBLISHED BY HARPER & BROTHERS, NEW YORK.

☞ *The above works are for sale by all booksellers, or will be
sent by the publishers by mail, postage prepaid, to any part of the
United States, Canada, or Mexico, on receipt of the price.*

By CONSTANCE F. WOOLSON

DOROTHY, and Other Italian Stories. Illustrated. 16mo, Cloth, Ornamental, $1 25.

THE FRONT YARD, and Other Italian Stories. Illustrated. 16mo, Cloth, Ornamental, $1 25.

HORACE CHASE. A Novel. 16mo, Cloth, Ornamental, $1 25.

JUPITER LIGHTS. A Novel. 16mo, Cloth, Ornamental, $1 25.

EAST ANGELS. A Novel. 16mo, Cloth, Ornamental, $1 25.

ANNE. A Novel. Illustrated. 16mo, Cloth, Ornamental, $1 25.

FOR THE MAJOR. A Novelette. 16mo, Cloth, Ornamental, $1 00.

CASTLE NOWHERE. Lake - Country Sketches. 16mo, Cloth, Ornamental, $1 00.

RODMAN THE KEEPER. Southern Sketches. 16mo, Cloth, Ornamental, $1 00.

Characterization is Miss Woolson's forte. Her men and women are not mere puppets, but original, breathing, and finely contrasted creations. —*Chicago Tribune.*

Miss Woolson is one of the few novelists of the day who know how to make conversation, how to individualize the speakers, how to exclude rabid realism without falling into literary formality.—*N. Y. Tribune.*

For tenderness and purity of thought, for exquisitely delicate sketching of characters, Miss Woolson is unexcelled among writers of fiction.— *New Orleans Picayune.*

MENTONE, CAIRO, AND CORFU. Illustrated. Post 8vo, Cloth, Ornamental, $1 75

For swiftly graphic stroke, for delicacy of appreciative coloring, and for sentimental suggestiveness, it would be hard to rival Miss Woolson's sketches.— *Watchman,* Boston.

To the accuracy of a guide-book it adds the charm of a cultured and appreciative vision.—*Philadelphia Ledger.*

PUBLISHED BY HARPER & BROTHERS, NEW YORK

☞ *The above works are for sale by all booksellers, or will be sent by the publishers, postage prepaid, on receipt of the price.*

THE ODD NUMBER SERIES

16mo, Cloth, Ornamental

BLACK DIAMONDS. By Maurus Jokai. Translated by Frances A. Gerard. With Portrait. $1 50.

DOÑA PERFECTA. By B. Pérez Galdós. Translated by Mary J. Serrano. With Portrait. $1 00.

PARISIAN POINTS OF VIEW. Nine Tales by Ludovic Halévy. Translated by Edith V. B. Matthews. With Portrait. $1 00.

DAME CARE. By Hermann Sudermann. Translated by Bertha Overbeck. With Portrait. $1 00.

TALES OF TWO COUNTRIES. By Alexander Kielland. Translated by William Archer. With Portrait. $1 00.

TEN TALES BY FRANÇOIS COPPÉE. Translated by Walter Learned. With Portrait and 50 Illustrations by A. E. Sterner. $1 25.

MODERN GHOSTS. Selected and Translated from the Works of Guy de Maupassant, Pedro Antonio de Alarçon, Alexander Kielland, and Others. $1 00.

THE HOUSE BY THE MEDLAR-TREE. By Giovanni Verga. Translated from the Italian by Mary A. Craig. $1 00.

PASTELS IN PROSE. Translated by Stuart Merrill. 150 Illustrations by H. W. McVickar. $1 25.

MARÍA: A South American Romance. By Jorge Isaacs. Translated by Rollo Ogden. $1 00.

THE ODD NUMBER. Thirteen Tales by Guy de Maupassant. The Translation by Jonathan Sturges. With Portrait. $1 00.

PASTELS IN PROSE, COPPÉE'S TALES, and THE ODD NUMBER—Three Volumes—White and Gold, in a Box, $5 25 per set.

PUBLISHED BY HARPER & BROTHERS, NEW YORK.

☞ *The above works are for sale by all booksellers, or will be mailed by the publishers, postage prepaid, on receipt of the price.*